DEFY YOU

REBEL INK BOOK THREE

Editing by Pinpoint Editing

Proofreading by Sisters Get Lit.erary

Cover and Formatting by Sammi Bee Designs

Andy and Amelia

CHAPTER ONE

KAS

THE BRIGHT LIGHTS heat my skin and cause my eyes to water as I reach the middle of the stage, ready for my first dance of the night. I can't see how many people —men—are currently staring at me. And that's a good thing.

As I glance down, my slutty little school uniform catches my eye and my stomach clenches.

I fucking hate this.

I should be at university right now, enjoying myself with everyone else my age, or at least spending my Saturday night out getting pissed.

But no, I'm here, selling my body to pay off debts that aren't even fucking mine.

I blow out a breath as the beat drops, the lights get brighter, and I have no choice but to jump into action.

I shut down my reality—helped somewhat by the generous amount of vodka I had before I left the dressing room—and pretend that I'm just at home, letting go.

I push aside the fact that men probably over twice my age are currently out there, staring at me and imagining doing all sorts of disgusting things to my body.

My stomach turns over with disgust.

It's a means to an end. It'll just be a few months, and I can move on.

I've barely started when the shadow of a person right on the edge of the stage catches my eye. My heart jumps into my throat as I picture some crazy drunk guy chancing his luck.

It's not until he's through the spotlights that I get a good look at him.

I recognise him instantly, but his familiarity does nothing to relax me at all.

I back away from him, praying that security will appear at any moment, but my short legs with the god-awful killer heels attached are no match for him.

In seconds, he's before me, my elbow in his grasp, steering me toward the stairs.

"Let's go." His voice is deep and rough. I've no idea if it's caused by alcohol or pure anger.

I fight the best I can, but seeing as I'm barely five foot to his six plus, I stand little chance. I'm like a fucking rag doll as I try to force my legs to keep up with him.

When we emerge from the bright lights, as I

suspected, every single person in the club is watching us with curiosity.

Where the fuck are the bouncers? I wonder once more. They're meant to be here to protect the dancers, not allow them to be carted off by mad men.

He continues forward until he pushes the staff only door open with such force it crashes back against the wall behind.

"Go and put some fucking clothes on. You've got five minutes."

"Wha—"

"Don't," he barks. The vicious bite to his voice has a shiver running down my spine, but it's not the same fear-filled one that I'm used to.

"Who the hell do you think you are?" I snap, turning to him and placing my hands on my hips.

I hate that I've got to look up at him, but being so small, it's something that I've always had to put up with.

His cold, dark eyes hold mine for a beat before they drop to my body. Goosebumps erupt across my skin from just his look alone. I cross my arms over myself in an attempt to cover up, but I'm already afraid he can see too much.

"You have five minutes," he repeats, dragging his eyes up to mine. "I'll be right here waiting."

"Who are you? My fucking brother?" I regret the words the second they pass my lips, because while they're not true, in only seconds he could be on the phone with my brother.

I hate what I'm doing, but it's a necessity. I'm making quick money the one way I know how, but what I really don't need is the drama of Zach finding out.

"No, Tiny. I'm most definitely not that."

I open my mouth to respond, but I don't get a chance because another female comes running over to rip Spike a new one.

"If it were anyone other than you pulling that stunt, they'd be in the back of a police car right about now," my boss, Dakota, seethes, stepping between the two of us and breaking whatever moment we were having.

"Five minutes, Tiny. Don't make me wait any longer."

My teeth grind with the nickname he gave me the first time we met. I fucking hate it.

"Stop calling me that."

"Stop defying me."

"Fucking pain in the arse," I mutter as I spin on my heels to get changed. I want to continue fighting him, but it seems pretty useless. There's no way Dakota will let me back out there after that. Hell, I'll be lucky if I still have a bloody job.

With anger filling my veins, I storm into the dressing room, ignoring the curious looks I get from the other dancers. I pull my locker open before impatiently ripping my tiny outfit from my body.

Dragging on a pair of leggings, I pull a loose-fitting tank over my head and stuff everything else in my backpack. I'll deal with it all later; I just need to get the hell out of here now the night has gone to shit.

With my bag over my shoulder, I march back out the way I came in less time than I was allocated. I almost turn back and make him wait just to prove a point, but I've still got the attention of the other girls and I need their curious, judgy eyes off me.

"You need to find a new girl. Kas won't be doing another shift here."

My chin drops at his words. How fucking dare he?

"That's enough. Where the hell do you get off trying to take over my life?" My hand lifts and I poke him in the chest with as much force as I can muster. Sadly, it does little against his hard muscles, and he just wraps his fingers around my wrist and stops me.

"This isn't up for discussion. You're not stripping here again. Fuck, you're not stepping foot back in here again."

"That's not for you to decide," I shout, ripping my arm from its restraint. "Dakota, I'm so sorry." I glance at my boss, who looks to be on the verge of laughing as her eyes flick between the two of us.

"Call me when you've sorted whatever this is out." She winks before spinning and walking away. She's the only one who knows how badly I need this job. She knows full well that I can't just give it up because this arsehole thinks he can control my life.

"She won't be calling. She's done."

I can't help but smile when Dakota's only response is to flip Spike off over her shoulder.

"Let's go." Wrapping his fingers around my upper arm, he all but drags me from the building.

"Get your hands off me," I grunt, fighting to get away from him.

Stopping dead in his tracks, he stares down at me. His jaw pops with irritation.

"What now?"

"Just do as you're told."

"By you? Never." Rolling my eyes, I storm past him and toward the exit.

His low chuckle sounds out behind me, and I try not to let it affect me as I push through the doors and smile at the security guys holding the fort. Although, I can't help being pissed off that they didn't try to rescue me from the caveman now following me out of the building.

"Spike," one says jovially, adding to my irritation. "Good night?"

"Something like that," he mutters.

There's a line of cabs waiting outside to take the drunken patrons away. The desire to jump in the back of one while he's distracted is strong, but I don't have anywhere near enough money for something as simple as a cab ride.

Instead, I take off down the street in the hope that I can hide in an alley or something before he notices.

I can't have taken any more than five steps when my feet leave the floor and I'm dragged around the back of the club, losing grip on my bag which falls to the ground with a thud.

My heart jumps into my throat.

This isn't Spike.

I don't need the dirty cigarette smoke or the stench of his body odour to tell me that. Everything about the touch, his movements, is different.

A blood-curdling scream is just about to rip from my lips when fat, sweaty fingers cover my mouth.

I fight to drag in the air I need through my nose as I'm thrown back against the rough wall of the club.

"Where's my fucking money?" Jet growls, his nose only millimetres away from mine and his dark, cruel eyes boring into my light blue ones.

I shake my head as much as I can.

I don't have his fucking money. Why does he think I'm working here, for Christ's sake?

"Y-you gave me to the end of the month," I say in a rush when he finally releases my mouth.

"Yeah, well. I changed my mind. I need a payment now."

Where the hell is Spike? He wouldn't let me out of his sight not so long ago, and now he's fucked off when I need him most.

Jet takes a step back, his eyes dropping to my body.

"My other offer still stands. We can come to *other* arrangements." He reaches out and cups my breast, squeezing just a little too hard and making me wince. "It would be such a shame not to put this body to use."

My stomach rolls like I'm about to puke at any moment.

"What do you say, slut? Wanna prove to me how much money you could make me? Let me test out the goods?"

"Fuck you," I spit at him. My head screams at me to fight, to run, but my body is frozen under his stare.

"No," he growls, reaching out and tearing the thin fabric covering me in one single move. The material rips, exposing my bare breasts to him. "Fuck *you*."

The next few seconds happen so fast, I'm not even sure if I imagine some of it.

What I can only describe as a roar sounds out from my left at the same time Jet reaches for me again.

One second, he's there, taking advantage, and the next he's flying away from me as two guys follow.

I watch in horror as fists fly, bones crunch, and grunts and groans sound out around the otherwise quiet alleyway.

I fight to catch my breath as I stare at the scene

before me, attempting to pull my ruined tank around my body to cover up.

"I've got this. Go get her," a vaguely familiar voice says before one of the shadowed bodies turns on me.

My instinct is to take a step back, needing to get away from whoever it might be, but I'm still against the wall and all I achieve is the brick tearing up my back some more.

I marginally relax when Spike steps into the light. I sag against the wall, but thankfully he's quick enough and catches me before I hit the ground.

"Fucking hell, Tiny."

His strong arms pick me up as if I weigh no more than a feather, and before I can blink, I'm cradled against his chest.

"It's okay. I've got you."

Resting my head against his shoulder, I can't help but breathe him in. He smells fresh, manly, sexy. The complete opposite of Jet, whose smell made me want to puke.

My heart continues to thunder in my chest as he walks us away from the scene and the moans of pain still coming from the darkness.

"It's okay, I can walk." I fight to get out of his arms, but he just holds me tighter.

"Who the fuck was that?"

When I glance over, I find Titch walking over to us, his breaths heaving as he looks down at his busted-up knuckles.

"Danni's gonna fucking kill me," he mutters to himself.

I flail about in Spike's arms once again, and thankfully he releases me. I wrap my ripped tank around myself in an attempt to cover up. "It was no one."

"Riiight," Titch says. "Well, he shouldn't be bothering you for a while. He's out cold."

"T-thank you." I hate that I sound unsure of myself. I'm just struggling to get my head around the last ten minutes.

They rescued me. No one ever rescues me.

I'm always the one who takes the fall, hence how I ended up on Jet's radar in the first place.

"We need to call the police," Spike states, making a whole new wave of panic roll through me.

"No, no, no," I chant. "Y-you can't do that."

"Kas, he just attacked you on the street. The fucker needs to be locked up." His eyes bounce between mine as he tries to read what I'm not saying.

While I couldn't agree more—Jet *is* the kind of man who needs to be locked up and kept off the streets—he's not the kind of man you deal with through the law.

It's just not how it works.

"Please, Spike. No police," I all but beg. "He's not that kind of guy."

Spike and Titch share a look.

"She's got a point, man," Titch says. I study him for a beat, wondering why he understands and how he had the skills to take Jet down like he did. Have I underestimated him?

"You're fucking kidding, right? He just attacked her."

"Please," I try again, running my hand over Spike's shoulder and gripping onto the back of his neck. The move works, and his eyes find mine.

Our connection holds for a second while I silently

beg him to just let this be. Titch taught Jet a lesson, and that'll keep him at bay. At least for a few more days.

"Fucking hell," he mutters. "Let's get out of here." Spike wraps his arm around my shoulder and pulls me into his side.

I try to shrug him off, but he just holds tighter.

"What are you doing?"

"Taking you home."

"No," I state, forcing my feet to lock onto the pavement.

He turns to me, his eyes hard and serious. "No?"

"You've already done enough tonight, don't you think?"

"Really? You want to go there?"

"If you hadn't stormed your way in and ruined everything, this probably wouldn't have happened," I say, flinging my arm out toward the back alley.

"You really believe that, Tiny? He was waiting for you."

"I can handle him."

"It didn't look like it."

"Fuck you, Spike. I'm not some weak and pathetic little girl."

"I... uh... I'm going to head home," Titch says, interrupting our argument. Neither of us look up at him, our eyes remaining locked on each other's. "A bit of advice, Kas. Just do as you're told, it'll be much easier."

The corner of Spike's mouth twitches up in the beginning of a smile, but he doesn't say anything to his friend.

Titch turns to leave, but he only gets a few steps away before I call out to him.

He looks over his shoulder as I rip my eyes from Spike's intense gaze.

"Seriously, thank you," I say, hoping that it sounds as sincere as I intend. I can't deny that what Spike said only a few minutes ago was true. Jet *was* waiting for me.

"You're one of us now, kid. Better get used to it. Especially with him around," he says, nodding to Spike.

I don't need to look at him to know that his eyes are still trained on me. His attention makes my skin tingle with awareness.

Titch makes his way down the street before jumping into a car that he must have called for and disappears, leaving just the two of us.

My heart continues to race as I wait for what he's going to do.

"Are you going to take his advice now and do as you're told?"

I think of my options, and as much as I want to fight him, following him is probably the best option.

CHAPTER TWO

SPIKE

THE IMAGE of finding him with his dirty hands all over her is burned into my brain, along with thoughts about what could have happened if I hadn't walked around the corner when I did.

Everything about this is wrong. We should be standing here now, waiting for the police to turn up and drag his arse away, yet somehow I've listened to both Kas and Titch and I'm walking away without doing anything.

A shudder runs through my body as I reach out, wrapping my arm around her waist and pulling her into my side.

"What the fuck are you doing?" she barks, grinding to a halt.

"I'm sorry," I say sarcastically. "I thought I was looking after you."

Her body is rigid as she stares up at me. "I don't need looking after."

"Really?" I ask, my eyebrows lifting. "Because you totally had that under control back there." I look down to where she's holding her ruined top around herself.

"I'd have figured something out. I always have in the past." She rolls her eyes like it's not a big deal. Like fuck it's not.

"This isn't the first time something like that has happened?"

"Spike," she says with a sigh. "My life is... different to yours. I know how to handle myself. I've had no choice but to learn to."

"But he—"

"Nothing happened. There's no point dwelling." She takes a step and continues walking down the street.

"W-wait," I call when she overshoots the entrance to my building.

She stops but doesn't turn.

"This is me."

She looks up at the building beside her before looking back to the club.

"You live next to a strip club."

"Where else would London's most eligible bachelor live?"

A laugh falls from her lips, and it does something to my insides. Thankfully, she doesn't give me the time to think about why that might be because she turns and walks to the door.

"So, what are you waiting for? Show me to your lair."

Shaking my head, I follow her before pulling my keys from my pocket and letting us both in.

Sadly, we don't have a lift, so I guide her toward the staircase and we make our way to the top floor.

"Whoa, the penthouse too," she mutters once we reach the top.

"Don't get your hopes up, I'm not some secret millionaire."

"It's more than what I'm used to," she says so quietly that I'm not sure if I'm meant to hear it or not.

Swinging open the door, I gesture for her to enter first.

I watch as she comes to a stop in the centre of the room and spins, taking everything in. I might have only met her a few times since she arrived, announcing that she was Zach's half-sister, but tonight she's different to what I expected. When I've seen her around her 'family' she's been shy, nervous. But tonight, she's confident, sure of herself, sassy.

I'm not quite sure how to handle it.

My flat isn't much, a relatively small two bed, one bath that Titch and I have shared for a few years. It's not exactly what you'd call a dream home, but it has everything we need, plus a bakery below and a strip club within stumbling distance. Life could be worse.

Dropping her bag to the kitchen counter, I pull the fridge open and grab a can of beer. The buzz I had from the whisky seemed to vanish the second I saw her up on stage, and I could really do with it back if I'm going to manage to rid myself of the images of him and what he was about to do to her, and the fact that I've allowed her to convince me to walk away.

The music I'd clearly forgotten to turn off before I left earlier plays away happily in the background.

"Do you want a drink?" I offer, but when she doesn't answer, I turn and look at her.

She's still looking about the place, her eyes wide.

"A-are you okay?"

She spins my way. "Why did you bring me here?" The shy girl I've previously met makes a momentary appearance.

"Because it was the right thing to do. You nearly just..." I trail off, not wanting to say the words out loud.

She stares at me, her face hard with her anger before she drops her eyes to my can.

"Do you have a real drink? One from a bottle."

I want to refuse and get her a glass of water, but after what she's been through tonight, I guess a decent drink is the least she deserves.

Spinning for the cupboard with the spirits, I pull it open and grab the bottle of vodka at the front.

I hold it up to her. She nods and releases one of her arms from around her body.

"Don't you want a glass?"

"No."

With a shrug, I pass the bottle over.

She opens her mouth to argue when she sees it's an unopened bottle, but after a beat she just releases her ruined top and twists the cap.

I should look away, I know I should, but the second the fabric parts I'm unable to rip my eyes away from the strip of skin it reveals.

It's no secret that she's an ink fan. They're visible when she's clothed, but the fabric reveals more, and I'd be lying if I said that I didn't want to find out what she was hiding. In more ways than one. She lifts the bottle to her lips and swallows a generous amount.

I know she's aware that I'm staring at her. It's impossible for her *not* to be, seeing as I'm only a few feet away, but still I'm unable to stop.

She's one of my best friend's sisters—my boss' little sister. I shouldn't be looking. Hell, I probably shouldn't have even brought her here. She's too young for me, too young for me to be looking at the way I am.

I lift my hand to my hair, sweeping it back from my face and tugging until it bites, punishment for everything I shouldn't have done tonight.

She pops her hip, resting her free hand on her waist, waiting for me to get my fill.

"I need that job, Spike. You can't just storm in and ruin it for me just because my brother won't like it." Thankfully, her words are enough to drag my eyes up.

"You don't need *that* job," I counter.

She lifts the bottle again and the fabric moves, revealing more of her skin.

"Ah," she says, as if she's figured something huge out. She lowers the bottle and stalks toward me. "This isn't about rescuing me, is it? You're not trying to be the big man, trying to protect me from myself."

I swallow, her sweet scent hitting my nose as the heat of her petite body seeps into my front where she's so close. "W-what do you mean?"

"If you wanted a private show, old man, you should have just said." She stares up into my eyes, her light blues holding me captive as my heart damn near beats out of my chest.

After long, excruciating seconds where I'm unable to find any words, she lifts the bottle once more. She swallows two huge mouthfuls without so much as a wince before slamming it down on the counter. "What's wrong? Cat got your tongue?"

My lips part but no words pass as she closes the space between us. All I manage is a step back that has me bumping into the counter behind me.

"I would offer you mates' rate, but seeing as I've got debts to pay, I'm going to have to ask for my full price. I hope you're good for it."

She shrugs off the ripped fabric that's doing a shit job of covering her, and I watch as it flutters to the floor.

"If you ask really nicely, I might even do extras."

"What! No," I say in a panic as she rolls her hips against me and runs her palms up my chest.

"It's okay, I won't tell him if you don't." She bites down on her bottom lip as one of her hands descends down my stomach.

My reactions are too slow to catch her, and by the time my fingers wrap around her wrist, she's already rubbing my cock through my jeans.

"Oh look, I'm right. I mean, it was kinda obvious. You know you've got a rep in Pulse, right?"

"Kas," I growl, my fingers tightening to stop her rubbing at me.

"Hey, I may as well find out what all the fuss is about, now we're alone."

"No," I bark, releasing her and slipping from my trap between her body and the counter.

Reaching behind me, I pull my shirt from my body and hold it out for her.

"Put this on, for fuck's sake."

Her eyes lock onto my abs, but I don't hang around long enough to hear what she might have to say, because I turn my back on her and march toward the bathroom, flipping the lock the second I'm inside.

"Jesus, fuck," I mutter to myself, standing with my hands on the basin and my head dropped between my shoulders.

Shame burns through me that I even allowed that to get so far. But fuck, her tits.

"Fuck," I bellow, willing the image of her standing half-naked and offering herself up to me from out of my head.

Zach would cut off my bollocks just for looking, let alone anything else.

I brought her here to do the right thing. To protect her. To do what he would do himself. But that... that wasn't meant to happen.

Deciding to make use of the bathroom, I toe off my shoes and drop my jeans before stepping into the shower. I turn it on and tense when the ice-cold water hits me. I fucking deserve it after what I just did, looking at her like that, letting her touch me.

I have a quick shower before wrapping a towel around my waist and pulling the door open.

The last thing I expect to find is Kas in the hallway, leaning back against the wall in only my shirt and the now half-empty bottle in her hand.

Her eyes lock onto mine for a beat before dropping down my practically naked body. Water droplets run down my chest and stomach before soaking into the towel, and fuck if she doesn't follow them.

"What are you doing, Kas?"

"Enjoying the view," she says, almost sounding bored. "Seems to be a little obscured, though." She lifts a brow as she stares at the towel like its mere presence offends her.

"I'm going to get dressed," I say, ignoring her burning stare and the need it creates within me. I can't lie, I was hoping to end tonight with a girl in my bed, but never in a million years did I think it would be Zach's little sister who ended up in my flat.

"Why? Things will probably be more fun if you don't." A smirk appears on her lips as she tilts her head to the side, looking me up and down and causing my temperature to increase.

"We're not going there, Kas."

"Why not?"

When I look over my shoulder, she's pushed from the wall and has followed me to my room.

"I've had a shitty night. *You* ruined my night, so it only seems fair that you make it better." She takes another drink, only she's had so much now that when she tips it up, too much comes out and it sloshes over her face and drips from her chin, soaking my shirt. "Whoopsie." She giggles, wiping her mouth with the back of her hand.

"I think you've had enough, don't you?"

Walking over, I wrap my fingers around the almost-empty bottle.

"See, you just can't stay away, old man."

"You need to go to bed, Kas. Sleep it off."

"I have every intention of making use of a bed, Spike. Yours, to be specific." She glances around me. "Don't you think those sheets need messing up?"

I pull the bottle, but she keeps her grip tight. "No, I don't."

"Jeez, I thought you were meant to be the fun one. The one who's up for anything."

"Not with you."

"Oh, ouch." Her lips turn down, doing her best impression of looking offended, but I know it's all a drunken act. "And here I was thinking you thought I was hot."

"You're drunk."

"I know." She giggles again, the light sound doing things to my insides. "It'll only make it more fun."

"Come on, you're going to bed."

I finally manage to get the bottle from her hand and lead her to the spare bedroom.

When Titch moved out, he left all his furniture behind. It's all ready for a new tenant when I find someone who can put up with me.

With my hands on her upper arms, I walk her into the room and to the side of the bed.

"Sleep it off, and tomorrow I'll take you home."

"Oh goodie," she sasses.

Pulling the covers back, I gently push her so she has no choice but to fall into bed.

She drops onto her back and brings her knees up, forcing my shirt to slide up her thighs, exposing her curvaceous, inked legs.

"Go to sleep, Kas," I warn, taking a step back. Only she's quicker than I gave her credit for, because she reaches out and catches my fingers.

"I don't want to be alone," she whispers, her eyelids hooded as if she's already half-asleep.

My heart aches for her. She's clearly in some shit if

the events of tonight are anything to go by, but that doesn't mean that I'm about to crawl in beside her. Having her here and wearing my shirt is bad enough. Zach would kill me for looking at her, let alone getting into bed with her, even if absolutely nothing happened.

"You're safe here, Kas. I won't let anyone hurt you."

"Please, Spike. I need... I need you."

My teeth grind at the vulnerability in her voice, but I can't break. For once in my life, I need to do the right thing where a woman's concerned.

As I slip my fingers from hers, her arm falls to the bed. She's already out of it.

I silently walk from the room and pull the door closed, heading to my room, discarding my towel and dragging on a clean pair of boxers.

I flop onto my bed and stare at the ceiling.

Well, tonight didn't exactly go as I'd hoped.

I just wanted a normal night out with friends, a night like we used to have before women turned up and stole my best friends' hearts.

I blow out a long breath.

I'm happy for them, of course I am. But equally, I can't help thinking that they're fucking delusional.

Women are great, don't get me wrong, but relying on one to make you happy for the rest of your life? Huge fucking mistake.

So while I'm happy for Zach and Titch, I'm also dreading the day they learn what women are really like. The day they have their hearts smashed and their worlds turned upside down. Because it'll happen. I'd put everything I have on it.

I lie there for the longest time, running the events of

the past few weeks, along with tonight, through my head.

I should be fucking some hot woman right now. I should be half-cut and having the time of my life. Instead, I'm lying here fucking miserable with an untouchable woman in the other room.

I think about the way that man put his hands on her earlier and my fists clench, my knuckles cracking open from the couple of punches I got in before Titch took over.

No man should get to touch any woman like that, but especially not one of us. Because Titch was right—she *is* one of us. Just another reason why I need to keep my eyes off her.

I'm just drifting off when a blood-curdling scream fills the flat.

I'm up and out of bed in a flash, racing toward her room.

There's only a sliver of light coming from the crack in the curtains, but it's enough to see her thrashing about under the covers.

Rushing over, I rest my knee on the edge of the bed and place my hand on her shoulder.

"Kas, Kas. It's okay. Wake up."

"No, no. No!" she cries. "Get off me, no."

"Kas, wake up." I shake her harder in an attempt to pull her from her nightmare.

The light catches the tears streaming down her cheeks, and my heart aches for her.

We all knew that she didn't have the best of lives from the little she's told Zach, but I fear he's barely scratched the surface based on the little glimpse I've had tonight.

Suddenly, she sits up, drops her head into her hands and sobs, heart-wrenching sobs that wrack her entire body.

Without thinking, I crawl next to her and pull her into my arms.

CHAPTER THREE

KAS

WHEN I COME TO, not only is my head banging, but I'm really fucking hot.

Stretching my legs out, I still, when what I thought was the pillow that I'm clinging onto also moves.

My heart jumps into my throat. What the hell did I do last night?

Then one face pops into my head.

Oh, fuck no.

Lifting my head, I drag my eyelids open and look up at my companion.

"Mornin', Tiny."

"Fuck. My. Life," I groan, dropping my forehead to his very naked and very sculpted chest.

"Well, that's the first time I've heard that so early in

the morning," he chuckles, sounding way too amused and way too awake for my liking.

"Why the hell are you in my bed?" I ask. "You'd better have some..." I lift the edge of the covers that are resting halfway up his belly and breathe a sigh of relief when I find he's wearing a pair of boxers, although it's impossible to miss the huge bulge of his morning wood.

Something stirs between my legs, despite the hangover raging in my head.

Running my eyes over the definition of his abs and over his chest, I finally make it to his eyes. They're darker than I remember from last night, and I can't help wondering if he's having similar thoughts.

"I'm certainly not here for the reason you're thinking."

"I'd really hope not, because I don't remember anything, and I'm sure that would be a hit to your ego."

"Tiny, Tiny, Tiny," he mutters. "Had I touched you, you wouldn't have been able to think about anything else for days."

"Days?" I ask, one eyebrow lifting in question.

"Daaays," he confirms. "But seeing as I refused all your offers last night, you didn't find out."

He rolls away from me and sits himself on the edge of the bed.

My eyes lock onto his tattoo. I immediately know who did it, because the detail in the wings is as intricate as the one on my shoulder blades that Zach did not so long ago.

Unable to resist, I reach out and run my finger over the edge of the feathers.

His entire body jolts at my touch.

"Shit, sorry. This is amazing."

"Well, that's your brother for you." His shoulders square and he pushes from the bed, stopping me from touching him any longer.

The atmosphere in the room immediately changes, making it hard to drag in the air I need.

"Get dressed," he says coolly. "I'm taking you home."

Sitting up, I watch him march from the room. The muscles in his back flex in the most delicious way as he moves, and it's not until he's disappeared from my sight that I'm able to look or even think about anything else.

What the hell just happened?

Swinging my legs over the edge of the bed, keeping my movements slow so the room doesn't spin, I stand and follow him.

His door is still open, but the sound of him moving around inside is clear.

Coming to stop in his doorway, I push the door wider and lean against the frame.

"Spike?" He's still just in his boxer briefs, and I can't help but allow my eyes to wander over his inked skin. He's got fewer tats than I was expecting, and my muscles twitch to add more. Not that I think for a second he'd let my amateur fingers anywhere near his skin.

"Get dressed, Kas." His eyes lift for the briefest moment, but the second they lock on me, he looks away again.

"For someone who was so adamant he wanted me here last night, you're pretty keen to get rid of me now."

"Yeah, well. Things change. Now, will you do as you're fucking told? Or I'll take you home like that."

I look down at myself wearing his t-shirt and shrug.

No one where I live would bat an eyelid if I turned up dressed like this.

"I can take myself home. I don't need you."

That stops him.

"Oh, like you didn't need me last night."

"Yeah, I did, but you denied me, remember?"

His lips purse and his eyes narrow. "*That* wasn't what I meant." A muscle in his neck pulsates as he stares at me, and I can't help but smile at him.

"Maybe not, but it seems like you might be regretting it now. Feeling a little frustrated, are you, old man?" I ask, flicking a look down to where his semi is still pressed against the thin fabric of his boxers.

His teeth grind and his muscles tense at my name for him. "Enough with the old man thing," he warns.

"Why? You're what... ten years older than me?"

"Yeah, exactly why we shouldn't even be having this conversation."

I cross my arms over my chest knowing full well that it will make the shirt rise, exposing more of my legs.

"Get. Dressed."

"Keep your fucking knickers on. I'll be out of your hair in a few minutes. Maybe then you should figure out a way to relieve that tension." I give him an insincere smile before spinning on my heels and walking back to my room.

I don't find any of my clothes or my stuff there, so I head for the living room. I find my leggings in a pile where I vaguely remember stripping them off, along with my ruined shirt on the kitchen floor.

The memory of letting it fall from my shoulders in front of him hits me, and I can't help but laugh to myself. No wonder he's feeling a little worked up this morning. I offered myself to him on a platter last night, and he turned me down. I probably should feel a little hurt about that, but it's like water off a duck's back. It only fires me up to keep pushing him. I need some entertainment in my life; fuck knows everything else I've got to deal with is too depressing for words.

Pulling on my leggings, I leave my ripped top on the counter and pull my bag over my shoulder.

"Thanks for last night," I call out before pulling the front door open and marching through it.

It slams behind me, leaving no question about the fact I just walked out. My head pounds as I begin to jog my way down the stairs and away from Spike and his morning attitude.

I need to go home, have a shower, and get ready for work again. I've got a debt to pay, and from the looks of last night, Jet isn't willing to wait any longer for what he thinks I owe him.

I can't afford it, but as I move, I pull up the Uber app on my phone and order myself a car. I just need to get out of here.

It seems that some luck must be on my side, because there's a car right around the corner and it's pulling up in front of me in less than thirty seconds.

I've got the door open and I'm about to climb inside when a voice behind stops me.

"Wait."

"What now?" I ask, my voice flat and unamused by the fact that he's just followed me.

"Let me take you."

"Why? So you feel better about yourself? So you can tell Zach that you looked after me? Fuck off, Spike." I flip him off and climb into the car, slamming the door behind me. "Go, please," I instruct the driver, and he pulls away from the curb.

I breathe out a sigh of relief and rest back, but it doesn't last all that long.

"Are you in trouble, miss?"

I open my mouth to respond with something along the lines of, 'I'm always in trouble', but I refrain from making this situation look worse than it already is.

"No, I'm good thanks. Just the morning after the night before, you know how it is." He glances at me in the mirror and I realise that I've not even looked at myself this morning. I probably look like a bus has run over me.

"Okay, well... you should probably know that he's following us."

"What?" I bark, twisting in the seat to look out of the back window. Sure as shit, there's a black bike right behind us. I narrow my eyes on his right arm and immediately recognise his tattoos.

"Motherfucker."

"I don't get paid enough to embark on a car chase," the driver mutters.

"He's not a threat to me," I say with a sigh. "Quite the opposite, actually."

Resting back, I close my eyes for a beat and think back to last night and the way he tried to rescue me from myself. Twice.

I'll be the first to admit that I don't want to be working as a stripper, but aside from properly selling my body or becoming a drug lord, I'm not entirely sure how I'm going to raise the money I need. And fast.

The threat of what will happen if I don't pay Jet is the only reason I stay up on that stage and allow the sleazy men to drool over me. Deep down, I was more than happy to be dragged away from it.

Equally, I can't deny that being in his arms after the incident with Jet didn't feel pretty damn good. I'm not sure I've ever been held quite like that in my life before.

For just those few moments, I felt safe, protected. Two feelings I really don't need to get used to, because where I come from, the only way to survive is to look after yourself.

"So, you still want to go to the same address?"

I consider my options. Wherever I go, I have a feeling that he's going to follow. And really, by not going home, I'm only putting off the inevitable.

"Yeah," I say sadly, once again resting my head back and closing my eyes. I need more fucking sleep.

I think back to what I remember from last night. I recall him turning me down, but how did he end up in my bed when he quite adamantly didn't want me?

The movement of the car eventually sends me to sleep, and it's not until the driver speaks that I wake up. My head is groggy from my impromptu nap and the lingering vodka in my system, but the second I look up at the dark and dingy building I live in, everything hits me once again.

"Thank you," I say, pushing the door open right as a rumbling engine pulls up alongside us.

"Fucking hell," I mutter to myself.

"What the hell is this place?" he asks the second he pulls his helmet off.

We're in one of the shittiest areas of London, one that I'd likely say he's not visited before, if the look on his face right now is anything to go by.

"This is my house." I refrain from calling it my

home, because it's the biggest shithole ever and doesn't deserve that label.

"Here? You live here?" We both turn when the door slams and we watch some junkie stumble down the steps and sway his way down the street.

Concern laces through Spike's eyes when he turns back to me. I fucking hate it.

Pushing past him, I head for the front door to let myself in—and hopefully shut him out.

"This isn't a house, Kas. It's a fucking crack den."

"It's not, actually," I bark over my shoulder. "It's a house share. Now, have you finished stalking me?"

"I'm not fucking leaving you here," he says, following me. His face is hard and the muscles in his shoulders are pulled tight as he takes in the rubbish, bottles, and other questionable paraphernalia littering the steps I'm standing on.

"You fucking well are." I spin at him and place my hands on my hips.

"Does Zach know?"

I open my mouth to respond, but no words come out. There's no point lying—he'll only go to my brother and ask.

"We haven't spent all that much time together yet," I mutter. It's the truth. Since I discovered he was my brother and plucked up the courage to speak to him, we've both been pretty busy. Plus, I'll do anything I can to keep him away from this place. I'd have happily kept Spike away from it too, if he hadn't insisted on following me.

"He won't allow you to live here."

"Well then, it's a good thing I'm an adult who has my own mind, isn't it?" I taunt.

"Tiny," he warns.

"Stop fucking calling me that. And leave me the hell alone."

Spinning on my heel, I rush into the house and go straight for the stairs.

The place stinks, and having spent the night in Spike's clean flat makes that fact only more obvious.

As always, there are people everywhere. It's meant to be a house share for a maximum of eight people, but most nights it feels like eighty instead.

I race up the stairs and toward the room I call mine, although in reality, it's not just mine.

There are three makeshift beds in here, and all my stuff is in a couple of cases and a box. It's a pretty shitty way to live, but it's all I've ever known.

Mum dragged me from shithole to shithole and introduced me to all the down and outs that live in this city.

Thankfully, no one else is actually in the room right now, so I drop my backpack on my bed and start rummaging for some clean clothes, hoping the bathroom is empty and in some kind of working order.

The creak of footsteps sounds out from behind me and my spine straightens. Jet knows where I live.

Just a few more shifts, then I can get paid for the month and get him off my back. For now.

Only, when my visitor speaks, I realise I'm not in danger.

"You've got to be fucking kidding me. You can't live here like this."

When I glance over my shoulder, he looks furious. As his eyes flit around the small room, they're filled with disbelief.

"It's done me okay for most of my life."

He opens his mouth to respond but clearly doesn't have any words because he just closes it again.

"Do you mind? I need to have a shower and get ready for work."

"I'm not leaving you here."

"Then it looks like you're moving in as well. Good thing about that is that no one will notice." I roll my eyes, going back to my bag to find some clean underwear. I really need to get my arse to the launderette.

A growl is emitted from behind me before large hands wrap around my waist and I'm moving.

"Do you fucking mind? Arsehole."

"No, I really fucking don't."

I watch as he bends down where I just was and starts shoving all the haphazardly strewn clothes inside before zipping it up.

"What else is yours?"

I stare at him as he picks up the two cases before flicking my eyes to the box beside them.

"That too?"

For fuck's sake. I chastise myself for not staying strong.

"You can't force me away from this place. I live here. I pay rent here."

"Well, then I'm about to save you some money."

"Uh—"

"Tiny, either follow me, or I'll carry you out like all your shit."

"It's not shit. It's my life."

He looks down at the pathetic number of

possessions I own, and a sadness I don't need to see washes across his face.

Looking away, my eyes land on my best friend's bed beside mine. Jodie and I have been friends for years. I can't just up and leave her.

"Let's go, Tiny."

"No." I stand firm with my hands on my hips, but I know it's a battle that I'm not going to win.

"You're a pain in the fucking arse, you know that?"

"I've been told a time or two."

He drops the cases and stalks toward me. I back up, but I only make it two steps before I hit the wall.

His palms plant themselves on the dirty paint either side of my head, and he bends his knees so he's at my eye level.

"I've got a perfectly good guest room with your name written all over it." His eyes hold mine, but I hate the pity I see in their depths.

Ripping my stare away, I look at his shoulder instead.

"There's no point in arguing with me on this. You send me away, and I'll come back with Zach. We both know he'll give you even less of a choice than I am right now."

I blow out a breath, an emotion that I don't want to be feeling beginning to burn in my eyes.

"Tiny?" His fingers connect with my chin and he forces me to look back at him. "Fuuuck," he whispers when he sees the tears filling my eyes.

His hand moves up to cup my cheek, and his thumb catches the lone tear when it drops. I hate myself for being weak. Living in places like this all my life has hardened me better than this. But one look in his chestnut eyes and I turn to mush.

Damn him.

"You hungry?" he asks, changing tack.

I nod. I'm starving after not having anything to eat last night and unable to turn down the offer of some decent food.

"Good." He reaches back down and takes my cases in one hand. By some miracle he also scoops up the box. "This everything?"

I nod, because I'm still very reluctant about this, but I don't think I stand a chance in hell of arguing with him right now.

I follow him out of the house. The pair of us get more than a few curious looks, but as is usually the way, people stay out of my business.

It never used to be like this, but the second people started to learn that I owed Jet, they started backing away. Everyone aside from Jodie, that is.

My stomach twists at the thought of leaving her here alone. Her life's about as screwed up as mine. I look back up the stairs, part of me longing for the only home I've ever known, while the other half of me screams that I should be happy about this.

I'm getting a chance at the only thing I've ever really wanted. A real home. I should be shouting and screaming in excitement right now.

Spike comes to a stop at his bike, looking between it and my limited possessions.

"Suddenly realising that this was a stupid idea?"

He thinks for a minute before pulling his phone out. He taps away at the screen before announcing that it's sorted.

I keep my eyes on him as he drops it back into his pocket, the denim of his jeans tightening across his crotch as he does so, giving me a hint of the bulge I was lucky enough to get an eyeful of this morning.

Maybe his idea won't be so bad. It'll give me the opportunity to torment him again. Last night might have been all kinds of fucked up, but I can't deny that I didn't enjoy teasing him.

I stand awkwardly on the pavement, waiting to see what his new plan is, suddenly achingly aware that I look every part the homeless girl standing outside the house share while he's looking insanely hot and put together in his dark jeans and white, long-sleeved Henley that shows off his muscular arms and sculpted torso.

My mouth waters as I look at him, thinking about the indents of his abs. I wonder if his muscles would twitch the way I'm imagining if I were to trace them with my tongue.

"You're staring."

My eyes fly up to his, my chin dropping.

"Sleep deprived," I mutter, trying to get out of being caught, but when I risk a glance up at him and find a smirk on his lips, I know he's not believing a word of it.

"Here's the car," he states, stepping forward when a black saloon comes to a stop before us.

"What about your bike?"

"Don't worry, I'm not leaving my baby here."

I raise a brow at him, firstly because he called his bike his baby, but mostly because of his accusation.

"Why? What do you think would happen to it?"

He glances back over his shoulder at either the

drunk or high guys hanging around. It's not even midday and they're all off their faces.

"I know this might have been where you lived, Tiny. But it's a fucking shithole."

My lips purse with my need to defend where I've lived for longer than I want to admit, but really, it's pointless. I'm not blind. I can see this place for what it is. Plus, there's a good chance that one of Jet's boys are watching us right now, and I'm sure they'd delight in riding the thing into the Thames the second we turn our backs.

"Here," he says, passing something over.

When I glance up, I find he's holding a helmet.

"Um... what the hell is the car for if you want me to get on that thing?"

"The car is for your stuff. One of my neighbours is going to collect it at the other end for you. You're getting on this, and we're going for food before I starve."

"Starve?" I ask, thinking it's a little extreme.

"Shall we?" When I follow his gaze, I find the car disappearing down the road with everything I own. His movement catches my attention as he throws his long leg over the beast of a machine and looks at me.

"Not scared, are you, Tiny?"

Truth is, I kinda am. Not that I'm going to let him see that.

"Scared? Puh-lease." Praying that I look like I know what I'm doing, I pull the helmet over my head and fiddle with the clasp until it's secured.

It feels weird as fuck. It's like I'm one of those bobble head things some of the taxi drivers have on their dashboards.

"Put your right foot there." He points to a little step

thing, and I do as I'm told before throwing my other leg over the machine.

My arse slides down the leather until my legs are spread wide around his hips.

Okay, so maybe this wasn't such a bad idea.

His body visibly tenses as we connect, making the muscles of his back even more apparent.

I wait for a few seconds as he takes the helmet that was hanging from the handlebars and places it on his head. In much less time than me, he has it secured before leaning forward and kick-starting the engine.

The vibrations race through my body, making my heart rate increase, knowing that it means he's about to move.

Shit, shit, shit.

"You might want to hold on," he shouts over the deep rumble of the engine.

"Oh, um..." I look at his body before me.

Without putting much thought into it, I slide my hands around his sides, brushing them over his abs and pressing my breasts into his back as I hold him. Just as I was imagining earlier, his muscles jump at my touch, and I can't help but smile inside the helmet.

He doesn't say anything else; he clearly thinks I'm ready for this, because he kicks the stand and takes the weight of the massive bike.

My mouth goes dry as I wait for what's to come next. The engine revs, the vibrations mixing with his heady scent and giving me a bit of a thrill before he pulls away.

I squeal as we fly down the road and away from my house.

I don't look back, there's no point. It's not like I'm

going to miss the place. It's just a shame I've got to leave one person behind.

I'll be back, I tell myself as he guns it out of the end of the street before turning left and really putting his foot down.

I panic for a second and squeeze my eyes shut, but after only a few seconds, I begin to feel brave and crack them back open. The second I do, I find the city flying past me in a bit of a blur, and a smile creeps its way onto my lips.

CHAPTER FOUR

SPIKE

THE SECOND HER small hands touch me, I know I should have sent her back to the flat, with the car.

I grind my teeth as I gun away from the place she called her house. I feel the eyes of all the people loitering around, enjoying the bit of entertainment as I take her away.

She doesn't belong here. Zach would go crazy if he knew this was where she slept at night. It makes me wonder how she's kept it from him. I know they've not spent all that much time together since she revealed who she really was, but still. He's gonna be pissed. Although, possibly not as pissed as when he discovers that her new lodgings are my place.

It's fine, I tell myself. I'm just helping her out.

Giving her a decent place to stay so she can have a chance at starting over. I might not have all the details about her past, but all the evidence only points toward a pretty shitty life.

I know her mum—their mum—died of an overdose earlier in the year. That alone is enough to screw anyone up, let alone having to live like that. I should know.

Thoughts of the way the guys in that house looked at her along with the lingering memories of that arsehole with his hands on her last night are enough to keep my muscles locked up with tension as we drive toward my favourite café.

"Off," I bark after killing the engine.

For once, she does as she's told, and I watch as she gets to her feet and undoes the strap under her chin.

I should look away, but I can't help myself. My eyes stay locked on her as she lifts the helmet from her head. Her almost black hair falls around her shoulders before she shakes it out. I swear the whole thing happens in slow motion, like in the fucking movies.

She's still got makeup all over her face, and she's still wearing my shirt, but fuck, she's hot.

"Here," she says, handing me the helmet, although she stills when she clocks the look on my face. "Oh, would you like me to do that again so you can record it?"

"Uh... funny." I snatch the helmet from her before climbing off the bike and removing my own. I place hers into the top box, but I keep mine with me and tuck it under my arm as I lead her toward the café.

"Well, I didn't have you down as a cute café kind of man."

"I'm not," I grunt as I push the door open.

As usual, a little bell rings, and one of my favourite people walks our way.

"Spike," Nina says, walking toward me with a soft smile on her face and her arms wide open.

I feel Kas' stare, but I ignore her as I wrap the other small woman in my arms. Her head stops at my mid-chest when I pull her into me.

"It's been too long, boy," she chastises when I release her.

"I know, I know." One word from her and I feel like a little boy again.

"And who is this young lady?"

"Hi, I'm Kas," Kas says politely, holding her hand out for Nina.

"Nice to meet you, dear."

Kas smiles, but her curiosity doesn't leave her face. "I'm sorry, could I use your bathroom?"

"Of course. Just down there on the right."

Nina looks almost as confused as Kas as she watches her walk through the café and disappear around the corner.

"Start talking then, boy. You never bring a girl here."

"Kas isn't a girl," I say, rolling my eyes as I walk to my go-to table next to the window.

"Oh?" Nina stands with her hands resting on the back of the chair, her grey eyes drilling into me.

"No. She's Zach's little sister. I'm just... helping her out."

"Sure, sure. So how have you ended up with her first thing in the morning with her looking like she's been dragged through a hedge backward?"

"Long story."

"Oh, sweetie. You know I've always got time for your stories."

I smile at her, a warmth I haven't felt for a while filling my belly. Nina is my grandad's oldest and dearest friend. She's also the only mother figure I've ever really known in my life.

"Nothing to tell. I'm just helping out a friend, and we could really do with some of your cooking."

"Well, you're in the right place. You want the usual?"

"You know it." I wink at her and she blushes like she always does.

"How's your pops doing?" she asks before turning away. "I've not got out to see him for a few weeks."

"He's good. Loving the easy life. You know, you should follow his lead sometime," I say, gesturing to her almost-full café.

I don't know exactly how old Nina is, but I do know that she's old enough and wealthy enough to have retired long ago. Yet, she's still here, sweating over the fryer every day of the week and filling her beloved Londoners' bellies.

"The only way to get me out of this place, my dear, will be in a box."

I laugh at her. If I've heard her say that once, then I've heard it a million times.

Chloe, one of her young waitresses, brings over a coffee, and we're busy chatting about the weather when a shadow falls over us. I don't need to look up to know that it's Kas. I feel it. My skin tingles with awareness and fire begins to smoulder within me.

I push it aside, just like I did last night and this

morning, in the hope it'll fade the more I tell myself that I'm just helping out my boy's sister.

Fuck knows that's all it can be. Not only is she forbidden, but she's way too fucking young for me.

"Excuse me," she seethes, pulling the chair out and forcing Chloe to back up a little.

The move has me stifling a laugh. That is, until I notice what she's wearing.

"You ripped my shirt?" I ask, staring at the now slashed open neck that's falling dangerously low over one of her shoulders.

"You gave it to me," she says with a shrug, holding out her mug for Chloe, who's staring at us with an amused expression on her face.

"To sleep in. Not to ruin."

"Well, you really should have clarified. To be honest, I think it's better."

"I guess you'd better keep it then," I mutter.

"Really?" she asks, her voice increasing a few notches like she's excited. "Wow, thanks." Those two words are accompanied with an eye roll, and I realise she's being sarcastic.

"You look better," I say, pushing aside the shirt issue and taking in her clear face.

Her skin is so fresh, so pale without the dark makeup that was coating it from last night. She looks so pretty, so... young.

It's the exact reminder that I need.

"I hope you don't mind, I've already ordered."

"I guess that all depends on if I like it or not."

"You'll like it," I say without a doubt. I don't think there's anyone on the planet who doesn't like Nina's cooking.

"So, who's she?" Kas asks, following my gaze to where we can see Nina through a little window, singing to herself as she cooks.

"My unofficial grandma." Kas screws up her face. "I'm pretty sure she and my grandad are soul mates, but they never quite got it together. Been by each other's sides for years though."

"Soul mates? I didn't have you down as the romantic type, Spike."

"I'm not," I grunt, "but their unrequited love or whatever the hell it is would turn a few cold hearts, I'm sure."

"Huh," she mutters, slouching back and sipping on her coffee.

"What?"

"Nothing. Just putting a few pieces together about my new roommate."

"So you're agreeing to this all of a sudden."

"You say agreeing, I say conserving energy for an argument I'm more likely to win."

"Like?"

She shrugs. "I'm sure one will present itself. I'm not really one for doing as I'm told."

"You don't say." I can't help but laugh at the hard expression I get in return.

Thankfully, Nina brings over our breakfast before we find something else to disagree about, and I watch as Kas devours the lot like she hasn't eaten in a week.

"When was the last time you had a proper meal?"

She glances up at me, a piece of sausage halfway to her lips. "No idea," she answers stiffly.

I guess that would explain why she's so fucking skinny then.

"You'd understand if you saw the kitchen in the place we just left. It's not exactly... hygienic."

I shake my head, hating how she's been living.

"Don't," she snaps. "Don't look at me like that. You know nothing about my life."

"I know enough to know I'm doing the right thing by taking you away from it."

"You're going to tell Zach, aren't you?" she asks quietly.

"Yeah. Unless you want to do it, save me the bother."

"Whatever."

"Don't do that, Kas."

"Don't do what?" she asks, sitting back and crossing her arms over her chest.

"Make out like you don't care. I know you do."

She makes some unintelligible noise.

"If you didn't need family, you wouldn't have reached out to him. There's no shame in admitting you need help."

"Who says I need help?"

I raise a brow at her. "Oh, I don't know. Maybe the fact you work as a stripper, or the guy from last night, or that you live in a squat."

Her lips purse in anger.

"Firstly," she snaps, holding up one finger to begin counting, "I might love being a stripper. It might be my dream job." I raise an eyebrow at her in question. "Second, I owe Jet some money. I can't help that he's trying to call it in early. And third, that place isn't a squat. It's a house share. I've lived in squats, and I can tell you that that house you saw this morning is like

Buckingham fucking Palace in comparison. So if you'd kindly stop judging, that would be smashing."

"I'm not," I say in defence, although really, I might well be. "I just want to help."

"By ruining my one job that will help to pay off my debts. Yeah, it's going great so far."

"How much do you owe?"

"Enough for him to come calling for it."

"How much?" I ask again.

"It doesn't matter. Even if it were fifty quid, I wouldn't be borrowing it from you."

"I've got some money, Kas. Plus, the second this gets back to Zach, you know he's going to hand over whatever you need."

"I don't need anything from either of you," she seethes. "This is my problem, not anyone else's."

"How'd you end up in debt to a man like that in the first place?"

"That's a story for another day," she mutters, no longer making eye contact with me.

It frustrates me to no end that she keeps me shut out, but then I'm not sure why I expected anything else. She's not wrong, I did drag her off that stage last night without much thought and probably ruined any chance of Dakota allowing her back.

"Come on, let's get out of here and we can get you set up at home."

She nods, and after saying goodbye to Nina—who, like always, refuses to accept any money for our short stay—we climb back onto my bike and head for my flat.

CHAPTER FIVE

KAS

I HATE the way he looks at me while trying to dive into the disaster that is my life. In truth, I'd fucking love for someone to hand me a pile of cash so I can get that arsehole off my back. But even if they did, I wouldn't accept it. It's my problem to deal with, not anyone else's, and certainly not Spike's. He's already done too much.

The second we're through the front door of his building, another door opens and a woman with a young child attached to her hip appears.

"Louisa, this is Kas," Spike says, gesturing between us. "And this cutie is Freddie," he says, reaching over and tickling the small guy, who giggles in delight.

Glancing at Spike, I find his eyes are softer than I'm

becoming used to as he laughs at the little man before him.

He said earlier that he wasn't a romantic, but from just the limited amount of time we've spent together, I don't believe it for a second. Even more so, now I'm watching him with a kid.

"Hey," I say when I remember I was introduced to someone.

When I look up, I find the woman's eyes locked on Spike. There's something a little more than friendly within them, and I wonder what the story is there. I won't ask, though. I don't want to look like I care.

"Kas is moving in for a bit. Thank you for taking her stuff in."

"No problem. There's not much though, so I'm not sure if it's all arrived yet."

"It'll be everything," I mutter sadly.

She allows Spike to step inside the door so he can collect my belongings, and before long, he's saying goodbye to his obviously interested neighbour and gesturing for me to go ahead and up the stairs.

"I can carry some of that myself, you know."

"I'm aware. But for once, just accept the help."

"Just this once. It goes against everything I've ever done in my life."

He doesn't respond, but I feel the sadness oozing from him.

When we reach the top, I'm forced to stop and wait for him to open the door.

"I've got a spare key inside. I'll find it for you in a bit."

I nod. All I want to do is get inside and curl up on the comfortable bed I passed out in last night. I might have been off-my-arse drunk, but it was still the best night's sleep I've had in... probably my life, to be honest.

The second he opens the door, I march through to what I'm assuming is my bedroom.

"I think Titch has taken everything, but if you find anything, just give it to me and I'll take it to work for him."

I nod, unzipping my suitcase the second he places it on the bed and rummaging through to find some clean underwear.

"Do you need me for anything or..." He glances down at the thong hanging from my fingers and his words falter.

"I think I can manage showering myself."

"Okay, that's... good. That's good," he says, stumbling over his words.

"Great. Do you mind?" I ask as I take a step toward where he's now totally blocking the doorway with his wide frame. He stands aside, but not enough, and as I pass, I brush up against him.

His breath catches the second we connect, and a small smile twitches at the corner of my lips.

"The woman downstairs wants you," I point out as I walk down the short hallway. He doesn't reply, and when I look over my shoulder, I discover the reason is me. His eyes are locked on my legs. "And it seems that you might need to get laid, so maybe you should pay her a visit at nap time."

"Huh? Oh... um... no. We're just friends."

"Well, trust me, she doesn't want to be 'just friends'," I say, mocking his deep voice.

"Too bad. I'm not interested."

"And here I was thinking the rumour about you

fucking anything that moves is true. Is that just a story to make you look good?"

"Louisa is my friend. Not only that, she's got a baby and is looking for forever after being screwed over. That's not my thing."

"No? So what is your thing?" I ask, turning on him and making a show of running my tongue along my bottom lip.

"I make no promises. To anyone. Especially not a single mother who deserves someone to take care of her."

"Who burned you?" I ask, narrowing my eyes at him.

"Who says I was burned? There are plenty of guys out there who don't want to settle down."

"Yeah, there are. But you're not one of them."

He opens his mouth to respond, but no words come out.

He might think I'm young and naïve, but he doesn't know me. He doesn't know that I've spent my life watching others, studying them and trying to work out what motivates them, what scares them. I see more than he thinks possible, and I know he's lying right now. Someone hurt him. Bad.

"So, were you planning on joining me, or…" I say with a laugh when he remains in the hallway, watching me.

"Uh… no. I'll just be in here." He darts for his room, and in the blink of an eye, he's gone.

"It's okay," I call out, "I wasn't planning on leaving the door open." Although, I must admit, it would be quite amusing.

He seems to be doing anything he can to prove he's

not affected by me in any way, but I see it in his eyes.

With a laugh, I walk into the bathroom and close the door behind me. I turn the shower on, and, after stripping down, I step into the bath and allow the hot water from above to wash over my body.

I can't remember the last time I had a shower that felt this good. The one at the house certainly wasn't. It also makes the ones at the club seem terrible, when I thought they were the best I was going to get.

This huge showerhead and torrent of water, is everything.

Realising that I only brought in a clean set of underwear and no toiletries, I make the most of Spike's that are littering the edge of the bath.

The second I open his body wash, images of him from this morning in my bed fill my mind and a smile forms on my lips.

I wonder how much it would have taken to make him stay and give in to what he was so obviously craving.

Picturing the impressive bulge behind the fabric of his boxers, I use my hand to rub the bubbles all over my body. I gasp when I brush over my pebbled nipples, not realising how much just thoughts of his body are turning me on.

Parting my legs, I drop my shower gel covered fingers to my clit and find I'm wetter than I probably should be.

Knowing that someone isn't about to barge through the bathroom as was a usual occurrence back at the house means I lean back against the wall, prop my foot against the edge of the bath and continue what I've started with his scent filling my nose.

As my muscles start to tense, I realise just how long it's been since I felt this. There's no privacy at all in that house, and I've witnessed one too many of my housemates openly taking what they needed to ever run the risk of getting caught doing it myself. They might have barged in and seen me naked in the shower, but I refused to give any of them that kind of show.

All too soon, my release rushes forward, making my knees want to give out as my hips buck against my own fingers.

As I come down from my high, I can't deny that it was needed. My muscles already feel a little more relaxed from it, but I want more.

I need a man to work me over good and proper.

I groan to myself, rolling my head and feeling my shoulders crack.

Making quick work of finishing up, I dry myself with what I assume is Spike's towel before pulling on my fresh underwear and dragging the door open.

He's crashing around in the kitchen, so I bypass my room and stop in the entryway.

"What are your plans for the rest of the day?" I ask, startling him.

He turns around and his eyes almost bug out of his head.

He clears his throat, but it doesn't work. His words still get stuck. "P-put some clothes on and I might be more likely to tell you."

"Jeez, are you always this much of a prude?"

"When it's my boss' little sister standing in front of me, yeah, I am."

"Zach doesn't give a shit what I do."

"You really believe that?"

I shrug. He's spent most of his life not knowing I even exist; he can hardly have an opinion on my life now.

"Well, let me tell you that he'll likely scoop my eyes out with a fork if he was aware I even knew what colour underwear you owned, let alone what you look like wearing it," he says, turning around and returning to what he was doing when I walked in.

"I get up on stage and dance for hundreds of men at a time, in less," I say flippantly.

"Fuck," Spike barks, dropping the knife that was in his hand to the floor and lifting his finger to his mouth.

"Shit, are you okay?" I ask, rushing over. "Please don't tell me you were hungry?" I ask when I spot that he was attempting to make a sandwich. He pins me with a hard look, but there's a fat chance of me being scared of the likes of him, not when I've got Jet and his crew on my back.

"Let me see," I say with a sigh.

Reluctantly, he pulls his finger from his mouth, although not before I notice just how his lips look sucking on it.

He holds out his finger for me, which immediately gets coated in a layer of red from his cut.

"Over here." I drag him using his finger to the sink, where I run it under some cool water to ensure there's no food in it before reaching for the kitchen roll sitting on the counter and pulling off a piece. I fold it a few times and then wrap it around his finger.

"I can look after myself, you know," he sulks.

"Says the one who cut himself chopping cucumber," I sass with a raised brow.

"I was distracted," he mutters.

"Does it hurt?" I tilt my head to the side, waiting for an answer.

"Yeah, a little."

A smile curls at my lips. "Want me to make it better?" I bite down on my bottom lip and take a step toward him, all the while keeping my hand wrapped around his injured finger.

"I-I think I'll survive."

I stare up at him, our eyes locked in our silent battle of wills.

He wants me, I can see it in his eyes, in the way his chest is suddenly moving at an increased rate.

I also know that at some point I'll win this game.

Looking away from me, he swallows, making his Adam's apple bob. "You need to stop this."

"Stop what?" I ask innocently. "I was merely helping you out in your time of need."

"That's not what this is, and you know it." He glances back down at me and to my breasts. "I'm trying to do the right thing here, Kas. Don't push me, or I won't bat an eyelid sending you back where you came from."

"Bullshit. You aren't sending me anywhere. You care too much. I like it, it's sweet." I step away from him, allowing him to release the breath he was holding. "It makes a change from no one giving a shit. Oh look, you dropped your knife." I bend over to reach for it, and the second I touch the cool metal a growl sounds out from behind me. "You really should be more careful. You could have cut a toe off."

I place it on the side and walk from the room. I don't look over my shoulder. I don't need to. I know he's watching my every move. I can feel it.

The second I close my door, I rest back against it and laugh to myself.

Tempting him is too easy. I can quickly see it becoming my favourite hobby.

Pulling on some clothes, I spend the next few hours in my room, unpacking the few possessions I have and having a much-needed nap on the incredibly comfortable bed.

I'd set an alarm to wake me so I can get to work—assuming I still have a job—but I'm woken by Spike's buzzer, followed by the low rumble of another male voice a few minutes later.

It's not Zach, I know that, and I'm pretty sure it's not Titch either.

Climbing from the bed, I check my reflection in the mirror. After fluffing up my hair a little, I pull down the neck of my tank and push the girls up a bit before going to see who's here.

"Have you got a girl here?" the deep voice asks the second I open the door.

"Uh..." Spike hesitates.

"Jesus, you're such a dog."

"Takes one to know one, man. But she's not that kind of girl."

"And here I was, thinking we could both make use of her."

I'm slightly taken aback by his words, although I'm not sure why. Boys will be boys. I know that more than most with the job I've been doing.

"You're really, really going to regret even suggesting that," Spike says, his voice harder, angrier even after the man's suggestion.

"Why? Who the fuck are you hiding back there?"

At that, I walk around the corner.

"It's not polite to talk about people behind their backs, you know that, right?"

The second I see him, I know who he is, and I understand Spike's warning a little more.

"D, how's it going?" I ask while he stares at me with his chin dropped.

"Spike." His voice is a warning as he looks between us. "Why the hell is Zach's little sister in your flat wearing... well, not a lot?"

"It's nothing like that," Spike argues. "I found her in Pulse last night."

D raises a brow at his friend, clearly not following his lead. "If you've touched her, Zach will kill you with his bare hands. I know he let Titch off lightly, but he won't do it again, and not with her."

"I am in the room, you know," I snap, but they both continue to ignore my presence.

"I haven't fucking touched her." It's kind of a lie, but I let it go. "She wasn't there on a fucking night out, she was up on the fucking stage." If I weren't so pissed off about them talking about me like I'm not here, I'd be amused by how wide D's eyes go at Spike's words.

"Nooooo. Zach will fucking—"

"Zach will fucking nothing," I bark, coming to stand between the two of them. "I'm a fucking adult. I can make my own choices. And right now, I need money, and that's the best way I know how, other than to—"

"Oh no, don't even go there," Spike spits. "Do not even consider whatever follows that sentence."

"Whatever," I say, waving him off. "My point is that it's my choice. My body, my life. I don't give a shit what either of you, or my brother, think."

"You fucking should. He's gonna lose his shit when he finds out you're flaunting it for the scumbags in that place."

I refrain from pointing out that they *are* two of the scumbags from that place.

"So, don't tell him. Let me do my thing, earn the money I need, and then I'll be done. Trust me, it's not a career that I want to embark on for longer than necessary."

D chuckles, causing my brows to draw together.

"What's so funny?" I cross my arms over my chest and don't miss Spike's eyes drop momentarily. Yeah, definitely one of the scumbags. He's trying to be all chivalrous, playing my protector, but really, he's just like all the others. I've heard the stories about his antics. It's one of the reasons I pushed last night. I thought he'd give in much easier though, I must admit.

"You really think we'll keep this shit quiet? You might be related to Zach by blood, but make no mistake that he's our brother in every other sense of the word. We look out for our own, and that, young lady, includes you."

"Don't 'young lady' me," I snap, unhappy with the way he's looking at me like I'm a little girl. "I'm younger than you lot, so what? I'm not the naïve child you think I am. If you'll excuse me, I've got a job to get ready for." Spinning on my heels, I storm back to my room and slam the door.

Okay, so maybe that was every bit as childish as they were making me out to be.

I can't help it though. Their condescending tone as they talked about me as if I wasn't in the room pissed me the fuck off.

I do my hair and makeup before shoving everything I'm going to need for my shift in my backpack and getting ready to leave the flat.

I'm earlier than I need to be, but right now, I'd rather spend time in the dressing room at the club with the other dancers than I would with those two judgemental arseholes.

Two sets of eyes leave the TV and turn to me the second I'm in the same room.

"Where the hell are you going?" Spike barks.

"Um... to work."

His lips purse as he sucks in a deep breath before he responds. "Have you heard nothing I've said to you? You're not going back there."

"Get over yourself, Spike. It's my job. You of all people know why I need the money." His face reddens in anger as I assume he thinks about what happened last night.

"Exactly the reason why you shouldn't go back there."

"Oh, so what am I meant to do? Sit here and wait to win the lottery that I don't play? Great idea, arsehole."

"I've told you the solution. You tell me how much, and I'll sort it. If you don't, it'll just get me to Zach's door quicker."

"Blackmail?" I ask with a sigh. "You're resorting to blackmail now? Let me just sort out my own life. Butt the fuck out."

"No can do, sweetheart." He shrugs, and all it does is infuriate me further.

Rolling my eyes at both of them, I march toward the door.

"Leave and I'll make sure Zach finds you up on that stage himself tonight."

I pause with my fingers wrapped around the handle.

"You think I caused a scene last night? Just wait until *he* finds you."

Blowing out a calming breath, I spin around and look between the two of them. D just looks amused that Spike seems to be winning this argument, whereas Spike looks about ready to combust.

"Fine," I sass, thinking of another option. "Fine. You win. Happy now? Just remember that you were the one to stop me when Jet catches up with me and forces me to make payment in *other* forms. It'll be your fault when he passes me around his arsehole friends for shits and giggles."

Without waiting for a response, I run for my room, once again slamming the door so hard that the floor vibrates beneath my feet.

Turning on the wireless speakers that were sitting on the chest of drawers when I got here, I sync my phone and turn up my angry playlist.

I can't help smiling as I wait to see if there's going to be a response from the arseholes in the living room.

When neither of them appear at my door after five minutes, I take it as my cue that it's safe, and stalk toward the window. Pushing it as wide as it'll go, I look down. It's a fire escape, so it's not the most dangerous place I've had to climb down from over the years, but equally, it's not a staircase either.

Pulling the straps of my bag higher up on my shoulders, I throw my leg over the windowsill and set about my secret escape.

CHAPTER SIX

SPIKE

"SHE'S AWFULLY quiet in there for someone who has so much to say," D comments as I make my way back to the sofa with a pizza for each of us.

"She's probably just sulking."

"Is she really stripping?"

"Yup," I mumble around a mouthful of steaming meat feast pizza. "I pulled her off the stage and demanded we leave. Dakota was pissed."

"That was brave of you. There's no way I want to be on the wrong end of Dakota. That bitch is scary."

"I decided I'd take my chances with her over Zach."

"He's gonna lose his shit, man."

"You don't know the half of it." I fill him in on what

happened once we got outside the club and then the squat I followed her to today.

"Jesus. He said her life was shit, but fuck. I don't think he knows it's that bad."

"Why do you think I dragged her back here?"

"To be honest, I'm just glad it's not to fuck her."

I raise a brow at him. "I am able to say no, you know." I roll my eyes and reach for another slice.

"You've had to say no?" he asks with his brows raised in suspicion.

I shake my head. "She was drunk. It was nothing."

"You need to watch your fucking back, Spike," he warns.

"What?" I ask innocently, because there's no fucking way I'm about to admit the less than innocent thoughts I've had about my latest roommate. Her presence makes me realise why I've only had male housemates to date. Even though she's forbidden in every sense of the word, she's still a temptation I really don't need.

"You think she's hungry?" he asks, glancing up at her closed bedroom door.

"How the fuck should I know? I'm not her keeper."

"I was thinking more of a fairy godmother."

"Fuck you."

"Kas," he calls, his tone much softer than a few moments ago. "Do you want some pizza?"

Silence greets him.

"And here I was thinking no one could turn down pizza." He shrugs and goes back to his puke-inducing ham and pineapple. There is something seriously fucking wrong with my friend.

"Kas," I call, trying myself when a feeling I can't shake fills my body. "You hungry? There's plenty here."

Silence once more makes me sit forward on the sofa.

"Why do you look so worried?"

"She wouldn't... would she?"

"What? Ignore us because we're arseholes? Yeah, more than likely."

"I have a feeling it's worse than that." Marching over to her door, I rain my fist down on the wood. "Kas, open the door."

Silence.

"Kas," I warn one more time. "If you're in there, I need you to open the door right now."

Nothing.

"Motherfucker," I mutter, pushing the handle down and shouldering the door open.

"Fuck," I bark, taking in the empty room and the window that's cracked open.

"What the fuck, man?" D asks when I storm back into the room and angrily shove my feet into my shoes.

"She's fucking gone. Come on."

"Gone? Gone where? How?"

"Out the fucking window. Move, or I'll go without you."

He's up off the sofa in a beat and joins me as I walk through the front door.

"She's a pain in the arse," D mutters as we descend the stairs.

"You got that fucking right."

As we turn toward the club that's only a few doors down, it doesn't escape my mind that we could just leave her to it, let her do her thing, allow her to get naked for all those sets of eyes, but I can't. The thought of them looking at her makes me want to lock her up in that bedroom properly this time.

She's too young. Too innocent. Too precious for the likes of the regulars in this place. The likes of me. That final thought is a sobering one as we greet Gary who's on the door tonight and enter the club like we would any other night of the week.

We go straight to the main room—it's where I saw her last night, so I have no reason to think she'd be anywhere else. Heaven forbid Dakota allows her to spend time one-on-one with guys in the private rooms. A shudder runs through me at the thought. Those girls in there can be... rule breakers, shall we say, and I've no doubt that Dakota knows every single thing that happens under this roof.

I squint as I step into the darkened room. Unlike usual, I forgo a trip to the bar in favour of checking out the girls on the stage, but again, unlike usual, it's not them I'm really interested in. I don't see the way their hips roll or what they're wearing, I just need to find her. But she's not here.

"I can't see her," D says when I find him back by the entrance.

"Me either."

"I need to find Dakota."

Stalking toward the bar, I lean over when the barman comes over and I shout in his ear.

"Where's the boss?"

He shrugs. "In her office. Why, who's asking?" I've not seen this guy before, and he clearly doesn't know who I am.

"Spike. Get her down here. I need to talk to her now."

His eyes widen a little in shock, but thankfully it seems to do the trick because he pulls his walkie-talkie from his belt and says something into it.

"She's coming. Drink?"

"Vodka, neat."

He looks to D who's standing beside me and he quickly adds a whisky to the order.

The second the glass is in front of me, I lift it to my lips and down it in one. It burns, but I need it right now.

"Well, well, what a pleasant surprise," Dakota shouts, making me spin to look at her.

"Where is she?"

To be fair to Dakota, she does a great job of trying to look like she has no idea what the fuck I'm talking about, but she knows. I can see the truth in her eyes. We may not have been friends all that long, but I can read her.

"Where's who?"

"Dakota," I warn, taking a step toward her. Not that it'll faze her, she's nothing if she's not a hard-arsed bitch. There's not many women I'd admit I'm scared of, but she's one of them.

"Spike," she sasses back with a smile.

"Tell me where she is, and I won't cause a scene."

"What are you really going to do?"

Honestly, I've no idea, but I don't want her to know that. "Test me and find out."

She pales ever so slightly, and I know I've got her. This place is her baby, there's no way she'd willingly risk losing out on a few customers because of me.

"If you tell me you've got her working one of the back rooms, I'll—"

My words are cut off when she starts laughing. "You really need to stop threatening me."

"Tell me what I need to know, and I will. She shouldn't be here, and you know it."

"I'm sure there are people out there who'd say that about every one of my dancers, Spike. But no one forces them to be here, and I pay them well for their work."

"I don't care about your other dancers. I just care about her." That admission rocks me slightly, but I tell myself that it's in a sisterly way because I'm such a loyal friend to Zach.

"Fucking hell. Follow me."

I look at D who nods at me to go. I spin and follow Dakota in her insanely high heels to the staff only door at the back of the room.

The second we're through it, the music instantly quiets down.

She takes two more steps before turning on me.

"Why do you care about this girl?"

"She's my best mate's sister and she's in trouble. Trouble I don't think you're going to want to bring into your club." Dakota narrows her eyes, encouraging me to continue. "Not my story to tell. I just need her out of this place and somewhere safe."

"You care too much about this one, Spike," she points out like I wasn't already fucking aware.

I haven't put this much effort into a woman since... nope, not going there.

"I just need her safe."

"Suuuure. I'll take you to her, but it's going to cost you."

"You want me to fucking pay?"

"You want one of my girls during working hours, and after the scene you caused last night, yeah, I want compensation."

"Fuck you, Dakota."

Her eyes run down my body and her lip curls in disgust. "I hear what the girls say. Apparently you're not all that."

My chin drops in shock before she starts laughing and walks away from me.

"Pay for her for the night and she's yours to do with as you wish. And," she adds, "should you not leave the room for a while, I won't even tell her brother."

CHAPTER SEVEN

KAS

"WELL, well, well, I didn't think you'd be stepping back in this place," Dakota says the second I step into the dressing room at the club after my less than glamorous escape from Spike's flat.

"He doesn't own me," I mutter, dumping my bag on the bench and shrugging off my zip-up hoodie.

"Are you sure about that?"

"Ugh, he's my brother's mate who thinks he can 'fix' me or whatever." I wave her off, really not wanting to go into this. "I need this job, Dakota, no matter what his opinion might be about it."

"I know you do, kid, but I can't risk him going all alpha on your arse like he did last night. It's bad for business. If the men start thinking they have a right to manhandle my girls, then I'm fucked."

"I get that, I do, and I'm really sorry he did that. But I need this. Please. Put me in one of the back rooms until he gets bored of trying to be my keeper."

"You know I can't do that."

"Why? Because I'm young? That's bullshit and you know it. I'm just as good as the rest of the girls, if not more desirable because of my age. Wasn't that what you said to me when you hired me?"

"Damn it, Kas."

"Just give me a chance. If you get any complaints about my... services, then you won't see me again after tonight."

A ball of dread explodes in my stomach at knowing what I'm offering. I know what some of the girls do in the back rooms, but fuck, I'm desperate, and it's either the guys who are paying for the privilege or it's Jet's guys. I know which is the better end of the deal, so I'll take it with both hands, thank you very much.

"I'm not happy about this."

"I don't need you to be happy, I just need you to let me do it."

She blows out a frustrated breath. "Alicia," she shouts to one of the other girls, "I need you out on the main stage tonight. Kas is taking over your room."

"What?" she barks, clearly pissed off. It's understandable; the back rooms are where the real money's at.

"Suck it up, Alicia. Now let's get sorted. Showtime in thirty, ladies." With that, Dakota flounces out of the dressing room, leaving hard, angry eyes on me.

"What?" I bark. All the women in here might be older and more experienced in this line of work than me but I've no doubt I could take each and every one of them if they were to try something. They look like the kind of bitches who'll slap and scratch with their fake arse nails. I bet they've never punched someone in their lives.

I make quick work of getting ready. I pull on a white lace underwear set, complete with stockings and suspenders and my heels. I always go for white, it helps to show off my 'innocence'. I laugh to myself. Innocent, what a fucking joke. I'm pretty sure my innocence was stolen before I even knew what the word meant with the life I've been forced to live.

"You got what it takes to be what the guys in that room need, kid?" Alicia asks, stopping behind me where I'm topping up my make-up in the mirror.

"More so than you, I'm sure." Her eyes narrow, but I don't give her the time of day and focus on my red lipstick.

"Watch your fucking back, kid. That room is mine, and everyone knows it."

"You do realise how that makes you sound, right? We all know what you do, in there. Just because it happens in a warm room with security on hand, it doesn't make you any better than the girls on the street corner."

Her face turns tomato red. "What the fuck did you just say to me?"

Pushing the stool out behind me, I turn to her. She's taller than me, no shock there, so I tilt my head to look into her eyes.

"Watch your back, Alicia," I seethe before throwing

my stuff in my locker and heading toward what she considers *her* room.

The room in question is dark. The walls are covered in black flocked wallpaper, the bench style seating wrapped around two of the walls covered in black velvet. There's a pole right in the centre up on a small stage, and the ceiling is mirrored.

But it isn't the decoration that I pay much attention to, because the second the door shuts behind me, a trickle of apprehension runs through me.

Being up on stage with loads of eyes on me is one thing, but being shut in a room with just one guy really is another.

Suddenly, I understand Dakota's reluctance to allow me to do this.

It's safer, I tell myself. I'm more likely to get through an entire shift without Spike—or worse, Zach—causing such a scene that Dakota does fire me.

After a few seconds, the low bass of the music fills the room, telling me that the night is really getting started outside the door.

I guess all I do now is wait for my first client.

I run my slightly sweaty palms down my thighs—not that it does much as I hesitantly perch my arse on the edge of the seat.

The lighting is so dim in here that I can hardly see the door at the other side of the room. I guess it's meant to heighten the sense of anticipation or whatever, but right now, all it's doing is making my heart gallop.

I have no idea how much time passes. It feels like a fucking lifetime, but the reality is that it's probably no more than ten minutes when the sound of the door opening cuts through the room.

My spine straightens as I push to stand. I give myself a talking to and take a step forward, waiting for the guy to show himself.

My lip curls in disgust as I think about the fact that it's probably some old, fat and smelly man who's coming in here for a special Sunday night treat.

My stomach turns over, but when the guy steps into the light, I realise just how very wrong I was.

Our eyes lock and his mouth opens, probably ready to rip me a new one, but before any words pass his lips, his eyes drop down my body.

"Motherfucker."

It might be dark, but I don't miss how his pupils dilate at the sight before him or the way his fists clench in what I hope is a move to stop him reaching for me.

"What's wrong? Cat got your tongue, old man?" I ask, taking a seductive step forward, putting as much swing into my hips as possible.

"Tiny," he warns. By some miracle, he keeps his eyes on mine, but I know it's killing him not to drop them once more. It's clear in the tightening of his muscles.

I step right up to him, delighting in the movement in his jaw as he tries to restrain himself.

"What's wrong, Spike? Is the temptation suddenly too much for you to handle?"

"I-it's time to leave." His voice is deep and husky despite the fact that he had to clear it before he managed to get any words out.

"And what would be the fun in that?" I forget all about my earlier hesitation when I was in here alone. Seeing his reaction to me has given me all the confidence I could need.

"We're leaving." His hand wraps around my

forearm and he tugs—only he's underestimating me, because when I move, it's to press the length of my body against his.

The feeling of his hard planes against my softness is enough for the temperature of my body to spike.

Reaching up on my tiptoes, I brush my lips against his ear lobe, enjoying the feeling of him shuddering beneath me. "It would be such a shame to waste the room, don't you think?" I whisper.

His fingers tighten for a beat as his eyes shut.

"You know what they say? What happens in the back rooms stays in the back rooms."

"Tiny," he warns again, his voice so deep it causes goosebumps to prick my skin. His restraint is starting to slip, I can sense it. If it weren't, I've no doubt I'd already be dragged behind him to the dressing room like I was last night.

He lowers his face, his breath tickling across my neck and down my back, making my entire body shudder.

"She made me pay for the room," he admits, making my breath catch.

"Well then, it would be rude not to use it."

As if someone is watching—to be fair, they probably are—the music increases, the sexy beat of the song unable to be ignored as it pumps though the darkness.

When his eyes come back to mine, they're blown with desire. I know there and then that I've won.

Taking a step back, he surprises me by releasing his grip on my wrist, but it's only for a second. The next thing I know, I'm moving and my back is pressed up against the soft wall.

With his height, he totally surrounds me as he steps

up to me and looks down. I'm pretty sure I've never felt so small in my life, yet so powerful at the same time.

I want to smile in accomplishment, but the intensity in his stare stops it from happening.

His chest heaves as his breath fans my face.

"Spike?" I ask when I start to wonder if he's in some kind of daze when he just stands there staring at me.

My voice must drag him from wherever he'd gone, because his eyes flash with awareness before he moves forward.

His lips brush my ear, and I swear my knees are a second from giving out.

"You're playing with fire, Tiny. And you are going to get burned."

"It's okay. I'm already going to hell. I like it hot."

He groans as if in physical pain, and after a beat, he pulls his head back but doesn't move far. His lips gently graze my jaw, his eyes finding mine and holding them as he moves.

"I-I'm meant to be the one teasing you," I stutter when he begins to hover over my own lips, close enough that I can feel his heat, but too far away to actually give me what I need.

"Oh, baby. Trust me, you're doing that."

"Spike," I moan, my body sagging back against the wall as my core floods with heat. My need for his touch is all-consuming. "Please."

His eyes harden for a beat.

"Why would I do anything you ask of me, Tiny? All you do is defy me. Did you think you were clever, sneaking out of that window?"

"Yeah, actually. I thought it was kind of genius."

"Did you really think we wouldn't notice?"

I shrug. Honestly, I'd not really thought much further than getting here and begging Dakota for my job back.

"You're trouble," he states.

"I could have told you that myself," I admit with a roll of my eyes. "So what are you going to do about it? Are you going to punish me? Show me what a bad little girl I've been?" I bite down on my bottom lip and roll my hips, ensuring I make contact with his groin.

His eyes darken and he growls once again before pushing away from me.

Coldness surrounds my burning skin and disappointment races through me.

I had absolutely no desire to do any of the usual things that happen in this room when I first begged Dakota to allow me back here. Hell, the first thing I wanted to do when I stepped foot inside was to run back out as fast as my heels would allow me. But now, surrounded by his woodsy, addictive scent and the memory of how hot his body is beneath those clothes, I'm suddenly more interested than I think could be deemed as healthy.

"Get a good look around, Tiny. This is the last time you're ever going to be in here."

"But, I–"

"No. The time to disobey me is over." His voice is harder than before, and I can't deny that it does make my argument die on my tongue. I don't think anyone has ever told me no before. It's kind of thrilling.

"But I hoped my first time back here would be more… satisfying."

I watch him as he spins around the pole before locking his eyes on mine once again.

"You mean, you've never worked one of these rooms before?"

"Nope. And guess what, you're my first client. So... *boss*, what's it to be?"

I push from the wall and stalk toward him, looking at his pained face through my lashes.

"You didn't really get to see me in action last night, did you? Did you just want to see if I'm up for the job, or..." Reaching out, I cup his already hard length though the fabric of his jeans. He gasps in surprise, his eyes going incredibly wide for a second. "Or would you like the full experience? This must be all kinds of uncomfortable right now."

Backing away from me, he falls down onto the bench and drops his head into his hands.

It doesn't escape my notice that he doesn't just bolt for the door.

As I stand and watch him, I realise he's fighting an internal battle with himself.

His body is screaming yes, that much is obvious. But his head, that's in a whole other place right now.

"You look tense. You should probably sit back and relax."

I gesture to the camera that I know is pointing at us and request that the music be turned up. I think our time for talking is over.

CHAPTER EIGHT

SPIKE

I KEEP my eyes locked on the floor as I ask myself why I didn't just walk out, dragging her barely-clad body behind me.

Some fucked-up part of me wants this torture to continue, although fuck knows why.

I shouldn't be in a room alone with her dressed like that, let alone one that's filled with low, sexy music and a fucking stripper pole.

This is wrong. So very wrong.

I can almost feel Zach's hands wrapping around my neck as I sit here, but still. I don't leave.

Suddenly the music gets louder and she moves before me.

Unable to resist, I look up.

I somehow manage to swallow down the groan as I take her in. Her back is pressed up against the pole as she slowly slides down, her knees widening as she hits the floor.

Fuck. Me.

Dropping my hands, my fingers wrap around the soft fabric of the bench and my nails dig into the wood on the underside.

Her movements are hypnotic, and as I watch her hips roll against the pole, I forget about who she is and all the reasons why I shouldn't be watching her move the way she is right now.

Sitting back, I rearrange myself in my trousers and keep my eyes on her, totally fascinated.

I've seen plenty of dancers in my life. Hell, I've spent more time and money in these back rooms than I'd admit to most people, but I can honestly say that I've never been quite as captivated as I am right now.

Her feet never leave the floor, but she doesn't need any of the fancy moves I've seen before.

My eyes find hers after she's spun around the pole once more, and I take in the accomplished smirk on her face.

I want to ask her if she's proud of herself, but I can't force my lips to move—not that she'd hear anyway over the volume of the music.

She takes a step toward me and my heart damn near jumps into my throat.

Her eyes hold an intent that equally excites me as it does scare me.

Dropping my gaze down her body, I run my eyes over her slender neck, down to her barely contained tits. Biting down on my bottom lip until I'm sure I'm going to break through the skin, I try to push the image of her perfect rosy nipples from last night from my mind.

My cock throbs as I recall quite how desperate I was to suck one into my mouth to discover if she tasted as sinful as I imagined.

I go lower, finding her slim waist and toned stomach before my eyes lock on the lace that's wrapped around her hips. Her thong is tiny, to the point it's almost not worth bothering with, but it's the garter belt and stockings that really have my mouth watering.

The second she's in front of me, her scent assaults my nose, ensuring that she steals all my senses.

Her delicate hands land on my shoulders, pushing me back until I'm resting against the bench.

I watch in a daze as she places one knee beside my thigh and then the other.

My arms remain useless at my sides, although my fingers itch to touch her. To feel how soft and warm her skin is.

But I can't. I fear that if I so much as reach for her then I'm not going to be able to stop.

I push back, melding myself into the bench in the hope that it puts an extra bit of space between us. But it's futile. I already know that.

Her core presses down against my solid length, and I'm powerless to stop my hips from lifting to get more.

"Tiny," I half-moan, half-warn.

I want to take everything she's offering. I want to claim her, mark her as my own so no other motherfucker in this place will touch her.

"You're going to need to sound a little less like you're enjoying yourself if you want to convince me to stop."

Her hips roll, her tits thrusting in my face. Finally, my arms move, but it's only to wrap my fingers around her wrists.

She stills the second we connect, and her eyes fly to mine. They widen in challenge, her defiance shining as bright as ever. For whatever reason, she wants to break all the rules tonight, and fuck if I'm not a few seconds from throwing caution to the wind myself.

Leaning forward, my lips brush her ear and she shudders.

"Tiny," I all but groan, "I need you to stop."

"What about what *I* need?"

"What you need," I grate out, "is to do as you're told."

"I'm not a fucking kid," she snaps, thrusting the evidence in my face once more.

"Oh, Tiny. Trust me when I tell you that I'm more than aware of that."

My eyes drop to her tits, which are only looking more tempting with the way I'm pinning her arms behind her back.

They're right there. It would be so easy to take what I need. What I know she also wants. But I can't. Being tempted is one thing, but betraying one of my best friends is entirely another.

When I look back up, her lips are pursed in frustration and her eyes are dark with desire.

"I think I've had my money's worth. You should go and get dressed. But make sure you get a good look at the place, because it's the last time you're going to see it."

She growls in frustration as she thrashes against my hold.

"Can you go and get dressed without getting into any trouble?"

Disobedience flashes in her eyes, and a smirk curls her lips.

"If you can't, I'll just carry you out like this."

"I need my stuff if I'm not allowed back," she sasses.

"Then I suggest you do as you're told. You've got five minutes. Do not test me, Tiny."

"That's the thing though, Spike. Testing you is my new favourite hobby."

"Brilliant," I mutter, getting the confirmation I didn't need that this thing between us isn't over.

"I will break you, Spike." She winks before moving from my lap.

Her eyes drop to my crotch and she smiles. There's no point trying to hide the fact that my cock is trying to push through the fabric covering it. She's already felt it against her.

Licking her lips, she backs away from me.

"And that wasn't a warning. It was a promise," she says before turning around and walking toward the door. Her hips swing from side to side, her round arse on full display, but it's the sight of the artwork adorning her shoulder blades that confirms that I did the right thing. Guilt hits me. I should have put a stop to this much sooner.

"If you're not interested, then you should probably stop staring," she warns without looking back to confirm that I am indeed looking right at her.

"Stop waving your arse in my face and I might."

She chuckles as she pulls the door open and finally looks back at me. "You've got five minutes to sort yourself out. Don't make me wait."

My lips part to respond, but she's gone before I manage to form any words.

The second the door closes behind her, I fall back against the bench. "Fuuuuuuuck," I bellow, my frustration over this whole situation getting the better of me.

I'm meant to be looking after her. Keeping her safe. I shouldn't need her this badly.

Scrubbing my hand down my face, I think of Zach. I tell myself that he was the reason I dragged her out of this place yesterday and then away from that squat this morning, but I fear that I may just be lying to myself.

After giving myself a severe talking to, I push up from the seat and head out to meet her.

I rest my back against the wall outside the dressing room with my foot propped up behind me.

It can't be thirty seconds later when Dakota appears. It's almost as if she were watching. My eyes narrow on her as I try to figure out if she was or not. It's no secret that they keep cameras on their girls at all times.

"I hope you've got a plan for her, because as much as you might not like her working here, she needs the money," Dakota warns.

"I'll figure something out," I mutter, not willing to talk about this with anyone but Kas.

"Just make sure you think with your head, not your cock for once."

"She's Zach's little sister. I won't be going there." Dakota's brows rise, convincing me that she did indeed see everything.

"Right, well, good luck with that. You got what you wanted. I've terminated her contract and ensured she can't go anywhere else. Congrats, you may just have ruined her life." She slaps me on the shoulder before disappearing down the hallway.

"Oh good, you're still here," a familiar voice snaps behind me.

"Did you really think I'd leave you here?" I ask, turning to look at her.

"A girl can hope." She tilts her chin up at me. There's not an ounce of embarrassment or regret on her face for what happened in that room.

My eyes drop to her hoodie and leggings. It's a damn shame, I must admit.

"You regretting your decision already?" she asks, stepping up to me until her breasts brush my chest. "Don't worry, I made it easy for you. I've got nothing underneath." A wicked smile appears on her lips before she ducks away from me.

I stay where I am for a second, willing my body to do the right thing.

"Are you going to hang out here all night, or are you still intent on escorting me home so I don't get in any more trouble?" She looks back at me with an expectant look on her face.

I can't help but laugh and shake my head at her.

I think I may have underestimated this girl when I suggested she move in with me earlier.

After telling D that we were leaving, Kas and I make the quick walk home. Thankfully, we're not accosted by a gangster, or drug dealer, or whatever the fuck that guy was last night. I'm grateful, because although I'd have done whatever it took to get his hands off Kas, I can't deny that Titch was the better man for the job.

But he shouldn't be fighting, and I'm pissed that he

was even put in that position after everything, but I knew there was no way to stop him after what we saw. I just hope Danni wasn't too hard on him when he appeared with busted-up knuckles once again. I'm surprised I've not had a phone call ripping me a new one, seeing as I was meant to be keeping him out of trouble.

It seems I may not be as good at that as I once thought I was.

"I'm going for a shower," Kas says the second we're inside the flat. She drops her bag in the middle of the living room and begins stripping out of her clothes before she even gets to the hallway.

I stand where I am and watch. I've already fucked up enough times tonight, what's once more?

As she drops the zip-up hoodie to the floor, I discover that she was telling the truth about having nothing on underneath.

"I can still feel you looking," she calls back over her shoulder.

"It won't happen again," I reply, before turning to the kitchen for a much-needed drink.

The sound of the water running is a tease I don't need. I may not have seen her naked, but I've run my eyes over enough of her skin now, to have a very good idea as to what she might look like with water cascading down her body.

Fuck. My. Life.

Forgoing the beer I was intending to grab, instead I reach up and pull a bottle of Jack down from the top cupboard. Something tells me that beer isn't going to cut it tonight.

I flop down on the sofa with the bottle and pull my phone from my pocket.

Finding Titch's number, I hit call.

It rings a few times before his voice comes down the line.

"Hey, man. How's it going?"

"It's uh…" I hesitate, and as I should expect, he sees right through me.

"What have you done?" he asks, suspicion obvious in his tone.

"I… uh… Kas is here."

"Here as in, in your flat?"

I let out a sigh, sliding down the sofa and stretching my legs out.

"Yeah, she's currently in the shower."

"Fuck, man. What the hell happened after I left last night?"

I think of all the things that have happened. Where do I even start? "A lot. She's in a really bad place. I've offered her your room so she can get herself sorted."

"Okay. Does Zach know?"

"Not yet."

"Spike," he warns. "Tell me you've got a fucking good reason as to why you didn't tell him the second she stepped inside your place."

I pause for a second. "It's her life, not mine."

"It's your flat. Telling him she's moving in, isn't telling her secrets."

I blow out a breath. I know he's right, and I know I need to confess.

"I guess. So what about you? Danni hit the roof when she discovered you'd been fighting?"

"Pretty much. She made me sleep on the sofa as punishment."

I can't help but bark out a laugh. "It's not fucking funny. She made a show of the fact that she wore my favourite lacy little thing to bed."

"Man, that's cold."

"Mate, there was nothing cold about it. She's still holding out on me."

Some sadistic side of me loves the fact that Titch is about as blue-balled as me right now. "I'm sure you can turn her."

"Yeah, she doesn't stand a chance when she gets home later. What about you? How are you gonna bang everything with a pulse with Zach's baby sister on the other side of the hall?"

"I'm pretty sure she wouldn't give a shit."

"She's a kid. She doesn't need to hear all of that. I'm a grown fucking man, and some of what you got up to traumatised me."

"Shut the fuck up. You loved it, and you know it." He mumbles some incoherent complaint down the line, but I just laugh. He makes out that I'm into all sorts of kinky shit. I might not be one to say no to much, but my taste isn't all that crazy when it comes to sex.

An awkward silence ensues. I'm just about to make my excuses and end the call when he speaks. "What aren't you telling me, Spike?"

Fucking Titch. I grumble under my breath. Always too fucking perceptive for his own good.

"N-nothing," I stutter as the sound of the water shutting off catches my attention.

"Spike," he warns.

"It's nothing," I repeat with a little more strength behind it.

"Okay… just… don't do anything stupid. I won't rescue you from Zach if you fuck this up."

"I'm not going to fuck anything… u-up," I hesitate as Kas joins me. Her hair is wet from the shower, her face clear of makeup, and her body clad in an almost see-through vest and a pair of tiny shorts.

She falls down onto the other sofa and props her feet up on the coffee table, putting her bare legs on full display. I can see all the way down to her… Nope. Do not look.

When I glance up, I find her amused eyes staring back at me. She winks before reaching for the TV remote and turns it on.

"Spike. Spike." My voice being called eventually drags me from my daze.

"Y-yeah."

"Speak to Zach before he has a reason to take you out, yeah?"

"I don't know what—"

"Go on, keep lying to me. I dare you."

"What! I'm not…"

"Watch your back, Spike. And keep it in your fucking pants." Without another word, the fucker hangs up, although not before I hear his laughter down the line.

"Arsehole," I mutter, ending the call and throwing my phone down on the sofa. I tip my head back and blow out a slow breath.

"Problem?" Kas asks innocently.

"Yeah… it started when I found you up on that fucking stage."

"Ah, you're welcome." She chuckles and continues flicking through the channels.

Dragging my head up, I look over at her. "Any chance you could put more clothes on?"

"Nope."

CHAPTER NINE

KAS

I WATCH Spike as he sits, uncomfortably tense, on the opposite sofa, and I can't help but smile.

"I could have taken care of all that, you know?"

His eyes remain on the TV, refusing to look at me. "We're not having this conversation. As far as I'm concerned, tonight never happened," he mutters.

"Think that all you like, but you're only lying to yourself."

Shifting, I lay out on the sofa, getting comfortable for the film I've just found to watch. My movement forces him to look over once more, and my skin tingles as his eyes run the length of me.

It was mean of me to come out here wearing quite so

little, but knowing how much it would wind him up made it too tempting.

"Who did your ink?" he asks suddenly. They're not the words I was expecting.

"Loads of people. As I'm sure you can see even from over there, some could do with a little work."

He continues to study me, his attention making my temperature soar. If it weren't for his interest, I'd probably be cold, wearing so little.

"I could definitely improve a few."

"You think you've got the skills?"

He chuckles. "Oh, Tiny. I know I have. No one's ever disappointed when I get my hands on them."

Heat floods my core. He may not have touched me yet, but I already know his words are true. I was desperate to feel his touch back in that room earlier, but the fucker kept his hands well clear of me.

He's impressing me with his ability to deny himself what he so clearly wants. It's admirable, it really is. And that only makes my need to win stronger.

"Maybe I'll get to find out one day, when you stop being such a stick in the mud." I keep my eyes on the TV, but it's impossible to miss him sitting forward in disbelief.

"Excuse me, I'm not a stick in the mud."

"Whatever you say."

His mouth opens to argue, but he must think better of it because he falls back against the sofa with his arms folded over his chest as he sulks.

We both remain silent as the film starts. I turn the volume up until the sounds of gunshots and people's screams fill the flat.

"I didn't have you down for a shoot 'em up fan," Spike says when the first advert break starts.

"Why, do I look like a rom-com kind of girl to you?"

"You're a girl. I thought it was in your genes or some shit."

"Stereotypical much?" I mutter as he pushes from the sofa and disappears toward the kitchen.

"I just thought all females wanted that, the happily ever after those kinds of films always give you," he says, continuing to dig himself into the hole he started before he left. "Drink?"

"Sure, whatever you're having." I watch as he grabs a glass and pours me a generous amount of his Jack. "In case you hadn't noticed, I'm not the hearts and flowers, must-have-a-happily-ever-after kind of girl. Don't tell me that you're that kind of guy." He's already tried to tell me that he's not. Although I don't believe it for a second, I can't deny that I'm not curious about his reasons for saying so—or more specifically, who turned him off the idea.

"Fuck no."

"And why is that, exactly? I thought a guy of your age would be all about settling down and filling a woman with his seed."

"I can get on board with the last part of that sentence, just not with one woman."

I study him as he focuses his attention back on the TV. He chews on his cheek as if he wants to say more but isn't allowing himself.

"Who was she?"

He gives me a double take before my words must register. "Who was who?"

"The woman who broke your heart." I try again.

"Who says there was a woman?"

"Your body language. Your refusal to answer the question."

"Whatever. The film's starting again."

I study him for a while longer as I sip my drink. He knows I'm looking at him, but at no point does he turn back to me.

"It's a shame, if you ask me. You're a catch."

"Oh yeah?" he asks with a smirk. "Is that why you're putting so much effort into *catching* me?"

A laugh falls from my lips. "Me? No. I just want a bit of fun, and I have it on good authority that you're an expert in that department."

His lips part, but he doesn't respond. Instead, we silently watch the film, the chemistry left over from the strip club crackling between us.

When the credits start to roll, I decide I've tortured him enough for one day and excuse myself to bed.

"If you're cold in the night, you know where I am," I say with a wink before I disappear from his sight.

"I'll keep that in mind," he calls behind me.

I HAVE no idea what the time is when I finally pry my eyes open the next morning, but I know it's late. The sun is already high in the sky, the strength of it warming my room nicely.

Rolling over, I find my phone on the bedside table and turn it on. I'd switched it off before my shift last night and never got around to powering it back up again after the drama that ensued with Spike.

The second it gets a signal, the messages start coming through.

"Fuuuuck," I groan to myself as message after message from Jodie flashes up on the screen.

I meant to tell her that I'd left, but I kind of forgot.

With a wince, I open the final message from her that demands to know if I'm still alive or not. Guilt eats at me that she'd have been awake all night worrying about me while I was here in the most comfortable bed I've ever slept in, getting well over my required eight hours.

My fingers fly over the keyboard as I reply to tell her that I'm fine and that I'll ring her once I've had coffee.

Pushing from the bed when I hear movement out in the living area, I pull my hair out of my face and secure it in a messy bun. After making sure my tits haven't escaped my vest during the night, I pull my door open.

The scent of breakfast wafts down to me and my stomach rumbles.

Spike can cook?

I nod to myself as I head for the kitchen. I could really get used to living here.

"This smells amazing," I say, stepping up to him and running my hand down his back where he stands at the cooker. His entire body tenses at my contact, and I smile.

"I'm glad you think so. Hungry?"

I press myself against his side and look up at him. "Sure am, the bacon will be perfect for after what I have in mind."

"Kas," he groans, unhooking my arm from around his waist and stepping away from me to grab two plates with buttered bread on them.

Resting back against the counter, I watch as he moves

effortlessly around the kitchen in his shorts and white shirt. I can see the darkening of the tattoos that are inked across his back and shoulder blades, not unlike mine. The muscles ripple making me wish I was still pressed up against him.

"Sauce?" he asks, holding out the bottle of ketchup for me.

Stepping up to him, I take it and flip the lid before aiming it at the bread.

I squeeze, but nothing happens. I put a little more force into it, and the sauce shoots out the end, covering the bread, plate and counter.

"They always blow their load too fast," I mutter, reaching for a cloth while Spike explodes with laughter beside me. "What are you laughing at?" I ask when I turn back to him. "I bet you're just as bad as the rest of them."

He puts his knife down from cutting his sandwich and turns to me. "Firstly, I'm concerned about the number you're talking about here."

"Do you hear me asking about the number of notches on your bedpost?" I ask, my eyebrow almost hitting my hairline.

"Noted. Secondly." He leans in, his breath tickling down my neck, making my nipples pebble against the thin fabric of my vest. "I can go all night long, baby girl."

I can't stop the shudder that runs the length of my spine at his words. I do, however, manage to swallow down the groan that threatens to rumble up my throat.

"I'll believe it when I see it, old man. Thanks for this." I swipe my plate from the counter, and with as much sass and swing to my hips as possible, I take it over to his small table.

After clearing his throat behind me, he follows, bringing his plate and two mugs of coffee, and drops down on the other chair.

"I really needed this," I mumble around a mouthful of delicious salty, smoked bacon.

As I take another bite, the sauce squirts out onto my lip. Spike's eyes lock onto it the second I move the sandwich.

"Whoops." I make a show of wiping it off with my fingertip and then sucking it into my mouth.

His eyes follow my fingers before they darken.

"Fuck," he barks, pushing the chair out behind him and walking away from me. "I'm going out."

"I hope it wasn't something I said." I can't help the amusement that fills my voice. He just makes all of this too easy.

Looking back over his shoulder, he narrows his eyes at me. "I can send you back to the squat as fast as I took you away, you know."

"Yeah, but you won't," I say confidently.

He leaves the room, and feeling like I should probably pull my weight, I set about cleaning up.

He's only gone a few minutes, and when he returns, his hair is styled—although still a total mess—and he's wearing fresh clothes.

"Hot date?"

"Something like that." He swipes his keys from the bowl and pockets them and his phone. "Do me a favour, yeah?"

"Depends what it is."

"Don't fucking leave this flat."

"Or what?" I sass.

"Tiny," he sighs, "just do as you're fucking told. I don't want to have to rescue you twice in two days."

"Huh, I thought that was Titch."

A wide grin covers my face, but all he does is shake his head.

"Just stay put. I'll only be a few hours."

I salute him as he leaves, but he doesn't see it.

After finishing up in the kitchen, I fall down onto my bed and grab my phone.

Jodie answers on the first ring.

"Where the fuck are you?"

"I'm not explaining over the phone. Coffee?"

"Sure, where?"

"The usual, thirty minutes."

"Okay, sure."

"Jo?"

"Yeah. Can you... uh... make sure no one follows you?"

"Why would they... shit. Is Jet still on your case?"

"Yeah, fucker decided I needed to pay up early. I'll explain all when I see you."

I SMILE like a naughty little kid as I pull the front door open and make my way down the stairs.

I almost expect my phone to start ringing and for him to demand I go straight back up. I've no idea how he'd know, but I'm sure he'd find a way if he could.

I glance at Louisa's closed door. That would probably be how he finds out.

I hot foot it out of the building and down the street a

little, just in case she chooses that exact moment to appear.

I jump in the Uber I'd ordered before leaving the flat and sit back with a sigh.

I shouldn't have allowed Spike to take me away like he did yesterday. I was too blown away by it all and then the drama that was my shift after to think of much else. But as the car heads toward our usual meeting place on the other side of the city, I remember the promise Jodie and I made each other not so long ago.

That when we left that place, we'd do it together.

My nails dig into the skin of my thigh as I realise just how much I've fucked up here.

"Shit," I bark, startling the driver. "Sorry," I mutter, feeling bad for giving him a heart attack.

"No worries, sweetheart. You need to get something off your chest?" he asks.

Great, I've got one of those drivers who thinks he should have been a therapist.

"No, no. I'm good, thanks."

I look out the window as the city passes by and think about my life. I'm unemployed and basically being babysat by my brother's mate.

I blow out a slow breath as I think about Dakota telling me in not so many words that there was no longer a position for me at her club. She also made sure to explain how she'd speak to the other owners she knew to ensure I couldn't go running straight to those.

I understand why they both did it. I don't want to be stripping any more than Spike wants me to be, but I have a debt that's not going anywhere anytime soon.

Finally, the car pulling to a stop drags me from my thoughts, and when I focus once again, I find Jodie standing by the entrance to our favourite waffle shop, waiting for me.

She smiles when she spots me, but my heart drops when I notice it doesn't meet her eyes.

I don't know why I'm surprised. She has every right to be pissed with me right now.

"Ah, so you really are still alive and in one piece."

"I'm so sorry, Jo."

"I need caffeine and sugar before we hit the heavy stuff."

"Let's do it then."

We order our usual and find a seat at the back of the relatively small café so that I can at least attempt to hide.

No sooner has my arse hit the chair than I've scooped up my first bit of waffle covered in vanilla ice cream and a lashing of salted caramel sauce. The bacon sandwich I had not so long ago is well forgotten as I savour the sweetness.

"I'm waiting," Jodie asks once she's swallowed her first mouthful.

"Ugh so... one of Zach's friends was at the club on Saturday night. He dragged me from the stage. It was mortifying. Anyway, after a dressing down from him, he walked me out so that I could head home, only guess who was waiting for me?"

"Jet?" she guesses correctly.

"Yup. He decided he wanted to take payment in another form." Jodie gasps in horror. "He didn't get very far, because Zach's mates beat the shit out of him."

"Fuck." The fear on her face matches what I feel beneath the surface. I might appear not to be fazed by this, but that would be a big fat lie.

I know that Jet is waiting for me and that he'll strike

when I least expect it. I've no doubt both Spike and Titch are on his hit list too, after what they did. Jet's not one to take that kind of thing lying down.

"Yep."

"So then what?"

"Spike took me back to his place. Then, because he's an interfering arsehole, he followed me home the next morning and point-blank refused to let me stay at the house. He made me pack my stuff and took me back to his place."

"Sounds like a white knight story if I've ever heard one."

"Funny you should say that, because he has tried locking me up in his tower."

"How'd that go?"

"I climbed out the window so I could do my shift." Her brow rises, sensing that there's more to the story, which of course there is.

I relay the rest of the night, much to her amusement.

"You fucked him?"

"No," I sulk. "He's too focused on being a good friend to Zach. He's getting close to breaking though, I can feel it."

"Sounds like you've had a good ol' feel." I can't help but burst out laughing as she waggles her eyebrows at me.

"Here's hoping," I say, lifting my mug to cheers with hers.

"This is probably a stupid question but... is he hot?"

"Fucking smoking," I admit with a smile.

"Zach will kill you, you know that?"

"Nah, he'll kill Spike for ever touching me. That's if Jet doesn't get to us first, of course."

The colour drains from Jodie's face at the mention of him again.

"You're not going to out-run him, you're aware of that, right?"

"Yep. I just need to figure out a way to pay him off."

"Talk to Zach," she says, like she hasn't already suggested it a million times since this all came about.

"Not happening. I sort my own problems."

"That's just it though, isn't it? It's not yours, it was your mum's. Please, just let someone help you before this goes too far."

I shake off her concerns, but I can't deny that they only fuel the fear within me. I know this isn't going to end well, yet I'm still not willing to take the easy way out.

We move on to safer topics, like her college course and the teacher she's lusting after, and by the time we leave, I'm feeling much more relaxed. Well, until I stop on the path to find my Uber because a shiver of awareness runs down my spine.

I shake it off as I say goodbye to Jodie, but the feeling never leaves.

CHAPTER TEN

SPIKE

MY FIRST DESTINATION as it is every Monday is to my grandad.

I climb off my bike, lock the helmet into the top box, and make my way toward where I know he'll be waiting for me.

A few friendly faces smile at me and say hello as I pass them. They might all live here, but I'm somewhat of a regular. Since my grandad moved into this place, it's like my family quadrupled overnight. I'm not complaining, seeing as most of my life he's been my only relative.

I duck into the summer room and look directly at his seat that overlooks the pond and water feature in the stunning gardens beyond.

My heart drops into my feet when I find it empty. My heart begins to race that something is wrong with him and he hasn't let anyone know.

This place isn't a nursing home, but there are always carers on hand should any of the residents need some assistance. If something was up with him, then they know to call me straight away.

"Ah, is it Monday already?" Maureen asks from her spot at the table where she's working on what looks like the world's most complicated puzzle. "Don't look so worried, sweetie. He's only visiting the bathroom."

Every muscle in my body relaxes at her words.

"Fancy giving an old lady a hand?"

"You're not old, Maureen," I say, pulling out the chair beside her. "You don't look a day over thirty-five."

"As much as I appreciate that, sweetie," she coos, tapping the back of my hand with her cool one, "you're a rubbish liar, and I can see right through you."

I chuckle at her as a shadow falls over us.

"How many times have I got to tell you to stop chatting up my ladies, son?"

"Gramps," I say, pushing the chair out and pulling him into my arms.

"Don't take away my eye candy, Phillip," Maureen complains behind me.

"I thought you'd popped your clogs, old man." As I say the final two words, all I hear is Kas' voice in my head.

Shaking the thoughts away, I follow my grandad over to his seat and pull up my own.

"So, what's new in the tattoo world then?"

I chat away about the clients I've had this week, along with the designs I've done. He listens to every word like I'm telling him the world's secrets. He's always been the same. Even when I was a kid and talked more shit than I can imagine, he always listened to every word, savoured every memory with me.

"When are you going to book me an appointment?" he asks, just like he has since the day I expressed my interest in my chosen career.

"Not gonna happen, old man," I joke.

"Why not? You know I want to die with your ink on my skin." My stomach twists at his mention of death. I hate that it bothers me so much. He's still relatively young but the idea of being left all alone in the world has always scared me. I guess it's just how it is when you're brought up by grandparents—you've got to accept that it might happen sooner than you'd like.

I think of Kas and how she lost the only parent she'd ever known long before her time, and my heart aches for her. She's too young to have been forced to deal with that. It's one thing having a parent die, but to overdose?

I blow out a breath, a move that my gramps doesn't miss.

"What's up, son? You look like you've got the weight of the world on your shoulders."

"It's nothing," I argue.

"Waaaaait," he says, a shit-eating grin appearing on his face. "Is it a girl?"

I open my mouth to respond, but apparently I'm too slow, because my slight pause gives him all the answer he needs.

"Oh, it is." He rubs his hands together in delight while I silently groan. "I've been waiting for this day for so long." The delight on his face makes my heart drop. He wants nothing more than for me to find a nice young lady to settle down with—his words, not mine.

"Yeah, it's to do with a girl, but," I say in a rush before he gets carried away with himself, "it's not like you're thinking."

"No?" he asks, disbelief written all over his face. "Enlighten me. I've got all day."

Knowing that there's no way out of this now, I sit back in my seat and reluctantly give him the basics of the situation with Kas.

"Well, that's quite a story," he says after a few seconds of silence once I've finished. "You need to talk to Zach. She's clearly not going to do it."

No shit.

"I know," I agree. "I'm heading there next."

"So… is she pretty?" he asks with a twinkle in his eye.

I roll my eyes at him. "Gramps, she's ten years younger than me. She's basically a kid."

"And yet, she's not. She's an adult, and as far as I'm concerned, age is just a number. You're only as old as how you feel."

"Around her, I feel as if I'm ancient," I mutter.

"Nonsense."

"She's Zach's sister. She's off-limits," I say, much like I did earlier—which he chose to ignore.

"That may be so, but I've not seen that look on your face when you talk about her for a lot of years. It would be a shame to see it go to waste."

"And, I think that's my cue to leave." I push to stand, ready to say goodbye, but as I get closer, he snatches up my hand, making me look at him.

"Stop being so scared. History doesn't always repeat itself."

I open my mouth to ask how he knows that, but I know it's pointless. I'll just get the same words he always says.

Stop writing things off before you've even given them a chance.

"Yeah, I know," I say weakly, hoping it'll get him off my case.

"Be honest with Zach. He'll appreciate hearing it now rather than later."

"Thanks, Gramps. Same time next week?"

"You got it. Unless you're otherwise engaged, of course." He winks, and a small part of me dies at what he's suggesting.

"Bros over hoes, Gramps. Bros over hoes," I mutter as I make my way out, much to his amusement.

I say goodbye to Maureen, who gives me a knowing smile—I'm assuming from having eavesdropped our entire conversation.

"She sounds like a firecracker, Spike. They're always the most fun."

With colour staining my cheeks, I make my way out of the building and toward my bike.

I guess there's no time like the present than to go and tell Zach all of his sister's secrets. I guess only time will tell as to which will cause me bodily harm first.

As is almost always the case on a Monday, Rebel Ink is in darkness as I pull up in front of the building and kill the engine.

I look up to the flat above, but I don't see any movement. A little bit of hope trickles in that he won't be here and I'll be able to get out of this.

I know it would make me a total pussy, but Zach's a perceptive little fucker, and I have a feeling he's going to see through me. I might have managed to resist so far, but fuck if I've not had plenty of less than admirable thoughts about his little sister, especially when her all but naked body was pressed up against mine.

"Fuck," I mutter, pushing my key into the lock and letting myself in.

My cock swells as I think about that white lace lingerie set she was wearing last night. I assume it was meant to make her look innocent, much like the school uniform the night before. But fuck, the way she moved... that was anything but innocent.

I clear my throat as I begin to climb the stairs to his flat. I need that image out of my head before this gets out of hand.

Rapping my knuckles against his front door, I wait for a response.

Nothing.

That little bit of hope I felt outside comes rushing back.

Pulling my phone from my pocket, I find his name and hit call.

He picks up after only two rings.

"Hey, man. I'm outside your place. Where are you?"

"I've had to come up to Manchester to sort some shit out in the studio."

"Oh, okay."

"I-is everything all right?" he asks, concern lacing his voice. I hadn't meant for my words to come out sounding quite so dejected.

"Yeah, yeah. I was just calling in on the off-chance. Any ideas when you'll be back?"

"I guess that depends on why you're so keen to see me. You're not about to hand your notice in, are you?" he asks lightly, but I hear the hesitation.

"What? No, never. You aren't ever getting rid of me, man."

"Thank fuck for that. So, you're good, yeah?"

"Yeah, man. I'm great. I'll see you when you're back. Biff with you?" I ask in an attempt to take the heat off me.

"Of course. I'm not about to leave her with you horny fuckers."

"Fuck off, man. Neither D nor I will be going after your girl."

"And for that, I'm fucking grateful. Titch is already playing with fire," he jokes.

"Nah, they're perfect for each other. In a weird kind of way," I admit. Seeing my boy so whipped by a woman has been weird. He always said he wanted something serious, but I guess my own fear of commitment meant I didn't really think he meant it. I don't trust women—not with my heart, anyway—and I kind of thought he was the same. Clearly not.

"Weird, yeah. That's one way to put it. Listen, I've gotta go, man. I'll see you in a couple of days, yeah?"

"You got it."

We hang up, and I rest back against the wall, kicking myself for being a pussy and not just telling him.

There's something fucking wrong with me.

Seeing as I've now got a house guest, I stop off at a shop on the way home to pick up food and other bits she's probably going to expect. I even go to the extent of getting her some girly toiletries, seeing as I noticed she's yet to litter my bathroom with the shit. I can only assume, knowing where she came from, that she didn't have any.

I grab something for dinner and a new bottle of Jack before heading to the checkouts.

Stupidly, I didn't think anything of it all day, but as I push the key into the lock of my flat, I'm suddenly very aware that she could have ignored my final warning.

I tell myself I'm just being paranoid. Kas might be many things, but I don't think stupid is one of them.

"Kas," I call the second I have the door open.

I look around the room, which is exactly as I left it earlier, minus her.

"Kas?" I ask again, dumping the bags in my hand on the kitchen counter.

My heart sinks as I push her bedroom door open and find it empty.

"Fuck," I bark, racing to the bathroom, followed by my bedroom on the off-chance this is another of her seduction techniques and she's naked on my bed. I find her in neither place, and I start to panic.

Zach will fucking kill me if I brought her here to protect her and still managed to get her hurt.

Pulling my phone from my pocket, I unlock it and open my contacts.

I haven't got her fucking number.

Furious with myself that I never bothered asking for it, I immediately pull up Titch's name and call him in the hope Danni will have her number, seeing as they're technically sisters.

It takes longer than I would like and more explaining than I have time for, but eventually I get her number along with a grilling from Titch about not telling Zach yet.

I know he's right. I should have just told him on the phone, but I didn't, and now here we are.

I hang up the second he rattles the number off to me and immediately dial it.

It rings and rings as I pace back and forth through the living area and kitchen, trying to dispel the dread that's sitting heavier and heavier in my stomach with each passing second.

Eventually, her voicemail kicks in and I hang up. I figure that there's no point in leaving one asking if she's okay when she clearly can't answer the fucking thing.

My fingers grip my phone painfully as I try to figure out what to do.

She's probably fine, a little voice in my head tries to convince me. But no matter how many times I hear the words, I don't believe them for a second.

I told her not to leave.

I told her not to fucking leave, yet once again she's done the fucking opposite.

My teeth grind as my nails dig into my palms.

What the fuck am I meant to do? Watch the news and wait to hear that a young woman's body has been found dead in the fucking Thames?

Falling onto the sofa, I try to come up with a plan, but short of searching the city with a population of somewhere near nine fucking million for one girl, all I can think is that I'm just going to have to wait.

Aside from Danni and Zach, I have no idea who any of her friends are... or where she hangs out, that's not the squat or the club.

That thought causes a lightbulb to go off. I call Pulse and ask to speak to Dakota, but she quickly assures me that she's not seen or heard from Kas since she terminated her employment the previous night.

I could go back to the squat, but then what if she turns up back here perfectly fine while I'm gone?

"Fucking hell." Why did I get involved in the first place?

It would have been so much fucking easier just to walk out of Pulse on Friday night and forget that I ever saw her there.

Sitting forward, I drop my elbows to my knees and shove my fingers through my hair.

This whole thing is a fucking disaster waiting to happen.

The clock on the wall ticks, taunting me with every second that passes and I don't know if she's dead or alive.

Dramatic? Possibly. I've no idea who that guy was the other night, or really why he's after Kas aside from wanting money, but one thing I do know is that his threat is real.

He was dangerous, I could sense it. I could see it in her eyes.

It must be well over two hours later when a key is pushed into the lock and the door is shoved open.

I'm on my feet in seconds.

I'm expecting her to walk in and wonder what the hell is wrong with me. That all of my stress has been unwarranted. But the second I get a look at her, I discover that I was very, very right to be concerned.

"Kas," I breathe, racing toward her.

"I'm fine," she argues.

"Fine?" I spit, allowing her to step farther into the flat and close the door behind her. I take in the bruises that are already colouring her face and the swelling around her eye. "You're black and blue. And fucking bleeding." Lifting my hand, I brush my thumb beneath her bottom lip to wipe away a trail of blood.

"It's nothing I can't handle."

"Bullshit." I follow her as she makes her way to the kitchen, dumping her bag on the counter.

"It was just a warning."

"Words are a warning, Kas. Someone raised a fucking hand to you. That's *more* than a warning."

She sighs, reaching for the drinks cupboard.

"No," I bark, my fingers wrapping around her upper arm and pulling her back to face me. "Tell me what happened. Why did you leave?"

She hesitates for a second, but in the end her lips part. "I just went to meet a friend. The one I lived with. To tell her what had been happening and why I'd suddenly abandoned her."

"I told you not to leave," I seethe.

"Yeah, well. I did."

My teeth grind as I stare at her.

"It was fine. We had coffee, and then right before I went to get in an Uber to come back, some guy grabbed me."

"Him?"

"No, one of his goons. He just reminded me that Jet is waiting. Made sure I'm not going to forget anytime soon." She gestures to her face and something explodes inside me.

"This is fucking bullshit, Kas," I bellow, the volume making her wince. I knew I should have called the police to stop it getting this far.

CHAPTER ELEVEN

KAS

I DON'T NEED to see Spike's wild, fury-filled eyes, or hear his angry tone, to know that I fucked up today. I can feel it.

"Spike," I sigh.

"No. Don't fucking *Spike* me. I've been sitting here for hours, wondering if you were dead in a fucking ditch somewhere, and how the hell I was going to explain to your brother that I allowed it to happen."

"It's not your fault."

"No? I'm meant to be protecting you," he shouts, making me rear back again.

"I never asked you to. You were the one who dragged me here. I was perfectly happy with my old life."

"Happy? Living in a squat and running from some fucking drug lord or whatever the fuck he is? Yeah, sounds like a great fucking life, Kas."

"Fuck you, Spike. I don't judge you."

He laughs, but it's low and menacing. "No? You judge me every time you fucking look at me. You think I'm easy, that I'm a man-whore. That's the reason you keep throwing yourself at me, right? You're testing me."

All the words I want to say to him stick in my throat as I stare into his dark eyes.

"Exactly," he spits when I fail to find a response. "Come on." His fingers wrap around my wrist, and I gasp in pain.

Lifting my hand, he pulls my sleeves up and stares down at the dark bruising that's forming from where that arsehole held me.

"Motherfucker," he grunts, but instead of him walking off and expecting me to follow, my feet are suddenly lifting from the ground.

"What the hell do you think you're doing?"

"Shut up, Kas."

"Why?"

"Because I'm fucking telling you to."

"And what if I don't?" I sass, unable, even now, not to taunt him.

"I'll make you."

I pull my head from where it was resting against his shoulder in shock, but when I look into his eyes, all I find is desire staring back at me.

My stomach clenches as heat races between my thighs. The need to keep defying him, to keep talking back fills me just so I can find out what it is exactly he'll do to keep me quiet.

Just as I'm about to part my lips to respond, he releases me.

The second I'm placed on the edge of my bed, I miss his contact. A shiver runs through me as he steps away, taking his warmth with him.

"Stay there."

My sudden coldness is forgotten the second I watch his denim-clad arse walk out of my room. My blood damn near reaches boiling point as my imagination goes into overdrive.

By the time he's come back, I've shed my hoodie and am sitting in my skirt and t-shirt. The fabric has risen up my thighs, exposing almost all of my legs, but he doesn't seem to notice as he lowers to his knees before me and drops his supplies to the floor.

"What are you—" His dark eyes look up at me through his lashes, and my words falter.

"I'm fucking looking after you. What do you think I'm doing?"

I watch silently as he dips a cotton ball into a small bowl of water and lifts it to my face.

I want to back away, to tell him not to bother. No one's ever done this for me before, not even Mum in her more lucid times. But I'm powerless to resist and stay exactly where I am, waiting for him to clean me up.

It might only be a cotton ball, but I can't help flinching when it connects with my cut lip.

"Shit, I'm sorry," he whispers, thinking that he hurt me.

How do I even begin to explain that the pain is nothing? I'm used to the pain. It's his soft, caring actions that are affecting me more.

His eyes hold mine, despite the fact that he should

probably be looking at what he's doing. I feel like he's trying to tell me something without actually saying the words, but I can't quite get a read on him.

"I'm so fucking mad at you right now," he finally grates out, breaking the almost unbearable silence that had fallen between us.

The overwhelming need to apologise to him comes over me, but I bite the words back. I don't owe him one. I'm my own woman and make my own choices. Okay, so today's choices may not have been the best, but I needed to see my friend, and it's not like I wasn't aware that Jet and his goons wouldn't be far behind. Sadly, it's currently a very real and almost normal part of my life.

I let out a sigh and drop my shoulders, suddenly exhausted from the day's events.

Spike never once takes his eyes off me. It's as unnerving as it is comforting.

"I'm fine," I say in what I hope is a reassuring tone.

"That's not the point, Kas."

"No? So what is the point?"

"I... I want to keep you safe." His voice is quiet, like he doesn't really want to say the words out loud.

"Why? Because you think it's what my brother would want?"

"Trust me, your brother wouldn't be too impressed with my thoughts right now."

"Oh?" I ask, tilting my head to the side, causing his hand to fall from my lip, the ball dropping from his fingers as he lowers it.

"How much does it hurt?" he asks, cupping my jaw and very gently rubbing his thumb over where that fucker hit me.

"Not enough to stop me from doing anything."

His eyes search mine as if he's trying to find a reason to put an end to this, to back away, but I fear we're both already in too deep.

When his gaze drops to my mouth, I can't help running my tongue along my bottom lip. I swallow the gasp I want to let out when I hit the cut and the taste of copper fills my mouth.

His own tongue sneaks out to match my own. The sight has my heart racing and my fingers twisting in the sheets beneath me.

His eyes drop once more and he locks onto something on my t-shirt.

"W-what?" I ask, wondering what's so exciting about the white fabric.

"Blood. You've got blood on your..."

Ripping my eyes from his, I glance down to see that he's right.

Without thinking, I wrap my fingers around the hem and pull it up and over my head.

"Jesus, fuck," Spike barks, standing from his crouched position on the floor.

I follow his line of sight to find purple bruises on my ribs.

"It's—"

"Do not tell me that it's fucking fine."

I shrug, not having any other words for him.

"Fuck. I shouldn't... fuck." He lifts his hands to his hair and tugs harshly as he stares down at me. His chest is heaving, the torment evident in his eyes, but clearly the reasons for holding back aren't quite strong enough, because not a second later he is on me.

His knee presses into the mattress beside my thigh,

his fingers wrap around the back of my neck before twisting in my hair, and his lips find mine.

The contact is light at first, and I start to think he's going to pull away, regretting this impulsive decision, but the second I reach out and fist his shirt in my hand and tug, he loses control.

His lips part, as do mine—greedily—and his tongue dives into my mouth. I waste no time in twisting mine with his as he begins to devour me.

All too gently, he lays me back against the mattress. His hand remains tightly in my hair while the other lands on my waist, dropping down to my arse then thigh so he can wrap it around him when he presses his weight on top of me.

His kiss never falters. It's dirty, wet, needy, and I fucking love it.

My fingers find the hem of his shirt and I slip my hands under, desperate to feel more of him than just his lips.

His skin is burning hot when I make contact, and I can't help wondering if he feels the same about mine because he flinches the second I touch him.

His lips pull from mine just a fraction as his dark, lust-filled eyes stare down at me. His kiss-swollen lips are parted, his breath racing over my face.

Panic starts to fill me that he's about to put the brakes on this, and I scramble to do something that's going to keep him here with his body pressed up against mine.

Gripping onto the bottom of his shirt, I pull, hoping he'll get the idea and take over.

Thankfully, after a second, he does. Reaching

behind his head, he pulls the fabric off in one smooth motion and drops it over the side of the bed.

He takes my face in both his hands, his thumb gently tracing the cut on my lip.

"Fuck, are you okay?" His eyes are full of concern, regret even, but his voice is deep and rough to the point that it sends shivers down my spine. He needs this just as badly as I do right now, and I'm sure as shit not letting him walk away now he's here.

"More than okay. Now, as you were." I might only be small, but when I push against his shoulders, he willingly falls back against the bed, allowing me to straddle his waist and take matters into my own hands.

A smirk tugs at his lips as he watches me. I can see the anger and concern racing through him as he drops his eyes down my body and takes in the bruises that today has left behind. He needn't worry though, because with his hands on me, I don't feel them in the slightest.

Needing to move things along slightly, I lift my hands behind me, ready to remove my bra, but the second they move, he sits forward, gently wrapping his fingers around them.

"No," he whispers in my ear, sending goosebumps racing across my skin. I tense, thinking that he's saying no to all of this, but I soon relax when he speaks again. "I undress you, Tiny."

"Oh," falls from my lips, but it's no more than a sigh of anticipation.

Flipping us once more, I land on my back with Spike straddling my body. When he lowers this time, his lips don't find my own. Instead, they go straight for my neck.

He kisses down until he hits my collarbone before licking back up again.

"Mmm..." he murmurs. "You taste like heaven." His words have heat pooling between my thighs, and I can't help squirming in an attempt to relieve the pressure.

It's a move he doesn't miss, and when he lifts I find that satisfied smirk firmly in place.

I only get to appreciate it for a flash, because no sooner have I recognised it then he's moved.

His soft lips kiss down my chest until he licks around the lace edging of my bra.

"Spike, please," I beg, arching my back and offering myself to him.

The slow pace he's setting is fucking killing me.

His eyes lock on mine as he tucks a finger inside the lace and tugs until he exposes my breast.

I hold his stare until he wraps his lips around my nipple. All I can do as the sensation overwhelms me is to throw my head back and moan in pleasure.

This has been a long time coming. I need him to take me, possess me, own me more than I need my next breath.

"Yes," I cry out when he gives the other the same attention. "More, please. More."

His hand slips around my back and makes quick work of the clasp of my bra before pulling the scrap of fabric from my body. The second it's gone, it's like he's everywhere.

One of his huge hands palms and squeezes my breast, pinching the nipple between his fingers while his mouth goes to town on the other.

He licks, kisses, sucks and nips at every inch of skin, driving me to insanity.

"Fuck, I need you. Please," I groan, my fingers sliding into his hair in an attempt to push him lower.

"What do you need?" he asks, flashing a look up at me. "Tell me exactly what you need."

"You. Between my thighs," I manage to get out between my already heaving breaths.

"Fuuuuck."

He drops lower, kissing down my stomach and dipping his tongue into my belly button. Tingles fill my body as my temperature soars for what's about to happen.

After popping the button on my skirt, Spike wraps his fingers around the fabric and tugs it over my hips.

The scratch of fabric on my over-sensitive skin only adds to my desperation.

The second I'm naked, he pauses.

His eyes burn a trail over me and I get a flicker of panic that reality has hit him and that this is over at almost the last hurdle.

Needing to do something just in case he's about to realise this has already gone too far, I bend my knees, planting my feet firmly on the bed while parting my knees.

Immediately, his gaze drops to my core.

"Fucking hell, Tiny. You're playing with fire."

"That's good, because I really like getting burned." I've barely got the words out before he's on his knees at the end of the bed and dragging me toward him.

The second I'm right in front of him, he dives for me.

I'm already embarrassingly wet for this man, but the moment he presses his tongue against me and I get the sight of his gorgeous face framed by my thighs, more floods me.

He groans, the rumble of his deep voice vibrating up my spine and pushing me closer to a release that I'm desperate for but equally not ready for. I need this to go on for longer than I fear I'm going to be able to hold out for.

His tongue licks slowly, circling my clit with just the right amount of pressure that has my hands shooting out so I can hold him to me.

"Oh fuck, Spike," I cry when he ups the speed a little and begins teasing my entrance with his finger. "Fuck, fuck, fuck," I chant, desperate for him to slide it deep inside and to find that magical spot. I've no doubt he will; I know all about his reputation from the girls at the club, and fuck if I don't need a bit of that right now.

"You're addictive, Tiny," he murmurs, the vibrations of his voice doing crazy things to me.

"Please," I practically beg as he continues teasing my body, holding me just on the edge of what I know is going to be the mind-numbing release and escape from the world that I really need, if only for a few seconds.

"You're impatient when you're horny."

"I'm always impatient." My grip on his hair tightens until I'm sure I'm about to start pulling lengths out.

He must sense my warning, because he plunges two fingers deep inside me, and in what feels like only a blink of an eye, he's caressing that magical spot.

"Yes, yes, yes," I chant as my release races to the forefront.

"Come, Kas," he demands, his face still firmly between my thighs.

His tongue continues to lick at me as I detonate beneath his touch.

My body locks up as pleasure so intense seems to hit me from every angle. I feel it right to the tips of my fingers.

He doesn't let up until the pleasure drains from my body.

Releasing my grip on his hair, he pulls away from me, wiping his mouth with the back of his hand.

He looks up at me through his lashes, his eyes impossibly dark, hair falling onto his face and lips swollen as his chest heaves.

Fuck.

Aftershocks from my orgasm awaken from the sight alone.

I don't move from my position as he stands to his full height, his eyes never leaving mine. He's trying to tell me something, but fuck if I can work out what it is.

All I can do is pray he's not telling me that was all I was getting. I need more. I need all of him.

I drop my eyes down over his chest, taking in each tattoo as I go, before I get to his waist and his very tented trousers.

Without thinking, I push up from the bed and slide toward him.

"Kas?" he whispers as if he's in a daze when I look up.

"I've got you."

Making quick work of his fly, I push the fabric of his trousers and boxers down his thighs. His hard cock springs free and bobs before me. My mouth waters at the sight. No wonder there was such a huge bulge.

With his eyes still boring into me, I lean forward and lick at the precum glistening at his tip.

"Fuck," he groans, pushing me closer.

I wrap my fingers around his wide length and lick him.

A groan of pleasure rumbles up his throat as I suck him back into my mouth.

His fingers find my hair and grip tightly, but at no point does he try to take control. He just lets me do my thing.

"Shit, Tiny. So good." I run my eyes up his exposed body until I find his own. The intense expression on his face makes me stop and pull back slightly.

"Spike?"

Before he finds any kind of answer, his hands wrap around my waist. I gasp as he presses against my bruises, but thankfully he misses it, and I'm thrown back onto the bed. He sheds the clothing that's been abandoned around his knees and settles between my thighs.

I perch myself up on my elbows and watch as he takes himself in hand and teases my clit with the tip of his cock. Pleasure races through me from that simple move alone, and I fall back to the bed, unable to hold myself up.

"Kas," he says, making me drag my eyes open once more. "I'm... clean."

I swallow as I take in what he's asking me. I should rib him about being a man-whore, but at this moment, all I want to do is believe him.

And I do. Nothing about Spike the past two days has led me to think he's a liar in any way. I'm not sure when it happened, but I realise in those few moments that I trust him implicitly. I also realise that it could be the stupidest thing I've ever done.

"Me too, and I'm on the pill."

"Okay?" he asks one final time, although it seems a little late as he pushes against my entrance.

"Yes, please."

At my request, he surges forward, stretching me open and filling me to the point of breaking. My eyes cross for a second as I still, attempting to get used to the invasion.

"Fuck," he grates out. "So tight. So fucking..." His words trail off, and I'm powerless but to look up at him.

"What's wrong?"

His eyes are wild as he looks back at me. Yes, they're full of desire, but there's so much more within them.

"You're not... not a v—"

I can't help but bark out a laugh as I realise what he's about to ask.

"No, Spike. I'm not a—" My words falter as he bends over me and takes my lips with his. His tongue dives into my mouth as his hips begin to move.

His kiss doesn't stop as his one hand begins to trail around my body, the other clamped onto my hip to hold me in place as he ups the tempo.

His fingers find my nipple, pinching and twisting, giving me just the right amount of pain to go with the pleasure.

"Oh God," I cry, my back arching as he continues to drive into me.

Ripping his lips from mine, he drops his face into the crook of my neck.

"Not God, baby. Just me."

I groan at his words, my hands finding the smooth

skin of his back, my nails raking across until he shudders with delight above me.

"Such a dirty little girl. You're so full of my cock right now."

My muscles contract around him at his dirty words, and another groan rumbles up his throat.

"You like that? You like hearing that my cock is deep inside you right now?"

I moan, his words fuel to my already out of control fire. "Spike," I cry when he sits up and slides his palms under my arse to change the angle. I'm so full of him like this. He's stretching me so wide, hitting places I didn't know existed as he continues to move within me.

"You feel that? So fucking deep, baby."

His fingers grip onto my arse with a painful force, but I don't complain. Instead I do the opposite.

"More, Spike. I need more."

Propping my feet on his shoulders, he begins to really pound into me.

My head hits the headboard with every thrust, but I barely notice as pleasure starts to build to the point at which I worry that I'm literally going to shatter into pieces when it finally hits me.

The only sounds that can be heard throughout the flat are that of our heavy breathing, our low moans of pleasure, and our skin connecting.

"Fuck, Spike. Fuck," I cry when it gets to be too much.

His fingers find my clit, and the sensation has me crashing over the edge.

"Oh fuck, fuck."

Pleasure like I've never known slams into me, pushing away anything other than this moment right here. None of my usual life stresses exist for long, euphoric minutes. It's a really dangerous place to be, and one I fear I'm going to crave a repeat of the second this is over.

I'm just coming down, disappointment already beginning to creep in, when Spike lets out the deepest, most guttural groan I think I've ever heard.

My eyes fly open so I get to experience what he looks like when he falls over the edge.

His head is tipped back, the tendons of his neck straining, his muscles pulled tight with pleasure as he slams into me, one, two, three more times before he growls. His fingers dig into my hips as his cock twitches inside me.

"Fuuuuuck," he cries.

After a couple of seconds, he drops his head, almost startling when he finds me watching him. His eyes run the length of me before locking onto where we're connected as he slips out of me.

"Fuck," he barks once again, but it's no longer filled with pleasure, just anger.

"Stay with me," I demand.

"We can't... I can't..."

"Life's too short for regrets, Spike. Now, stay with me."

It takes him a couple of seconds to make a decision, but I can't help feeling accomplished when he drops down onto the bed beside me.

"Hey," I say, cupping his rough cheek in my hand. "It's okay."

His entire body tenses at my words.

"Stop fucking saying that. Nothing about this is

okay. Look at you. Look at this," he says, gesturing between us.

"I think that... *this*..." I say, scooting closer until the fronts of our bodies are connected from our stomachs down, "looks pretty good right now."

"Damn it, Kas."

"You worry too much."

He shudders as my fingers begin walking over his shoulder and down his arm. When I get to his elbow, I tug until he has no choice but to wrap it around my waist.

"Tiny," he growls. "He's going to kill me."

I assume he means Zach, because no one else in my life would give two shits about this right now.

"Well," I say, pressing a kiss to the side of his mouth, "then we don't tell him." My lips run down his jaw, and despite his pathetic excuse to put an end to this, he tilts his head up to give me access to his neck when I get there.

"That's not how things work between us."

"Then I'll call him tomorrow and explain."

His hand tightens on my waist. "No, it needs to come from me."

"Fine. Whatever. You're not planning on doing it right this second though, are you?"

Slipping my hand down between us, I find his already hard length and wrap my fingers around it.

"N-no. Not right now."

"Good, because I have other ideas."

CHAPTER TWELVE

SPIKE

MY CHEST HEAVES with my exertion as I fall back down on the bed, my muscles lax and my entire body exhausted. It's been a while since I've been worked over quite so well. I guess that's what happens when you end up in bed with a pocket rocket who's ten years younger than you.

Fuck.

I place my arm over my eyes as regrets begin to flood me.

I shouldn't have touched her. I really shouldn't have fucked her, over and over. And, I really shouldn't want to do it all over again.

The patter of her footsteps coming back from the bathroom sound out, but I refuse to move my arm and look at her. I don't want her to read the thoughts that I know must be clear in my eyes and for her to think they're about her. I mean, they are, but she's not the one I'm angry at. That's me. I'm the one who fucked up here, I'm the one who touched the forbidden fruit, and I'm going to have to take the punishment like a man. Once I confess, that is.

The bed dips beside me before her hot little body presses up against my side.

"Spike." Her voice is barely above a whisper. It causes an ache within me that should be long satisfied after the past couple of hours, but it seems my body, or more so my cock, didn't get that message.

Her fingers tangle with mine and she pulls my arm away from my face and around her waist. Her arse presses against my quickly growing cock, and my front presses against her back.

"I should go," I say regretfully.

"Talk to me," she demands, sounding much more put together than I am right now.

Silent seconds tick by as I try to form the words I need to say, but all of them fail me. Being here right now just feels so… right.

I'm not a cuddler after sex.

Well, once I was, but that's a time in my life I refuse to revisit, especially right now.

"I shouldn't be here," I admit eventually.

"But you are. Morals didn't seem to stop you earlier."

"Yeah, well. They should have."

She shrugs in my arms. "Do you hear me complaining?" She wiggles her arse against me, my cock standing to attention at the movement.

"Oh, I heard plenty of moaning, little girl." My lips press against her shoulder and she moans lightly.

She chuckles, the sound making my chest swell.

"I know you keep saying it but... are you really okay? Some of your bruises look pretty painful."

"I'm used to pain, Spike. This is nothing unusual for where I'm from."

I tense, the thought of this happening often making me want to go and hurt someone. "That's bullshit," I spit.

"It is what it is." She sighs.

"Why did it happen? I know you owe him money, but what for?" I ask, it's been eating at me since discovering that motherfucker with his hands on her, but I didn't want to push her for an answer she wasn't willing to give up. Well, things have changed now she's naked in my arms. It's time for a few home truths to come out.

"He's a dealer."

"I guessed as much. But you're not a druggie, so why?"

"Mum." She falls silent for long seconds, and I start to think that's all she's going to say when she eventually speaks again. "She was a mess. I hardly remember a time where she wasn't dependant on either drugs or alcohol. She always made these crazy promises to me. She was going to get clean, we were going to move to the country, she was going to get a good job, and we'd never worry about money again.

"When I was little, I fell for it. But as the years went on, she broke every single promise again and again, I started to realise it was all bullshit. That was our life, and the only one who was going to get me out of it was me."

"I'm so—"

"Don't," she snaps. "I don't want your pity."

I refrain from telling her that I'm not pitying her. I don't think she'd believe me if I did, anyway.

After another long stretch of silence, she begins speaking again.

"She'd pissed off more than a few dealers before she got tangled up with Jet. She had a bad reputation, but he still decided to give her what she needed. He knew he could get payment in other forms, and she was mostly more than willing to do whatever was needed. But then she was gone, and her debt was left unpaid. It fell to me. It took Jet less than a week after she died to send one of his goons after me, demanding money or... other services. Thankfully, I managed to make an agreement that would allow me a little time. Only, it seems that Jet got bored of waiting, because he's calling it in early."

"How much?"

She shakes her head, not willing to tell me.

"Kas," I warn. "How. Much?"

"Thousands," she says on a sigh. "Even with the job at the club, I was never going to pay him back. Not for years, anyway. But now... I've got no chance. I may as well let him do his worst and just hope I come out the other end alive."

"No," I bark. "We'll sort it."

"This isn't your issue, Spike. I'm not a charity case."

"Just let me help," I say, dropping my lips to her bare shoulder once more. "You can pay me back. It can be a loan."

"Not happening."

"Then you leave me no choice." Flipping her on to her back, I pin her hands above her head and stare down into her blue eyes. "I'll tell Zach everything, whether you like it or not."

"No, Spike." She wiggles beneath me, but her strength is no match for mine.

I continue to hold her stare so she can see the strength behind my next words.

"Tonight, we take whatever we need. But tomorrow, everything changes. We put this behind us, we talk to Zach, and we allow you to restart your life."

"And what if I don't want that?"

"You have no choice. I should have done the right thing from the beginning, but it seems I was incapable of denying you."

"And wasn't it worth it?"

My teeth grind with my need to tell her that it was. That tonight has barely scratched the surface for me. But I know it can't happen again. Well, not after tonight.

I've got to do the right thing... tomorrow.

"Spike," she cries as I drop my head and suck her nipple into my mouth.

"Get your fill, little girl. You've got until the sun comes up."

I'VE no idea what time we finally fall into her bed and drag the covers over our bodies. All I do know is that I feel like a damn teenager again. Every inch of her body is imprinted into my memory. I'm not sure if it's a good thing or not, because I fully intend to see through my warning. The second I step from this bed, whatever was between us tonight is over.

I've already betrayed Zach. I won't do it again. I might not be all that choosy when it comes to women, but friends' sisters and exes have always been no-go.

Until now.

Until her.

Fuck.

Kas almost instantly falls asleep. My body is willing me to do the same, but my head spins with all the mistakes I've made over the past few days.

I lie there, tracing one of the tattoos on her arms. It's rough, clearly done by an amateur, and it really needs redoing, but I already know that I can't be the one to do it. Getting her on my chair would be just one more mistake to add to all the others.

I have no idea how long I stay there, telling myself that I need to move and put an end to the night before, but when I do finally make it to the door, the sun has long risen.

My eyes run over her sleeping form. The sheets expose her back, and the sight of Zach's artwork is the last reminder I need of why I'm doing the right thing.

Pulling her door shut behind me, I make my quick walk of shame back to my bedroom, via the bathroom to shower her scent from my body.

Eventually my exhaustion drags me into slumber, and the next time I wake, it's to a pounding on the front door.

Not hearing any movement from Kas' room, I climb out of bed and pull on a pair of boxers.

The house is still silent as I make my way to the front door, so I can only assume she's still passed out.

Without looking through the peephole, I pull the door open to find a concerned looking Zach on the other side.

"What fucking time is it?" I grunt, seeing him totally put together while I feel like I've just been dragged out of bed by my little toe.

"Almost eleven. Busy night?" he asks, looking around me—I'm assuming expecting to find a half-naked woman waiting for me to come back to bed.

The reality of the situation makes my stomach drop.

"Um… something like that." Lifting my hand, I run my fingers through my hair in an attempt to brush out the freshly fucked look that I can only assume I'm rocking. "Is… uh… everything okay?" I ask, my brows pulling together.

It's not all that unusual for him to turn up unannounced, but combined with the look on his face and I'm on full alert.

"I don't know, you tell me. You sounded weird on the phone yesterday, so I…" His words trail off as a door opens behind me.

CHAPTER THIRTEEN

KAS

I KNOW exactly what I'm going to find when I wake up and look at the other side of the bed, but that doesn't stop the rejection setting in when I see that it's empty.

Last night was... I blow out a long breath. Amazing.

I wanted a bit of fun with someone I was confident could do the job right, but what I got was so much more than that. It was everything I needed, and it made me want things I have no right in wanting.

I want more.

I want him.

"Shit," I mutter, shoving my face into the pillow. I instantly regret it because it smells of him. It's bad enough that he's all I can think about, that his touch is all I can feel, his dirty words are all I can hear. Now his scent surrounds me too.

I lie there, staring at the ceiling, when a knock sounds out through the flat.

My eyes go to the door, but I make no effort to move. This is his flat after all, I've no place opening his door and inviting people inside.

When his footsteps eventually plod down the hallway, I sit on the edge of the bed, my feet landing beside his discarded shirt.

Reaching out, I pull it up to my nose and breathe him in. I know it's a mistake the second I do it, but much like the man himself, I'm powerless to resist.

Every part of my body aches as I stand and pull it over my head. I've no idea where the pain from my beating starts and the side effects of a delicious workout end.

Deep male voices ring out, and I run my fingers through my messed-up hair and pull the door open.

I don't even think about who it could be, and the second I step out of the door, I feel instantly stupid for not even considering this as a possibility.

My eyes lock on to Zach's the moment I appear. His chin drops, cutting off whatever he was saying mid-sentence before his eyes harden and his entire body tenses.

"You motherfucker," he roars, and before I can react, he's pulled his arm back and his fist is flying at Spike.

"Zach, no," I cry, racing forward, but it's too late.

Zach's knuckles connect with Spike's jaw, and he goes stumbling back until he collides with the wall.

Not content on just hitting his friend once, Zach growls and races toward him.

He takes another shot. The crunch of Spike's nose fills the flat before blood spurts out of it.

"Zach, that's enough," I cry. "It's not what it looks like." Okay, so that's a total lie and this is exactly what it looks like, but it's all I can think to say.

Zach ignores me, instead focusing his efforts on Spike's ribs until he's doubled over in pain.

At no point does he fight back. I know the reason why, but damn it, I wish he'd help put an end to this.

"Zach," I scream when he pulls his arm back once more. I fly at him, wrapping my hands around his arm in the hope of stopping him.

The second I touch him, he relaxes.

"Stop, please," I beg, quieter than before.

Assuming it's over, Spike slides down the wall, hunched over in pain as blood continues to pour from his nose.

Zach's angry stare turns on me. I swallow nervously. I've only connected with him recently. I have no idea what his temper is like or how he handles situations like this, and I've been in one too many where the guy is a fucking cunt who takes it out on anyone in the vicinity.

"Tell me he didn't do this to you." He points at my lip, and it's the first time I realise just how bad this looks.

"What? No. He would never. Fuck, Zach."

"Then why are you here?" I blow out a breath and look up to the ceiling. "If you fucking tell me you're a couple then I'm gonna—"

"No, no. We're not. He's just been helping me out."

Zach's eyes run down my barely-clad body before turning on his friend, who's still on the floor in just his boxers. Feeling his stare, Spike lifts his head up and I get my first taste of how he felt when he saw me last night.

Zach might be my brother, but right now I want to hurt him.

"Sit on the sofa, Zach. And don't fucking move. I'm going to sort him out."

Zach's lips purse, clearly not impressed with what I'm suggesting, but he can go suck it.

"It's either that or you leave," I spit, taking a step closer to him. I don't for a second think it's threatening in any way—I just hope it shows I'm serious.

His eyes narrow at me before he nods. "Then you'd better start talking. Both of you."

I watch as he backs away from me and falls down onto the sofa. I can't help but smirk when he lifts his hand, inspects his knuckles, and flexes his fingers.

"I really hope that hurts."

He cuts me a look that I'm sure would have others quaking in their boots. I guess it's a good thing that I'm not most people and my big brother doesn't scare me one bit.

Without missing a beat, I run for the bathroom to find the stash of first aid stuff Spike keeps in the cupboard.

I return to a very tense living room a few seconds later, and after collecting a bowl of warm water, I set about doing the same thing for Spike as he did for me last night. Sadly, though, we both already know it's not going to end in the same way with Zach's stare burning into us.

"Spike," I whisper once I've crouched down beside him, "look at me."

He keeps his face away like a petulant child.

"Don't be a prick, let me clean you up."

"I deserved it," he says so quietly that only I will hear it.

"Bullshit. Now, do as you're told."

After blowing out a long breath, he lifts his head, rests it back against the wall, and his eyes find mine.

My breath catches at the pain and regret in them.

There's so much I want to say to him, to reassure him, but while we've got an audience, I think bringing anything up from last night would be an epic mistake.

Silently, I clean him up while the tension hangs heavy in the room. We don't lose Zach's attention, my skin tingles with his stare the entire time I'm on the floor with Spike. I'm not sure what he's expecting us to do, but his warning is more than clear.

After picking everything up, I take it all to the kitchen.

"I'm assuming you'd like a coffee?" I ask Zach. "Not that you deserve it," I mutter, but it's nowhere near quiet enough for him to miss it.

"Please."

I don't bother asking Spike—we all know he needs one right now.

As I put the first mug under the machine, I watch as Spike hauls himself from the floor, and, clutching at his ribs, he moves over to the sofa.

Nothing is said between the two friends. I know Spike is waiting for me to do all the explaining, and although I understand why, I kinda wish he'd just do it for me.

All too soon there are three coffees on the table, and I'm sitting before Zach, who's not so patiently waiting for some answers.

"So..."

This is exactly what I wanted to avoid. I didn't want to drag anyone else into this bullshit with Jet, because I know for a fact that he won't think twice about using others to get to me. The last thing I need is for him to hurt the only remaining family I have.

"Mum was in some trouble." Spike scoffs behind me, but I ignore him. "You know she was an addict, that's no secret. She got involved with some shady dealer when all the others cut her off. She racked up a shit ton of debt with him with no way to pay. Well, long story short, she died, and I inherited her debt and the shady dealer."

"Right..." The vein in Zach's forehead pulsates with frustration as I talk. If the situation weren't so dire, I might laugh at it.

"So, I needed to earn good money, and fast—"

"If you fucking tell me that you're a hooker and that motherfucker has paid for you, I'll lose my—"

"Calm the fuck down, man. You know I don't pay for it."

Zach's face turns damn near purple at Spike's words. I don't think they had quite the effect he was hoping for.

"I got a job as a dancer at Pulse." Zach's mouth opens to say something, but I cut him off. "It's not the first time I've done it, and no one forced me, if that's what you're thinking. Anyway, I'd been there a few weeks, was starting to build up a little cash, and then this motherfucker turns up on a night off and drags me off the fucking stage."

"What?" Zach barks.

"What? I wasn't going to let her stay up there and have all those arsehole guys staring at her like that."

Zach nods at his friend before turning back to me

"Go on," he encourages.

I tell him all about Jet waiting for me and how Spike and Titch saved me, before I explain the house share I was living in.

"It wasn't a house share. It was a fucking squat, Kas," Spike complains. "There was no way I was leaving you there."

"It had done me fine for the previous few years. You might not like it, but I can look after myself, you know."

Zach sags back on the sofa, and Spike and I continue bickering.

"Shut up," he barks eventually. "You're like an old married couple."

We both halt and turn to him.

"Oh no, no. That's not what this is." Spike tries arguing while Zach drills him with a death stare.

"I might be more relieved to hear that if I didn't turn up to find you both looking like this." He gestures between the two of us.

"I can explain," Spike starts.

Zach raises a brow and sips on his coffee.

"I told her to stay put, but your sister doesn't do as she's fucking told, so she went out, got accosted by the arsehole who's after her, and turned back up here looking like that."

"Wearing your shirt?" Zach asks.

"Well, no, but—"

"I borrowed it to sleep in. It's nothing, Zach," I add in the hope that I can dig Spike out of the shit.

I'm not stupid, I knew last night when he told me that everything would change today, he meant it.

"You expect me to believe that?" Zach asks, his eyes trained on Spike.

He shrugs. "Believe what you want. I was trying to help." We both watch as he pushes from the chair and leaves the room. The sound of his door slamming shut vibrates through the flat before it falls silent once more.

Zach turns his blue eyes on me and sits forward, resting his elbows on his knees.

"How much?"

"How much what?"

He rolls his eyes like I'm an idiot. "How much do you need to pay this guy off?"

"I'm not telling you that. It's not your issue."

"Damn it, Kas," he snaps, making me jump. "Let me fucking help you. You don't have to do this alone now."

"And what if I want to?"

His teeth grind, his jaw popping with frustration. "Why would you? This guy is going to seriously hurt you if you don't just pay. I can give you however much you need. Just get the fucker off your case."

"I'm not taking your money, Zach."

He opens his mouth, but no words come for a few seconds. "Fine. Work for it."

"What?"

"Work. For. It."

"Don't be stupid, Zach. What the hell am I going to do at your studio to earn that kind of money, aside from turning one of the back rooms into a den of tricks?" I wink so he knows what I'm getting at, and his face starts to turn purple once more.

"Aside from that suggestion, I don't give a shit what you do. You can clean the place every day if you like or, we could train you up."

"What?"

"Don't even try to pretend that you're not interested. I know you always wanted to go to art school. I saw the drawing of your wings, remember? And as much as I hate to admit it, I think some of our clients would love you."

"You want me to be one of your artists?"

"Why not? I pay off your debts, and you sell your soul to me instead of some drug lord cunt. Sounds like a pretty winning deal, if you ask me."

I sit back, crossing my arms over my chest. "I'll think about it."

His eyes widen in shock. "You'll think about it?" What the fuck is there to think about?"

"Maybe I wanted to be a stripper, did you ever think about that?"

"Does anyone ever *really* want to be a stripper?" he asks so seriously it makes me want to burst into laughter. "You're not stripping, Kas. No fucking way."

"Jesus, you two are a pain in my arse."

"I'm your big brother, it comes with the territory. Just ask Danni."

"Great."

"I need you to do three things for me."

"Go on," I say hesitantly.

"Tell me how much you need." I roll my eyes, but he continues nonetheless. "Do as you're fucking told so you don't end up in a worse state."

"Sure thing, *Dad*."

Zach's teeth grind at my sarcasm.

"And?"

"Don't fuck Spike. I'd hate to have to kill him for touching you."

I swallow nervously, but thankfully he's too busy pushing from the sofa to notice my reaction to his words.

"Zach, I really don't need—"

"Stop being so fucking independent and accept some help, Kas. Just this once. I can make this go away, so let me."

"Fine. I need fifty G."

"Fuck me, Kas. What was she snorting, gold?"

"He's a businessman. He knew no one else would supply her with what she needed, so he tripled the price."

"I'm assuming you need cash?"

"I'm not sure any banks dish out business accounts to drug dealers and gangsters."

"Smart arse. I'll get it as soon as I can, then you'll tell me where to meet this motherfucker and we'll get it sorted."

"You're not meeting him," I say in a rush. "I'll do it. I'm not dragging you into this any more than necessary."

Zach stares at me for a beat, clearly not happy about my suggestion, but eventually, he lets it go—for now, at least.

"We'll talk about it once I've got the money. Come here." He reaches out for me and pulls me into his arms. Unable to resist, I wrap my arms around his waist. "We'll sort this, Kas. You're not alone now, okay?"

I nod against his chest. "T-thank you."

"It's what I'm here for, kid. I'll see what I can sort out for a place for you to stay, too."

"No, Zach. You're already doing enough. I'm okay here." As soon as the words leave my lips, reality hits me. Spike probably needs a paying housemate, not a scrounger. "Actually, yeah, that would be great. But the cheapest you can find, yeah?"

"We'll see." He winks as he steps back. "Call me if you need me. I'm only at the other end of the phone, okay?"

"Sure," I agree, although I have no intention of putting anything else on his shoulders. I didn't even want him having to deal with this.

He walks toward the front door, but before he opens it, he turns and looks down the hallway.

"I'm out, Spike. Sorry for the nose, but take it as a warning. Do not touch my fucking sister." With his warning hanging in the air around us, he pulls the door open and disappears. I quickly close it behind him and lock it.

CHAPTER FOURTEEN

SPIKE

I DON'T LOOK over as my bedroom door opens. I was expecting her, although that doesn't mean I know what to say as she stands there, still dressed in only my t-shirt and waiting for me to respond.

This morning has been fucked up beyond belief.

When I said to her last night that everything would change again today, that wasn't exactly what I had in mind.

My face aches from where he hit me, and my skin burns as her stare continues.

I can't look at her. I can't see the concern that I know is going to be written all over her face. I lied to one of my best friends because of her. Guilt eats at me and swirls around in my gut like an angry tornado. I should have told Zach the truth. *But what good would have come of it?* a little voice says. *There won't be a repeat, so just forget it ever happened.*

"Spike?"

"Leave me alone, Kas."

"W-what?" she stutters, like she might have misheard me.

"You heard me. Shut the door and walk away." My voice is cold, harsh, and I hate it, but it's what needs to happen.

"But—"

"There's no but, Kas. I told you that last night was a one-off. A mistake that never should have happened. An error in judgement. It's best if you forget it happened and just focus on your life."

"An error in judgement?" she asks, an astonished laugh falling from her. "You seemed pretty invested for an error in judgement."

"We all make mistakes, kid." She gasps at the word. I know how much she hates any reference to her being young and naïve. I understand it, but I need her to back off right now so I'm more than willing to use it.

"What if I can't forget, Spike? What then?" she asks, her voice more hesitant than a few moments ago.

"You don't have a choice. Close the door on your way out."

An unbearable tension fills the room as she continues to stare, and I fight like hell not to look back at her.

I might have been getting beat on by Zach, but that didn't mean I missed how fucking hot she looked when she emerged with her messed up bed hair and my shirt skimming her thighs.

"Fine," she huffs after long, uncomfortable seconds, "but this isn't over," she warns, finally slamming the door and leaving me to my misery.

Seconds later, hers slams so loud that the entire flat vibrates with the force.

I can't lie here long, I need to get myself patched up and head to work. Lifting my hand, I rub my thumb over the split in my lip. It's a mistake, because the only image that fills my head is me doing the exact same thing to her last night.

I was out of my mind by the time she appeared, and then to see her looking like she did, knowing that some guy had touched her, hurt her... It stirred something within me that I thought I'd locked down years ago. My need to protect, my need to keep what's mine close and out of harm's way just took over. And it really shouldn't be Zach's little sister.

"Fuck," I whisper-shout into the silence of my bedroom.

Dragging myself so I'm sitting, I catch sight of myself in the mirror propped up against the wall. I look a fucking mess.

The guys at the studio are going to have a fucking field day with this.

Pushing my hair from my eyes, I stand, grab some clean clothes, and slip down the hall toward the bathroom to shower.

The water stings, but the warmth helps soothe my aching muscles, especially my ribs. I know he's not broken any—they don't hurt that bad—but shit, he really went to town.

I understand why. If I had a little sister, I wouldn't want her anywhere near the likes of me either.

Kas doesn't emerge before I swipe my keys from the kitchen counter, so I'm forced to walk to her door.

I might not want to look at her right now for fear of even more vivid reminders of last night—my memories are already bad enough—but I need to tell her I'm leaving and attempt to get her to stay put this time so we don't all spend the next few hours worrying about her.

"I'm going to work. Can you do me a favour?"

"No." I want to laugh at her defiance, but knowing it could end up getting her killed stifles my reaction somewhat.

"Kas, please. Just stay here while I'm gone. I don't want to spend my entire shift worrying about you."

"That's sweet and all, but I didn't think you gave a shit."

My forehead hits the wood of her door. *Of course I give a shit. I give a little too much of one, that's the problem.*

"Please, Kas. For me, for Zach, for your friend, just stay here and keep the door locked. Zach's going to make this go away. Just give him time, and then you're free."

"Great, so in the meantime I'm locked up like your fucking sex slave. I don't think so."

I try to shake the images of us rolling around in her bed out, to forget but I'm afraid I'm not going to be able to. Her taste is still on my tongue, and fuck if my mouth doesn't water for another round.

"You're not a prisoner. We both know you can get out of this place of your own free will. I'm just asking you not to." I don't reference her sex slave comment for fear of me begging her to be just that.

"Whatever. I'll see how I feel."

I open my mouth to argue, but I swallow down the

words. What's the point? She's already made it abundantly clear that she'll do whatever the hell she wants.

"Okay, well, I'll probably be back about ten-ish. I'll bring dinner."

I get no response, so after waiting a few seconds too long for one, I turn and walk away.

I don't bother double locking the door. If she wants out, she'll just go through the window again.

The second I'm out of the building, I'm on high alert. I know they're waiting for her, so it seems likely that they'd have followed her back here. If Jet is the kind of man she makes him out to be, then he'll have his assets covered at all times.

I just have to hope he's not desperate enough to force his way to her.

A shudder runs down my spine at the thought of coming home to find her gone—not because she willingly walked out, but because she was forced.

Climbing on my bike, I rev the engine and allow the vibration to flow through me, to ground me, to push everything away so I can at least attempt to focus on work for the next few hours. Pulling the helmet down hurts like fuck, and as I cuss Zach out, I tell myself that I deserved it anyway.

The drive to the studio isn't all that long, and it's nowhere near enough to help clear my mind. It's still spinning with images of last night and this morning long after I've parked up and pushed through the front door.

"Whoa, what the fuck happened to your ugly face?" Titch asks the second he looks at me from his spot on the sofa in reception.

"Do we have to?" I ask, walking straight past him and out to our little kitchen.

"Biff's gone for coffee," he calls out to me.

"Where's Zach?"

"No idea, upstairs maybe. D's in his room already, if you need a full run down," he jokes.

"Fuck off," I mutter when I emerge with a steaming mug of coffee.

"Well, aren't you in a delightful mood this afternoon. Your clients are in for a real treat."

I cut him with a scathing look.

"Is this what happens when you don't get laid?"

"Who says I haven't got laid?" I regret the words the second they fall from my lips.

"The fact that you've got boss man's little sister living in your flat. Unless..."

"Whatever." I hold up my hand to cut him off and walk down toward our rooms, ignoring mine and going straight for D.

"Spike," he barks behind me. "You'd better not be holding out on me, man."

Letting Titch's voice fade into the background, I knock twice on the door before D calls out for me to enter.

"Whoa, shit. I knew Kas was a feisty one, but fuck, man."

Rolling my eyes, I close his door behind me and fall down on the old sofa he has in the corner.

"What the hell happened?"

"Zach happened," I state.

"Oh shit."

"He turned up this morning and flew off the handle.

I mean, I get it. I'd just stumbled out of bed and so had Kas... wearing my shirt." I wince as I say the words.

"Wearing your shirt. Tell me you didn't, man."

My eyes stay locked on the coffee that's being cradled by my hands.

The silence is all the answer he needs.

"Fuuuuuuck. I thought you were stronger than that, man."

"So did I. Zach doesn't know anything happened, though. I didn't sleep next to her."

"But you fucked her?" he confirms.

"Keep your fucking voice down." My eyes flick to the door in panic.

"Jesus. You need to tell him."

"Yeah, I also kinda like my face." He raises a brow. "It was a one off. It won't be happening again, so it can just be forgotten."

"You really think that's possible? You weren't able to resist her for forty-eight hours."

"I know," I groan, "but you didn't see her, man. She snuck out and he got his hands on her. She looked so beautiful, so broken."

"You're fucked, mate," he says, dropping down onto his wheeled stool and rolling over, a mixture of sympathy and amusement on his face.

"Where is she now?"

"In the flat, I hope."

"You need her to move out."

I open my mouth to agree, but even his suggestion of it sounds wrong. "Where would she go?"

"I know you're trying to do the right thing here, but maybe it's time you took a step back. You clearly don't just have her best interests in mind."

"Ah, fucking hell," I complain, rubbing at my rough jaw in the hope it'll give me some clarity.

"What's different about this girl? You usually move on without so much of a second glance."

"If I knew that, I might not be in this situation."

"Is Zach gonna pay off her debt?"

"I think so."

"Well, let's just hope that happens sooner rather than later, so she can get out of your hair."

"What if I don't want her out of my hair? Shit." I don't mean for the words to come out loud.

"Fucking hell," D chuckles. "You've got a serious problem here, mate."

Thankfully, a knock sounds out on D's door, and I'm forced to get up and head to my own room as he welcomes his first client of the day in.

"You know where I am, man," he says before I disappear from sight.

As I close the door behind me, locking myself in my little sanctuary, I wonder if D might like a new housemate. I'm just not sure if I should be the one to take up residence in his spare room or if I should ship Kas there. D's got more morals than I have. Hell, he's got more than the three of us put together. He'd never touch the forbidden. Unlike me.

My first two clients of the day drag. The tattoos they want aren't half as intricate as I need to fully lose myself in. Every time I hear footsteps or a door opening and closing, I wonder if it's Zach coming to continue our conversation from this morning, but he never shows his face.

That is, until sometime after six o'clock. I've got a break in clients so I can grab some food, and I'm just about to shove my wallet into my pocket to head out when his knock comes. We've worked together long enough to identify each other by that alone.

"Yeah," I call out, somewhat hesitantly.

"Hey. I'm uh... sorry about this morning," he says, gesturing to my face with a wince.

My eyes widen in shock. I was sure he was going to come flying in to deliver another painful message.

"I should be thanking you for taking care of her."

"Um... I didn't really do anything."

"Mate, you dragged her off that stage. Titch said it was pretty epic."

"I'm not sure your sister or Dakota saw it that way."

"Meh, don't care what they think. You did the right thing."

If he knew the whole story, I'm sure he'd be saying something else entirely.

Guilt threatens to engulf me, but I tell myself over and over that it was a one-time thing and it's better for everyone if it's just put in the past and never mentioned again.

"So, are you going to pay this motherfucker off or what?"

"Yeah, I'm sorting it."

"She hasn't told me how much, but that's gotta hurt."

He shrugs. "She's my sister. She's already had a shitty life. She deserves this."

"Couldn't agree more. You should have seen where she was living."

"You should have called me sooner."

"She was too busy giving me the run around. She's a defiant little bitch, your sister."

He chuckles, telling me that he's more than aware.

"She's something, all right. I wish I had a chance to meet the woman who gave birth to us," he says, a sombre expression passing over his face.

"From what I've heard, you didn't miss much."

"She deserves so much more," he repeats.

"There's plenty of time for her to turn it around. She's still young," I add, more to remind myself than Zach.

"I've offered her a job."

"Oh?"

"She's a kick-arse artist. She could do really well here, with the right training."

I swallow at what he might be implying.

"I've already got my hands full with Biff."

"You said it, man."

"Fuck off. You seem to know how to handle her, so I wondered if you wanted to take her under your wing."

"M-mentor her?"

"Yeah. You up for it?"

Fuck.

My heart races as I try to come up with a response that might get me out of this, but if I refuse, he's going to want to know why. If I say yes then... *fuck.*

"S-sure. If you think she's got what it takes."

"I do. Plus, she owes me a few quid now, so she hasn't got a lot of choice."

"When's she starting?"

"The second it's safe for her to step outside of your flat."

"She probably already has," I mutter.

"Oh, she's there. I sent Biff to babysit her."

I can't help but laugh at the serious look on his face.

"I'm not sure she'll take too kindly to that."

"Well, sadly for her, she hasn't got a choice until this motherfucker is dealt with."

"W-what are you planning?"

"Nothing for you to worry about." He winks, causing dread to settle in the pit of my stomach.

"Zach, you can't go up against this fucker. He'll kill you without a second thought."

"Don't worry. I've got it handled."

I narrow my eyes at him. "How?"

"Seriously, just make sure she doesn't fuck off."

"I've been trying."

"You worry about that, I'll worry about how I'm not about to lose fifty big ones to this cunt."

"Fifty grand?" I balk.

"Yeah, seems Mummy was a right fucking junkie."

"Jesus."

"I might have had a lucky break when she handed me over, but a little of her blood runs through my veins. I can end this." With that said, he spins on his heels and walks for the door.

"Zach, don't die. Biff would fucking kill me."

He chuckles. "No one is fucking dying. Well, maybe Jet and his goons."

"W-what?" I stutter out, but it's too late. He's already gone.

I fall back down onto my stool, my head spinning.

When did my life get so dramatic?

When you locked eyes on the pocket rocket.

"Fucking hell." I rub my hand down my face and tilt my head back to look at the ceiling.

This is going to be a fucking disaster.

CHAPTER FIFTEEN

KAS

THE KNOCK on the door scares the shit out of me. I like to pretend that this thing with Jet doesn't bother me, but when I'm alone with just the creaks and cracks of the building around me for company, I'm bordering on a nervous fucking wreck.

I might have been let off with a painful warning, but I've no doubt Jet and his men aren't too far away.

A suspicious looking black car followed me all the way back yesterday. It was almost enough to stop me from coming back here. But where the fuck else was I meant to go?

I laugh at my own thoughts as I slowly step toward the door.

I'm expecting to see one of his guys when I peer through the peephole, so I'm pleasantly surprised when I find Biff, my brother's wife, on the other side.

"Kas, open up. I brought cupcakes." She holds them up as if she knows I'm looking at her.

"Okay, but only because you have cake," I say, pulling the door open.

"And coffee."

"My hero."

I reach for one of the takeout cups before she's even inside the flat.

"Whoa, you must be a good influence on Spike. I'm used to this place resembling a dump."

"I cleaned," I admit, much to her surprise. Well, what did she expect me to do while locked up in here like fucking Rapunzel? Okay, so that's not quite true. It's hardly a tower, and really, I could have just walked right out the front door.

"So... how's it going?"

"Oh, just great. I've got a drug lord gangster on my back and I've had to resort to my big brother paying him off to stop him from taking payment in other ways. He beat me yesterday to prove a point, and thanks to Spike I have no job. You know, just a regular Tuesday."

I drop down onto one of the sofas with my coffee, and after toeing off her shoes she drops onto the other.

"You don't have to do that, you know?"

"Do what?" I ask, my brows knitting together.

"Try to play it off like it's nothing."

I shrug. "It's the only choice I've got. I can hardly let it break me."

"It would break most people."

"I'm not most people." The shit I've lived through over the years would harden even the softest of hearts.

"You're not alone anymore, Kas. You've got us. All the guys love you. We're all here to help."

"I know, it's just..." I trail off, not all that comfortable with this kind of girl chat unless it's with Jodie.

"You're not used to it," she finishes for me.

"Yup."

Silence descends as we sip at our coffees before Biff turns to me, her eyes shining with excitement.

"Zach said you're joining me as Rebel's newest apprentice."

"So it seems. I didn't get much choice in the matter."

"Did you want one? He said you've got mad skills."

"He's seen one sketch. I think he could be exaggerating a little."

"Don't tell him I said this, but most of the time, he's right. Let's see what you've got, then."

"Um... I don't have a portfolio or anything."

"Just a few scraps of paper is fine."

"Okay..." I push from the sofa with a sigh and head for the room to pull out my notepad. "Here." I pass the battered old thing to Biff before falling back down.

I can't look at her as she stares at it, firstly because I'm embarrassed that it's just a dogeared old notebook I found in a café I was working at a few years ago, and secondly, I don't show anyone my art, ever. It was only Mum who ever knew I could draw, but seeing as it wasn't going to put a roof over our head anytime soon, or pay for her habit, it got brushed aside so I could work whatever job I could find.

Zach was right, though; my dream was always art

school. I used to see some of the students heading to the universities throughout the city with their huge arse sketchbooks, and I'd be overcome with jealousy. I couldn't think of anything better than spending my days lost in art.

It was just a dream, though.

"Kas, these are amazing."

I shrug off the compliment like it's nothing and reach for a cupcake.

"Spike's going to have an easy job on his hands."

The mention of his name has me pausing mid-bite. "Spike? Why?"

"Zach's going to ask him to mentor you."

"He's what?" I splutter.

"Going to show you the ropes, get you trained up."

"So... I'll be working closely with him?"

"Yeah, why? Is that a problem?"

"No, I'm just surprised is all."

She stares at me for a beat, and I fear she can read everything I'm trying to hide.

"Something has happened, hasn't it?" she asks, causing all the blood to drain from my face. "Kas," she warns.

"It was my fault. I pushed it—him. You can't tell Zach, he'll kill Spike."

"I'm not getting involved in any of the dirty secrets that go on under this roof. And clearly, you already know the risks."

"It was a one-off. Tensions were running high."

"How do you know that won't happen again? You're going to be working together now."

"It just won't. He told me as much."

"I'm sure he said that when you first got here too, didn't he? Look how that turned out. You're playing a dangerous game here, Kas."

"I know. None of this was meant to happen. I was just... lonely. He's so sweet and... hot. I know it was wrong, but I needed it, the distraction."

"I can't tell you what to do and what not to do in this situation. Really I've no clue how you're dealing with it all, but I won't allow you to come between Zach and Spike, or the others. They've all been friends too long to have things ripped apart by you." Her warning sends pain through my chest. I don't have any intentions of ruining anything for either Spike or Zach.

Her warning comes from nowhere, but I feel its seriousness right down to my toes.

"I have no intentions of hurting them. Spike's done more for me in the past few days than anyone ever has in my life. I guess I just got a little carried away with myself."

"I won't lie to Zach. If he asks me about this, I will tell him the truth. But that being said, I'm not going to go out of my way to hurt him, either. So, if you say it was a one-time thing and really mean it, then I'll let it go. Just make sure it was, or you need to be honest. Those boys are my family now, and I won't have anyone hurting them."

"It's not going to happen again," I say, although even thinking the words feels wrong. I might want him back in my bed, I might want to feel his touch burning against my skin, to feel his body working mine to ecstasy, but I know I can't—we can't. Not now Zach knows, and not now he's offered me a job. It would be the ultimate fuck-you to my brother when all he's tried to do since I ambushed him and told him who I am, is help me.

"Okay," she says, nodding before leaning forward and swiping a cupcake of her own.

"I don't need a babysitter, you know? I am actually capable of following orders and staying put."

"I'm not babysitting, I'm keeping you company."

"Bullshit," I say with a laugh. "They all think I'm a flight risk. Well, contrary to popular belief, I don't actually want to walk out that door and be swiped by that arsehole."

"Do you think it'll be over once he's been paid off?" she asks. And if that isn't the million-dollar question. "I've seen enough films to know it's often not that simple."

"We can only hope, right? What else are we going to do, take them all out with the guys' tattoo guns? Hardly."

Biff snorts a laugh, but I can see the concern in her eyes.

"I didn't want to bring any of you into this. It's why I'd never told Zach. The thought of putting you all in danger because of me terrifies me."

"We're family, Kas. Danger or not, we're all in this together."

"You won't be saying that if he swipes you and uses you as bait."

"I'll be fine," she says, sounding way too confident. There's no way she can appreciate what Jet and his guys are capable of—she's grown up with wealth and privilege. The idea of London's dark underworld is like a myth to the people she grew up around. They all stick their noses in the air and pretend that the drug rings, the fighting, the gangs, the MCs don't exist. But I know differently. I see the evidence, the violence, the death that happens at the hands of all of them. It is very, very real, and equally as terrifying.

Biff ends up hanging out with me for a few hours before she makes her excuses and heads back to the studio and the guys.

As much as I appreciated her visit, I couldn't shift the feeling that Zach was trying to mollycoddle me. I'm the last person who needs treating like a child. I'm not sure I ever really was one, and I'm certainly not now.

Once she leaves, my notebook that she left on the coffee table taunts me until I pick it up. I find an abandoned pen inside a magazine beside it and lose myself in putting ink on paper. I don't think about what I'm drawing, I just let my hand move and forget about the world around me for a while. It's a similar feeling to what Spike gave me last night, although that one came with a hell of a lot more pleasure instead of a stiff neck.

My muscles pull uncomfortably from where I've been sitting hunched over for God knows how long when the sound of a key pushing into the lock startles me.

My breath catches as I wait for Spike to emerge. I haven't seen him since he sent me away from his bedroom this morning, so I have no idea what kind of mood he might be in or if he even knows about the fact that he's my new mentor.

"I brought pizza," is the only thing he says as he walks inside, his voice flat, cold even, totally unlike anything I'm used to from him. I swallow down my apprehension and follow his movement as he walks to the kitchen.

He doesn't once look up at me, instead just focusing on what he's doing.

He drops two boxes on the counter, along with his keys, before going for the fridge for a beer.

Much to my disappointment, he doesn't get one for me. I've been craving something all evening, but I didn't want to just help myself to his stuff, so I stuck with a glass of water.

"Here," he grunts, holding out the boxes and waiting for me to take the top one. "I took a guess. I hope you like it."

"It's pizza, what's not to like?"

He shrugs, but that's all the reaction I get as he places his can on the table and falls down with his own box, opening it up and immediately digging in.

I watch him, a little shell-shocked by his attitude.

"What?" he barks, still refusing to look up.

"Bad day at the office?"

"Something like that," he mumbles around a mouthful of what looks like meat feast pizza.

"Biff told me about you training me up."

"Can we not?"

"Can we not what? Talk?"

"Yeah."

I narrow my eyes at him, wondering what's turned him from the sweet guy he's been over the past few days to the prick sitting before me now.

I don't have to wonder for long. The answer is right in front of me. Well, it is me. Last night ruined everything, and although my body might have other ideas about a repeat, my head knows that he was right all along. It never should have happened.

"Okay, well. I'll just..." Standing, I take myself, my

pizza, and glass of crappy water to my bedroom and kick the door shut behind me.

I know when I'm not wanted, and I've already learned my lesson about forcing myself on him. If he needs space and to pretend that I'm not here, then he can have it.

CHAPTER SIXTEEN

SPIKE

"FUCK," I mutter as she shuts her bedroom door.

I don't want to be a prick, but putting some kind of barrier up between us is the only way I can see us getting through the next few days without doing something else we're going to regret.

The second I walked into the flat, all I could think about was dragging her from the sofa and showing her exactly what had been in my head all day. But I can't. I made Zach a promise—a promise that I've already broken. I need to stay away from her.

The thought of him finding her somewhere else to live doesn't sit right with me. I like her being here. She makes this place feel more like a home than any other housemate I've had before, but I know it can't happen.

The second all of this is over, she needs to get out of here so that I can continue with my life.

She makes me think back to a time I've fought hard to forget about, and she makes me want things that are just not a part of my future.

Forevers and futures don't exist with me. Been there, done that, got the shattered heart to prove it. I'm done with that bullshit.

If Zach and Titch think they can commit to one woman and that it's not going to end in disaster, then that's fine for them. They can't say I didn't warn them about it. But that shit is not for me. Not again.

I only eat half my pizza before I give up. It's unlike me, but my head's spinning so much with everything going on right now that I just can't stomach it.

Throwing it down on the other end of the sofa, a notepad on the one Kas was sitting on catches my eye.

I tell myself to leave it, but eventually my curiosity gets the better of me and I reach over for it.

My breath catches when I flip the page open. Zach was right, she really is quite talented. I flick through page after page of her drawings until I come to the last one.

"Fucking hell," I whisper, my cock swelling as I stare down at her sketch of the two of us. We're in her bed like last night. I'm between her thighs, my face in the crook of her neck. It's erotic as fuck.

The longer I stare, the more my temperature increases as I vividly remember just how hot her skin was when I touched her, the little sounds she made as she was heading for release and just how tight she was when I finally pushed inside of her.

Fuck. Fuck.

Slamming the book shut, I place it back where I was. I dump my half-eaten pizza in the kitchen and march straight for the bathroom for a shower. A very cold shower.

My footsteps falter as I pass her door. I want to know what she's doing, to say something, to apologise, but I know that doing any one of them is a bad idea. If I open that door, her scent is going to surround me and I know I'm not going to be able to remain standing in the doorway to have a conversation with her.

Lifting my hand to my hair, I run it through my messy locks, tugging until it bites and I'm safely locked in the bathroom.

Just a few days and she'll be gone, and I can get on with my life without the constant reminder of how easily I played her body.

Just a few more days.

THINGS CONTINUE the same way for the next two days. Kas clearly got the message on Tuesday night when I came home, because she's done her best to avoid me ever since. If I'm in the flat, she keeps herself locked in her room out of the way, and when I go to work, I can only assume that she stays put and keeps herself safe.

Biff goes both afternoons while we're all working and talks to her about starting at the studio. She might have only just started being trained up herself by Zach, but she knows the basics and can talk Kas through the process. I'm happy if it means I don't have to do it.

I've yet to come up with how I'm going to get out of being her mentor, but with each day that passes, I know my time is coming to an end. Zach was out this afternoon—I can only assume he's got the money Kas needs and this is all about to come to an end.

I'm glad; she doesn't need this hanging over her head any longer than necessary. But equally, it's going to mean she's leaving soon. And although she might have spent the past forty-eight hours avoiding me, I can't deny that I'm going to miss her when she moves on.

I shake my head at my thoughts as a knock sounds out on my studio door.

"Boss wants us all upstairs," Titch says when he pushes the door open a little.

"On it."

I drop the pencil in my hand and push back the sketch I was working on before following him up the stairs to the flat Zach and Biff share.

Biff's nowhere to be seen—not that it's a surprise. She'll be on her afternoon babysitting visit. Plus, I know that Zach doesn't want her anywhere near any of this. I can tell by the tense look on both his and D's face that shit's about to get real.

I've had a fair bit of drama in my life, starting with my mum fucking off and leaving me in the care of my grandparents and then the one who shan't be named shattering the life I thought I was going to have, but all of that pales in comparison to this.

This shit is the stuff movies are made of, not our lives. Well, maybe D's at times, but not the rest of us. We spend our days inking the people of London and mostly get on with our fairly mundane lives.

Zach looks between Titch and I and a ball of dread settles in my stomach. What the fuck is this motherfucker planning?

"Sit," he demands.

"Zach, what the fuck are you doing?" I ask. Possibly naïvely, I assumed we'd give this fucker the money he's owed and just put it behind us. But the hunger for vengeance oozing from Zach tells me otherwise.

"This ends tonight."

I swallow down the anxiety that statement drags up and look to D.

He's one scary motherfucker when he's angry, and right now the muscle in his neck is pulsating with the need to hurt someone.

"What the fuck?" Titch barks, clearly having similar thoughts to me.

"Kas is going to take this guy his money tonight."

"Kas is doing it?" I ask, shocked that Zach is going to let her anywhere near that fucker.

"Yeah, she's the one who owes him. He wants it from her."

"You've spoken to him?"

"No. Kas has."

"What?" I bark. "You let her contact him?"

"What the fuck else am I meant to do? She's the one he wants, not any of us," Zach says, his own concern becoming obvious in his tone.

"So why the hell are we here right now?"

"We've got a few hours yet. Calm down. I've got the address in my phone. We're going to follow her there, let shit go down, and then get her the hell out of there. Safe."

"Have you got a fucking death wish?"

"No. D's brother has it covered."

I drop my head into my hand. This is a fucking

dream right? This isn't actually my life right now? "So why the fuck are we going?"

"For Kas."

"If they see us, she might not be alive for us to rescue." All the blood drains from his face at my words. "This guy isn't playing, Zach. It's not a fucking game."

"I know that. I fucking know that," he says, scrubbing his hand down his face. "Cruz has it under control," he says, and I look at D. I know Cruz is his brother, but right now I'm not feeling much like trusting anyone.

D nods. "They've had this guy in their sights for a while. He's been dealing on their patch. They've been waiting for the right opportunity to meet with him."

"Fucking hell. What is this?" I ask, tipping my face to the ceiling in disbelief. If I knew that pulling Kas from that stage that night would drag me right into the centre of a drug lord/MC battle, then I might have had second thoughts about it.

Who am I kidding, there was no chance of me allowing her to stay up there any longer than she already had.

"We're not doing anything other than getting her out safely. Cruz's boys will sort everything else."

My eyes bounce between Zach and D's.

D's connection to the Royal Reapers isn't a secret. Hell, there's at least one of them in here daily to get some more ink, but he always stays at arm's length from that life. He has too much to lose to get involved. Well, that's what he's always told us, anyway.

Cruz, on the other hand, is a fully-fledged member along with their father.

I've heard D talk about that life, time and time

again, and it always sounds like he's talking about another world, or at least a film he watched.

"When and where?" I say after a long silence. I might not be totally okay with all of this, but at the end of the day, it's for Kas. And for her, I'm realising, I'll do more than I would for most.

"Kas is meeting Jet at eight," D says without looking at me. He's got his eyes trained on his phone. "I've just sent you the address. Zach's right. We're not doing a fucking thing. We're just going to collect her and get the fuck out of there. This is Cruz's battle, not ours."

"Are you actually going to pay this motherfucker?"

"The less you know the better."

"Jesus."

"Biff's rearranged our late appointments, but we will be back here on Saturday like nothing ever happened. Kas too, if she's up for it. Drink?" he asks, placing a bottle of whisky on the table in front of both him and D as if this is just a usual Friday afternoon.

"Does Kas know what's going on?"

D's eyes finally lift to mine. "No. She doesn't need the details."

I nod back at him before taking the glass when Zach holds it out for me.

With it in hand, I rest back in the chair and knock it back in one. It burns, but fuck do I need it right now.

The silence surrounding us is heavy. Zach might say all the right words and trust D with his life—hell, we all do—but saying it and having it actually happen are two different things.

CHAPTER SEVENTEEN

KAS

MY HANDS TREMBLE as I stare down at my phone.

Unknown: A car will pick you up at 7:45. Get in it.

I look at the other unread message I have from Jodie. My thumb hovers over it, but I fight my need to reach out. If she senses something is wrong, then she'll start trying to talk me out of it. But this needs to happen. It needs to come to an end.

Well, if that isn't the most ominous message I've ever received, I don't know what is.

The black bag that Zach dropped off earlier taunts me from beside the dresser where I dropped it. My fingers twitched to unzip it and see exactly what that amount of money looked like, but I didn't. I trust Zach. He's my brother. But if I were to open that and not find a stash of cash, then I don't know what I would do. At least while I'm in ignorant bliss believing that it's what Jet wants, I can act innocent.

I shower, dress, blow dry my hair, and apply my makeup, but I do all of it in a daze. Part of me expects the message to be a hoax and that someone will come crashing through the door any minute.

I'm not stupid. I know the chances of Jet taking that bag and letting me go scot-free are slim.

Two minutes before my pick-up time, I give myself one final once-over in the mirror.

My makeup is dark, my lips bright red. It might mean nothing to Jet, but it's my fuck-you makeup. It makes me feel powerful and in control.

I glance down at myself. It's been a scorching hot summer day, but there was no way I was dressing for the weather. I don't want to give Jet any ideas by wearing a short skirt or exposing too much skin—not that motherfuckers like him wait for any kind of invitation to take what they want.

I should know, he's tried.

Shoving my feet into my biker boots to finish off my dark, edgy look, I pick up the incredibly heavy bag and head for the door.

The flat is unbearably empty. I kind of hoped Spike would be home for this to make sure I'm okay. I'm not sure if his presence would have made this any easier.

Seeing him, knowing what we had for those few hours, it's fucking torture. Almost as painful as his closed-off attitude and general arseholeness ever since.

It's stupid, but I miss him.

It may have only been a couple of days, but I miss the man I was able to have a laugh with, who didn't take life too seriously. Not to mention his stupidly handsome face, the way his eyes softened whenever he looked at me. Like I was someone important, someone worthy.

I've always just been a means to an end to most people, my mother included. It was nice to feel special for once, even if he was only protecting me as a favour for Zach.

"Hi, Kas. How are you?" Louisa asks the second my foot hits the ground floor.

Glancing out the window, I see a black car pull up.

Fuck. Fuck.

"I'm good, thanks. I'm just off for a night out. Meeting a friend," I lie, hoping that she'll let me go.

"Aw, that sounds nice. I'm jealous. Since having this one, I can't remember the last time I went out without him, let alone a night with the girls."

"You should get Spike to babysit one night, go and have some fun."

I move to the door, but she still doesn't let me escape.

"You think he would? I've wanted to ask, but I didn't want to look like an idiot if he said no."

"All you can do is try," I say, my fingers wrapping around the door handle, ready to make my escape before I piss off whomever is waiting for me.

"I guess you're right. The next time I see him, I'll ask."

"Go for it. I'm sorry, I really need to..." I gesture over my shoulder, and her smile drops.

"Oh, I'm so sorry. You go. Have a great night."

"Thank you. Y-you too," I say with a wince as I take in her dirty shirt and the equally dirty kid attached to her hip.

"We had beans for dinner," she says as an excuse for the mess.

With a nod of acceptance, I push through the door and hotfoot it toward the idling car.

"You're late," a deep voice barks the second I pull the door open.

I don't bother responding. These aren't the kind of guys who accept a simple 'I'm sorry' and move on. And I'm proved right when I climb in and immediately get backhanded across the face by the guy sitting on the other side.

He reaches out and pulls me across the seats before the door slams shut behind me.

"Do you want your fucking money or not?" I spit, lifting my hand to where the prick just split my lip open again.

"Shut your mouth, bitch."

Rolling my eyes, I slide as far away from him as I can and keep my stare on the passing buildings.

I try to memorise where he takes me, but we're soon in an area I don't recognise, and I know I have no hope of making a smooth escape.

I don't bother glancing up at the goons up front. I don't need to. I can feel the passenger's stare drilling into me through the rearview mirror.

Without looking, I flip him off, much to the shock and amusement of the guy next to me.

"No wonder Jet loves you so much. Feisty little bitch, aren't you?"

"Bite me."

"With fucking pleasure, sweetheart. Only, Jet made us promise not to touch. It seems he wants a piece of you first."

My stomach rolls. "The only thing that cunt is getting from me is what's in the bag. Then I'm out."

An evil chuckle falls from him. "Yeah, that's what they all think, sweetheart. Jet will get a nice little price for you." His fingertip runs down my arm, and I flinch away.

"Get your fucking hands off me." I turn to him, my teeth bared in warning, and the fucker just laughs in my face.

"Jet owes me a favour. I call dibs on you."

Curling my lip in disgust, I turn away from him once more. I'd sooner allow them to kill me before they pass me around like a fucking rag doll.

The sun is starting to set as we pull up into what looks like an industrial estate and come to a stop beside a nondescript warehouse.

"What is this place?"

"If Jet wanted you to know, he'd have given you the address himself, don't you think?"

The front two get out before opening the back doors from the outside.

Before I even get a chance to move, a hand wraps tightly around my upper arm and I'm hauled out and to my feet.

"This way."

His fingers bruise as he drags me along behind him, my feet unable to keep up with his pace while the guy beside him carries the bag Zach gave me.

I'm pushed through a doorway and then dragged down a hallway until the very last door.

The minute the second guy swings it open, I'm not too gently thrown through it.

"Ow. Fucking cunt," I scream as I land on my hands and knees with a thud. Pain jolts through my kneecaps and up my arms, but I refuse to show these motherfuckers any kind of weakness, so I suck it down and stand, brushing myself off as I do.

In the centre of the huge office is a massive walnut desk with none other than Jet sitting behind it. He's leaning back in his chair with his feet up on the wood, like he hasn't got a care in the world.

The goon dumps the bag on his desk before shoving me toward the empty chair and pushing on my shoulder until I have no choice but to sit opposite.

"Well, well, well, what do we have here?" Jet sings in his slimy, puke-inducing voice.

He unzips the bag and peers inside.

His brows rise, but he doesn't say anything.

My lips remain sealed. It shouldn't matter to him where it came from. It's there, and my debt is paid. Deal done.

"You think this is the end?" he asks, almost like he can hear my thoughts.

"It's all there. The whole amount. We're done now," I state.

He chuckles, and it makes the ball of dread sitting in my stomach grow. "You really think your darling mummy only owed me money? Oh no, no. After I cut her off, she made me a deal. One that would keep paying over and over." I swallow my apprehension, my hands beginning to tremble.

"No," I spit. "She wouldn't."

"Oh, but she did. And I'm cashing in. So, thanks for

the money," he says, pushing the bag from the desk as if it's nothing more than a bag of rubbish. He drops his feet to the floor and stands, rounding the corner with his eyes trained on me.

"You're mine now, Kassie. I gave your mother an endless supply to do with as she saw fit, and in return, I get her daughter."

An evil smile curls at his lips, and I bolt—only he's expecting it, and his arms wrap around me from behind, pinning my arms to my sides and putting a halt to any fight I might have in me.

"We're going to have so much fun. And then I know my boys are desperate for a go." One of his hands grasps my chin, and I'm forced to look at his henchmen who are standing guard by the door, their sick eyes undressing me. "What do you think, boys? Worth the wait?"

My stomach turns over as Jet lifts my shirt, pulls out a pocket knife and slices through the thin bit of fabric holding my bra cups together, then slicing through my shirt like it's made of nothing more than tissue.

The fabric falls away from my breasts, but I refuse to react and give this prick the satisfaction of knowing he's getting to me.

"You just love putting on a show, don't you? I watched you at the club, you know. That little school girl uniform used to get me going just right. So innocent, yet so dirty. Knowing all those men were watching turned you on, didn't it?"

I twist my head from where he's breathing in my ear, keeping my lips sealed.

"Just like you're going to enjoy it when I fuck you

with them watching, waiting their turn to break you in for the rest of my boys."

Before I know what's happening, his hand is pushing at the waistband of my jeans. The shock of his touch forces me to react before I've even realised I said anything.

"No," I scream, bucking against him.

"I love it when they fight. It makes the prize so much sweeter."

"Get your fucking hands off me." I slam the heel of my boot down into his foot.

"Fucking bitch," he grunts, his grip on me tightening. The guys watching our exchange only get more excited, their eyes are dark with hunger, their fists clenched at their sides.

I thrash about the best I can in the hope of somehow getting away from this, from the inevitable.

Somehow, he manages to manoeuvre me so that my back is flat against his desk with both of my hands in one of his much bigger ones, pinning them above my head.

"Fighting won't get you anywhere with me, sweetheart."

The coolness of his blade connects with the soft skin of my cheek before he runs it down over my jaw, my neck, and between the valley of my breasts.

His dark, hungry eyes stare down at me as bile rises up my throat.

All my years with this shitty life, and it's when I'm almost free that this happens. I've had friends who were raped by scumbags from the age of twelve, but somehow, I managed to escape. I guess fate had bigger ideas for me. It saved me from the drugged-up arseholes from the squats and handed me straight to the devil himself.

The blade circles my navel and I have to fight not to move for fear of it plunging straight into my stomach.

The thin fabric of my jeggings is no task for the knife, and the second he tucks it under the waistband I feel the material loosen.

"Aw look, you even dressed up for me," he says, taking in the red lace of my thong.

"Fuck. You," I spit.

"Oh sweetheart, you're going to regret that."

His knife is under the lace, ready to rip it from me, when there's a commotion out in the hall.

He flinches as his guys move to see what's going on and the knife cuts into my skin. His eyes drop to where he's caught me, and an evil smirk appears on his lips.

"Looks like you'll have a permanent reminder about tonight."

This time, when my throat burns, I'm unable to stop it. I twist my head to the side and chuck up the contents of my stomach.

Jet's grip on me never loosens.

The next few moments happen in a blur. We're joined by others who clearly aren't part of Jet's little gang, because seconds after the crash of the door being forced open sounds out, what I can only assume is gunshots and a load of shouting fills the room.

As the commotion continues, Jet releases me, pulling a gun from his waistband, and turns toward the action. That's as far as he gets. The next thing I know, I'm sprayed with blood and his dead weight crushes me to the desk before we both fall to the floor.

CHAPTER EIGHTEEN

SPIKE

"WILL YOU CHILL THE FUCK OUT?" Zach barks as he watches me in the rearview mirror.

Both of my knees are bouncing nervously as we sit outside the warehouse where fuck knows what is happening inside, like we have for the past ten minutes.

Watching those guys frog-march her inside tested my restraint in a way I've never experienced before. I thought it was hard denying her every time she tempted me, but sitting there and watching as they roughly manhandled her was fucking painful.

"Cruz has got this," D says encouragingly from the passenger seat.

"How aren't you worried about this?" I snap at Zach.

"What the fuck good is worrying going to do?"

Our eyes hold in the mirror for a few seconds before I lose my fight.

"Fuck this," I bark, shouldering open the door and launching from the back of his car.

"Spike, no. Wa—" I don't hang around long enough to hear the rest of Zach's warning. I can't just sit out here while she's going through whatever might be happening inside.

"Fucking hell, Spike," D calls, jogging up next to me.

"You can't tell me that you're happy just waiting."

"Fuck no, but it's what we agreed."

"Fuck what we agreed. She might need us."

He glances at me briefly. "Fucking hell, Spike. You've got it bad."

"I've got nothing other than a need for this to be over."

"Riiight."

Thankfully, Zach and Titch catch up with us, stopping him saying any more, but I don't miss his knowing look as he continues to keep his eyes on me.

"You sure about this?" Zach asks, glancing between me and the door keeping us from seeing what's going on inside.

"Nope. But it's not stopped me in the past." Okay, so I've never been outside a warehouse with basically two gangs inside holding a girl hostage, but I'm sure it'll be fine.

I pull the door open.

The second we step inside, the sound of gunfire stops us in our tracks.

"Fucking hell," Titch mutters behind me. "We should maybe wait a few."

"Fuck that."

Ignoring their hesitation, I rush forward, focusing on the door at the very end where it seems the gunfire is coming from. Before we get there, everything goes quiet.

Peering around the doorway, the scene before me makes my breath catch and my stomach turn.

Bodies litter the floor, blood seeps from them while guys in cuts stand over them with their guns still poised.

Dragging my eyes from the guy closest who's face-down in his own blood, I scan the room looking for her.

At the other side of the room, I find a desk with two people lying on the floor beside it.

Racing over, I spot an arm with tattoos I instantly recognise.

"Kas," I cry.

"What the fuck are you—" I glance up to see Cruz staring down at the two of them. Recognition flashes in his eyes when I look up at him, and he lowers his gun.

"Fucking help me then," I bark, wrapping my hand around the body covering Kas.

He's dead weight, and the second we pull him off, I recognise him instantly as the guy who had Kas pinned up against the wall outside the club last weekend.

"Shit." Dropping to my knees, I take Kas' face in my hands. "Kas, Kas." I rub my thumbs over her eyes, wiping the blood away that I hope to fuck isn't hers. "Tiny?" I whisper, my heart racing as I search for signs of life.

A noise rips from her throat, and I swear the world around me comes to a stop right there and then.

"I-I'm okay."

"Fuck. Fuck." I drop my head to hers as relief floods me.

I give myself two seconds to get it together before I pull back. My teeth clench to the point at which I think I'm going to crack one when I look down to find her clothing ruined and her body on display for all the cunts in this room.

Without putting any thought into it, I reach over my head and pull my shirt off. I'm just pulling it down over her torso when feet come to a stop beside me.

"Is she okay?" Zach asks in a rush.

She's fallen limp in my arms. Honestly, I have no idea.

"She spoke to me. She was awake."

I watch as he bends down and attempts to scoop her up into his arms. He's almost lifted her from the floor when she starts to fight.

"No, no," she wails, her arms flailing and legs kicking.

"Whoa, Kas. It's okay, it's just me."

"No," she cries, the broken sound to her voice ripping me open, but that's nothing compared to what happens next.

She relaxes slightly, enough that she can reach out. Her eyes are still shut, so it's just chance that her hand connects with my arm. Her fingers tighten around me, almost pulling me to her, although she's not got the strength to actually do it.

Zach looks from her to me, his eyes tormented and torn about what's best to do for her, but I don't miss the anger and accusation within them. I fear that whatever act we've been putting on might just have been shattered.

"Spike?" he asks, fury dripping from his words.

"Not now," I snap, standing closer to take the decision out of his hands. I pull her to me and she immediately wraps her arms around me, tucking her head into my shoulder.

Zach's jaw pops with frustration, but he doesn't say anything. Not that anything he could say would make me give her up right now.

"Let's go." I take a huge step forward, more than ready to get away from this war zone. I turn back at the last minute and plough my booted foot into Jet's ribs. He might already be dead, but my need to get my own bit of vengeance for how he's treated Kas gets the better of me.

I pass D, who's talking to his brother while his men begin to clean the place up. I don't bother to attempt to hear what they're saying, I just need to get her away.

We're already in the back of Zach's car by the time the three of them join us a few minutes later. Kas is curled up on my lap. She's not said anything since her refusal to have Zach hold her, and she still hasn't opened her eyes. She's breathing, though, so I take that as her telling the truth earlier and that she isn't hurt. Not physically, anyway.

"Where to?" Zach's voice is rough, his eyes zeroing in on me through the rearview mirror.

"Home."

"But—"

"No buts, Zach."

"Okay, I'll call Biff to meet—"

"No," I spit out. "I've got this."

"But—" He starts to argue, but as our eyes hold in the mirror he backs down.

The drive back to my flat is in silence as we all

digest what happened tonight. Anger comes off Zach in waves, but I really couldn't give a shit about anyone but the girl in my arms right now. It's not an everyday thing for the four of us to go running into a room full of dead bodies.

When we pull up outside my building, everyone moves to get out with us.

"I'll call you," I say harshly.

"Spike, I need—"

"I know, Zach. But right now, we should be worrying about what Kas needs. I'll call you as soon as I know she's okay, and then I'll get her to call you when she's up to it."

His jaw pops as his teeth grind. He's not happy about this, I don't expect him to be, but it's the right thing to do. Kas doesn't need an audience or a whole room of people fussing around her right now. I might not know her all that well, but I can say that with confidence.

Titch insists on helping us up and opening the doors. I'm grateful, because I have no idea how I'd have done it alone, but the second he drops the keys to my kitchen counter he turns to leave.

"Thank you, Titch."

"Anytime. Message us later, just to let us know she's okay. Danni's going out of her mind."

I nod at him and he slips out of the flat without another word.

Kas stirs in my arms the second we're alone, and when I look down, her blue eyes are staring right back at me.

"Kas," I breathe, relief flooding me.

"I'm okay."

Glancing at the sofa and then back to her, I try to decide what to do next. But when my feet move, they must decide for me because I find us in my bedroom.

Gently, I lower her down. Her dark hair fans out over my light sheets, her makeup is smeared over her face, and she's got a trickle of blood running down from the split that's opened back up on her lip. Her skin is splattered with that cunt's blood—the only good thing about that is that it's not hers.

"Tiny," I breathe, shaking my head. I have no words to say to her right now that will make any of this any better, but she seems to perk up at just the sound of my voice. "What do you need?"

I stand awkwardly beside the bed, not knowing what's best to do. I desperately want to crawl in with her, but I have no idea if she wants that or not.

Looking to the door, I wonder if I should have taken her to her own room. She might not even want to be here at all.

Shit. I'm totally out of my depth.

My eyes run the length of her once more, taking in her ruined jeans, and I make a snap decision.

"Where are you going?" she asks in a panic when I march from the room.

"Just to the bathroom. I'm not going anywhere."

She nods, and I keep going.

Pushing the plug in the bath, I turn the taps on before rummaging around in my cupboard for the bubbles I know Maureen bought me for Christmas a couple of years ago.

I find them, twist the top, and pour a generous amount into the running water.

The room almost instantly fills with the floral scent before I check the temperature and rush back to Kas.

She's exactly where I left her.

"I'm running you a bath," I explain in case the sound of running water wasn't enough of a giveaway.

Resting on my knees beside her, I lift my shirt and take in her ruined trousers. "Okay?" I ask when I grasp the fabric. She nods once again and lifts her hips to help me. "Fuck, you're bleeding."

"It's just a scratch."

"Kas," I warn, flashing a glance up at her, but the second I find her sad eyes, I lose the words. I want to tell her not to try to make out like she hasn't just been through something huge, but then I realise it's not for me to tell her how to cope. I just need to be here for her. And the reality is, I've no idea *what* she went through in that room. She might not have been there all that long, but it was long enough… too long.

"He didn't actually mean to do it. He was going for my underwear."

My lips part, but once again I swallow down the words.

"Let's get it cleaned up and see how bad it is."

She nods once, and I rush to get the first aid kit, turning the bath off while I'm there. It's never been used so much since she moved in. Actually, I'm pretty sure it had never been used at all.

The second I wipe the blood away, I see that she's right. My panic and the amount of blood covering her makes it look worse than it really is.

"I-is the bath ready yet?"

"But—" I say, looking down at the knife wound on her hip.

"It's hardly going to kill me."

My eyes fly up to her. *No, but that cunt and his knife could have.* "Let me dress it. I know it'll come off, but it'll make me feel better."

"Whatever," she sighs, her body relaxing back into my mattress.

I put a sterilised pad over the wound before covering it in as much tape as possible.

"Okay, good as new." I look at her and wish I could eat my words. "Come on, let's get you cleaned up."

I hold my hand out for her, and almost immediately, she slips her small one into it.

She allows me to lead her to the bathroom before coming to a stop in front of the bath full of bubbles.

"Okay?" I ask when she just stands there, doing nothing.

"Are you... are you leaving me?" Her voice is low, and the chill within it guts me.

"I'll do whatever you need me to do," I say, taking her hand back in mine and squeezing in support.

She nods but remains silent for a second as she thinks.

"Help me?" Her words are almost a whisper, and for a moment, I think I misheard her. But when I look into her eyes, I know she said them. She's running on empty right now.

I check if she's okay with it before lifting my shirt up over her head. The second I discard it on the floor and look back, I'm reminded of what happened tonight. Her own shirt and bra are ruined and hanging from her shoulders. She's got red scratch marks running from her neck all the way down to her waistband.

My fingers clench with my need to go back and hurt

him. It doesn't matter that he's already dead. No man should ever do this to a woman.

"Please... don't look at me like that." She twists her head to the side so I have no chance of making eye contact with her.

"I'm not looking at you like anything. I just want to make sure you're not hurt anywhere else."

"You are, you're looking at me with pity, with disgust that I let him do that."

"What? No." Taking her chin gently between my fingers, I encourage her to look back at me. She resists for a moment but soon gives in.

"I'm in awe of you, Kas. Your strength, your ability to cope with this fucked-up situation. You blow my mind."

"I'm nothing, Spike. I just do what I've got to do to survive."

Anger swells in my belly that she doesn't see even an ounce of how incredible she is.

"That's bullshit. You're... You're..." Her eyes fill with water as I search for the right word. Lowering down, I press my forehead to hers and continue staring into her eyes. "Amazing, Kas."

A sob rips from her throat, and I gather her up in my arms as her small body trembles with her cries.

"It's okay, Tiny. I've got you, no one's going to hurt you now."

After long, agonizing minutes, she eventually pulls her tear-stained face from my chest. Her eyes hold so much pain when they meet mine that it makes my breath catch.

I cup her cheek, my fingers threading into her hair as our connection holds.

Every muscle in my body tenses with the need to lean down and kiss her, but I can't. That's the last thing she needs right now.

"Come on, let's get you cleaned up." She nods and takes a step back. I miss her warmth immediately, but I'm not the one who needs the support right now, and I remind myself that I have a job to do.

Pushing her ruined clothes from her shoulders, I drop to my knees and pull her ripped trousers and knickers down her legs. I run my fingers over the bandage I taped to her hip to ensure it's still secure before leading her to the bath.

"Okay?" I ask, holding her hand as she steps into the warm, bubbly water.

I watch her until she's submerged, and then I turn around to pick up her clothes. She doesn't need to sit there staring at them as a reminder of what happened.

"Spike?"

"Yeah?"

"Will you..." She shakes her head. She's trying to be strong and hates that she's so vulnerable right now. I understand it must be a bit of a shock to the system after taking charge for so many years.

Dropping her clothes once more, I fall to my knees beside her and plunge my arm into the water to find her hand.

"Anything, Kas. Anything you need."

She nods, accepting my words.

"Will you get in with me?"

My lips part, but no words make it past for a good few seconds.

"Sorry, I shouldn't have—"

"No, no, it's fine. I meant what I said, anything you need."

Standing, I make quick work of shedding my clothes before stepping into the bath behind her.

"Shit, this water is hot," I say, as it burns my skin.

She didn't so much as wince when she got in. She shrugs, and I realise that she probably didn't even feel it.

My legs encase her body before I pull her back against my chest, my arms wrapping around her waist.

"Better?" I ask once she's snuggled back against me.

"Hmmm..." she moans, twisting her head to the side and placing a kiss to my chest while lacing her fingers through mine.

We lie there in silence for the longest time, her soaking up the support she needs from me and me trying not to think too hard about the fact that her hot, little naked body is pressed up against mine. I'm sure she really doesn't need my cock poking her in the back right now.

After a while, I sit forward slightly and grab the shower puff and gel from the side. I lather it up before starting work on her arms. She moans in pleasure as I rub at her skin, clearing away the visible reminders tonight has left on her.

As I brush the puff over her breasts, her breath catches, and I fight like hell not to let it affect me. I drop lower, not wanting her to think that I have any intentions other than to look after her right now.

I finish over her belly before encouraging her to sit up so I can wash her hair.

She moans as I massage her head, her muscles relaxing under my touch. It's intoxicating to watch.

Once she's clear of bubbles, I drop my lips to her shoulder. Her body shudders, and I can't help but smile.

"Turn around, Kas."

She startles at my words, but after a second, she does as instructed. She lifts her legs over mine and scoots close, too close. My teeth grind as the heat of her pussy brushes against my quickly hardening cock.

"Tiny," I warn.

She looks up at me through her lashes, and my mouth waters.

Swallowing down my need, I focus on her. Reaching over, I swipe her washcloth from the basin and her bottle of makeup remover and set to work.

As gently as I can, I wipe at her eyes, clearing the mixture of dark makeup and blood away.

"There she is," I say softly when her face is clear. Her skin is pale but flawless, and her lips naturally full and red.

"Hey," she whispers, placing her hands on my chest. "How are you doing?"

"I'll be—"

"Don't say okay, Kas. Tell me the truth."

She lets out a sigh, averting her eyes from mine. "My head really hurts. I think I might have hit the desk on the way down... I don't remember," she says quietly. "My ribs hurt, the cut on my hip stings. Every time I shut my eyes all I can see are the evil intentions within his, and I can't get his scent out of my nose."

Cupping her cheeks in my palms, I swipe away the tears that drop with my thumbs.

"It's over now. He's gone."

"W-what happened? One minute he was about to..." she trails off, but I don't think either of us need her to say the next words to know what his intentions were. The state of her clothing tells me everything I need to know. "And then there were gunshots and he fell on me. And then there you were."

I know Zach and D don't want everyone knowing about what happened tonight, but something tells me that Kas is about as trustworthy as they come.

"D is connected to an MC. Turns out they were after Jet as well. So, when D mentioned him to his brother, they used it to set him up."

"Wow." She falls silent for a moment. "So it was them who came in, all guns blazing?"

"Yep."

"That explains a lot," she says, a small smile twitching at her lips. The sight makes my chest tighten.

"Why's that?"

"I just couldn't picture you, Zach and Titch taking down all the baddies." She chuckles, and I can't help but smile.

"What are you trying to say? I'm hard."

"Sure you are," she muses, tapping my chest patronisingly and making my eyes narrow in mock annoyance.

"Hey, I carried you out of there looking like the hero, didn't I?"

"My hero," she whispers, dropping down onto my chest and once again snuggling against me.

I wrap my arms around her and hold her until the water starts to cool around us and I begin to wonder if she's drifted off to sleep.

CHAPTER NINETEEN

KAS

THE SAFETY and contentment of being surrounded by Spike is more than welcome after the events of tonight.

I know the water is cold and that we really need to get out, but I can't bring myself to push away from him.

His support right now means everything.

I've lived almost all my life looking after myself. I was always the one Mum leaned on if she needed someone, but until I connected with Jodie, I never had a go-to person. As I lie here, soaking up everything he's offering me, I wonder how I ever coped without someone.

"We need to get out, you're shivering," he whispers

above me, his deep, husky voice causing a shudder to run down my spine.

"Just a few more minutes."

"Come on, Tiny. Getting pneumonia won't help anyone."

He stands, lifting me with him as if I weigh no more than a feather. My legs automatically wrap around his waist, his cock once again teasing my entrance.

I'm sure I should be numb after everything that's happened tonight, but I can't help just that little bit of contact sending a thrill through me.

Our night together is still at the forefront of my mind, or more so his ability to be able to make me forget everything.

I want that now. I need that now.

"You need to let go," he chuckles, and after another two seconds, I reluctantly allow my legs to drop. The second he releases me, he wraps a huge fluffy towel around me before grabbing another and tucking it around his waist.

After gently squeezing out the excess water from my hair, he guides me from the bathroom but comes to a stop outside both of our bedrooms, not knowing which way to turn.

Making the decision for him, I turn toward his room and walk through the door. My need to be surrounded by his scent, to feel safe, gets the better of me.

Stopping at his chest of drawers, I riffle through until I find his t-shirts. When I do, I drag one out, drop the towel around me and pull it over my head. I can feel his stare burning into my skin, and when I turn, I find I'm right.

"My clothes look better on you," he says after clearing his throat.

I smile weakly at him before heading for his bed. After pulling the sheets back, I climb in. I have no idea what time it is; all I know is that I want to be in a bed, preferably with him beside me, and I'm hoping that by choosing his, I've left him little choice.

"Are you hungry?" he asks, still hovering in the doorway, wearing only his towel that's wrapped deliciously low on his waist. It shows off the deep V that disappears beneath the fabric and the top of the colourful dragon tattoo that wraps around his hip and left thigh.

My fingers twitch to reach out and pull the towel from his body. If only I were a little closer.

"Something like that," I mutter, my eyes tracking back up to his face. His chin is covered with almost a week's worth of fuzz, his hair is damp and sticking up in all directions, and he's got rivulets of water running over his tanned skin. You'd have to be blind not to notice how hot he looks right now.

"I can order whatever you fancy."

I make a show of licking my lips as I focus on him, it's so much better than thinking I'm still back in that room like my brain keeps trying to tell me. I need him to make it all go away.

"Kas, you need to eat something. Did you even have any dinner before you went out earlier."

I shake my head. I was too nervous to eat.

I want to tell him to forget it, that I'm fine, but I know from the hard set of his jaw that he's not going to let this go.

"Chinese, and a bottle of Jack."

"You got it." He spins on his heels, and in a blink he's gone, leaving me alone for the first time since he went to run the bath. I begin to panic.

I hate that I feel so weak, so unsure of myself and my surroundings, but the second I can no longer see him, my heart starts to race, and the walls begin closing in on me. The images of his face that I'm trying to banish assault me immediately, and I squeeze my eyelids closed in an attempt to force him out of my head.

In a matter of seconds, his footsteps sound out over the blood racing past my ears, and his large frame fills the doorway once again.

I smile when his eyes land on me once more, but there's no way he misses my anxiety.

"I... uh..." He holds his phone out, clearly not knowing what to say about my obvious panic. "I thought you might like to choose." He drops onto the bed beside me and hands his phone over.

I stare at the menu before me, but the words just spin. I'm unable to focus on anything. My head pounds, reminding me once more that I clearly hit something hard when that motherfucker fell on me earlier.

"It's okay, you choose. There's not much I don't like." I hand it back, but he doesn't take it for a few seconds. Instead, he just studies me.

"Okay. Do you need some painkillers or anything?"

"Yeah, that would be great."

"I need to redress your cut, too."

I nod, knowing he's right. I can feel water trickling down from where the bandage has soaked up a load of bath water.

He makes quick work of ordering some food before placing his phone on the bedside table and standing.

He swaps his towel for a pair of boxer briefs—all too quickly, I might add—before disappearing from the room.

I focus on the noises he makes in the hope it keeps the panic and memories at bay, and thankfully when he reappears once more, I'm in a much better state than last time.

"Here, take these." He passes over a couple of tablets and a glass of water.

"Thank you."

"Throw the covers off, let's get a look at this cut."

I do as I'm told and happily lift the hem of his shirt. Sadly, he's too concerned about the blood that's dripping from the bandage to notice that I'm bare before him.

"Ouch," I complain when he starts pulling at the tape.

He glances up at me briefly, but he soon continues.

"You'd never make it as a nurse, you know. You're not exactly gentle."

"Hey, I'll have you know that these hands can do all kinds of gentle things."

"Oh yeah, want to start proving it?"

I breathe a sigh of relief when he finally pulls the last bit of tape from my skin.

"This might need stitches," he says, cleaning it up.

"It'll be fine. We can get some of those sticky things if need be."

"Kas," he warns.

"Spike," I counter.

"It'll leave a nasty scar."

Not as bad as the ones on the inside. I just about manage to stop that thought from spilling from my lips.

He knows tonight was bad. He's already seen me at my lowest; he doesn't need to hear things like that when he's trying so hard to put me back together.

"I've already got a plan for that."

"Oh?"

"Yeah, it might even involve your gentle fingers."

His eyes fly to mine. "You going to let me ink you, Tiny?"

"Damn right I am. I'm hoping you might let me return the favour, too."

"Err… I don't let just anybody at this work of art," he says seriously, gesturing to his half-naked body.

"You let my brother. That's all I need to know."

"Hey, it's not like that, Tiny. He's got skills."

"Of course he does." I wiggle my eyebrows and laugh, and fuck, it feels so good.

"I'll have you know that Rebel Ink is an upstanding studio. There's no dodgy dealings or extras going on under that roof."

"Of course there isn't." I wink, enjoying winding him up too much to stop. "So, would you let me? I am going to be mentored by the best, after all."

"Yeah, I might. I mean, you're not a terrible artist."

"How do you know?"

"I… uh… might have looked through your notebook the other day."

"You might?"

"Okay, so I did."

"I see."

"That last sketch you did. It was… graphic." His darkening eyes look up to mine from where he was focusing on cleaning me up.

"Like that one, did you?"

"Hmmm," he mumbles before going back to patching me up, his warm fingers brushing against my skin and causing goosebumps to erupt.

"You know, I can always use some more inspiration." Moving the leg he's not resting on, I bend it at the knee, giving him a taste of what I'm hiding.

He clears his throat, his lips parting and about to say something when the buzzer goes off.

"Ah, saved by the bell," I joke.

"Perfect timing, I'm all done here. We'll check it again in the morning and see if it does need stitches."

As quick as he can, he climbs from the bed and goes to get our dinner.

I've pulled his shirt down and am sitting myself up against his headboard when he reappears with a bag, a bottle of Jack, knives and forks.

"Picnic on the bed?"

"Sounds perfect."

The second the scent of the Chinese hits me, my stomach rumbles, reminding me that I haven't eaten for hours. I cast my mind back to my day before things got dramatic, and I can't actually remember the last thing I ate.

By the time my stomach is full and I've had one too many shots of Jack, it's all I can do to keep my eyes open.

"What time is it?" I ask, scooting down into Spike's bed and sucking in a deep breath that smells purely of him.

"Almost midnight."

"Hmmm."

"Just relax, Tiny. You're safe now."

The bed dips as he climbs off to discard what's left of our dinner in the kitchen and then use the toilet.

I have no idea if I drift off, but it seems like only seconds later he's crawling into bed behind me and pulling my body back into his. I sigh with contentment and almost instantly fall asleep. It's the most relaxed I've felt in months. Tonight might have been all kinds of fucked-up, but it's over. The weight of Mum's debt, of Jet catching up with me again, it's all gone.

I HAVE NO IDEA HOW, but the next thing I know, I'm waking after a peaceful night's sleep. Moving into this flat has changed my life in more ways than one—feeling safe enough not to have to keep one eye open at night is an even bigger relief than I thought possible.

Stretching out my legs, my entire body aches, and memories from why hit me like a fucking truck.

Jet forcing me against the desk, ripping my clothes from me, his knife, and then the dead weight of his body as he crashed back against me, pinning me to the floor.

I shudder as I think about the fact I had a dead, bleeding body crushing me.

Then my mind wanders to the slightly more positive parts of the night. The feeling of being in Spike's arms as he carried me away, the way he looked after me, how gentle and kind he was.

A light snore comes from beside me, and when I look up, I find him sleeping peacefully. His dark eyelashes are resting down on his cheeks, his full lips slightly parted. My eyes travel down onto his chest and abs that are exposed.

Unable to stop myself, I prop myself up on my elbow and reach out. My fingertip traces over the lines of the dragon tattoo that wraps around his hip and disappears under the sheets. It's bright, colourful, and so unbelievably intricate.

He doesn't react to my touch, so I continue my secret exploration, pushing the sheets lower so I can see more.

I'm totally lost to the lines of the artwork, and possibly the fact that I'm about an inch away from exposing a part of him that's equally as exciting, when he speaks, scaring the crap out of me.

"Careful, Tiny. You might get more than you bargained for in a minute."

"That's where you're wrong. I totally bargained for it. Studying your tat was just an excuse."

He chuckles, and I glance up at him. He looks incredibly sexy with his sleep-mussed hair and soft, just awake eyes.

With my eyes holding his, I continue moving the sheet.

"Kas," he warns.

"You really should have worn something if you didn't want me looking."

"It's uncomfortable."

"Sure it is."

Just before I expose him, his fingers wrap around my wrist.

"How are you feeling?" he asks, concern filling his eyes as they bounce between mine.

"Hot," I say, biting down on my bottom lip.

He stares at it, his tongue sneaking out to lick across his own. His chest heaves, and it's impossible to miss the tenting of the sheet beside me.

Sitting up, I take matters into my own hands and

wrap my fingers around the hem of his shirt and pull it up over my head, knowing that I'm bare beneath. I throw my leg over his waist and pin him in place.

His eyes lock on my breasts as I slowly grind down on him.

"Get out of your head, Spike. I need you."

Taking one of his arms lying limply at his side, I lift it, guiding his hand toward my chest, but just before he makes contact his phone starts ringing beside him.

Faster than I thought possible, I'm thrown off of him and he's standing from the bed.

"It's your brother," he states, keeping his back to me as he swipes the screen and puts it to his ear.

I watch the muscles of his back ripple and his round arse as he walks from the room. "She's okay, Zach. Yeah, she slept all night and seems fine this morning." He continues talking, but I zone him out as I slide back down where he just was, his heat surrounding me as if he's still here.

My core aches for more of what I started, and I just about resist the urge to give myself what I need. I already know it won't be enough.

The coffee machine comes on, drowning out the deep timbre of his voice. After a few seconds, my need for caffeine gets the better of me and I climb out of bed, making a quick pit stop in the bathroom to freshen up.

The bandage on my hip is a harsh reminder of everything that happened the night before, but I force the images from my head. I've got other, more fulfilling intentions to think about right now.

I make quick work of brushing my teeth and running my fingers through my sleep-dried hair and make my way out to join Spike.

"Yeah, I know..." His words trail off as he looks over to find me walking in as naked as he is. "Just leave it for now," he growls while shaking his head at me in warning.

Walking over to him, I don't stop until I'm right in his space, my eyes locked on his, both reading and ignoring the warning written in his.

The sound of Zach talking on the other end hits my ears, but I don't let it stop me.

Ripping my eyes from his, I briefly run them down his body, taking in his already hard length that's standing to attention.

I lick my lips before pressing them to his chest. He flinches at my touch, his hand finding its way to my hair, but to my surprise, he doesn't pull me back.

"Well, I guess you'll just have to find out for yourself if you won't listen to me."

I don't even try to bother attempting to figure out what they're talking about. It's obvious it's to do with me. I've got every confidence that I'll get it out of Spike once he hangs up one way or another.

"No, no. You don't need to. We'll come to you."

He pauses while I make my way down his stomach, his eyes locked on mine. The warning that was there morphs into a look of desire and need as I descend.

"Why not? Today seems like as good a one as ever."

I couldn't agree more.

"Fuck," he barks once I'm on my knees before him and my tongue licks at the end of his cock. "Yeah, yeah, sorry. I... uh... spilled my coffee."

Smiling to myself, I part my lips and suck him into my mouth.

A groan rumbles up his throat. It's low enough that

Zach would never hear it, yet I feel it all the way down to the tips of my toes.

His fingers tighten in my hair as he encourages me, his fight for this not to happen long gone.

"O-okay. Uh huh. Yeah."

Pulling back, I flatten my tongue and lick up the underside before swirling it around the head.

The muscles in his neck pull with his restraint, and his jaw pops as Zach says something else in his ear.

"Fine. See you soon."

Pulling it from his ear, he shoves his finger into the screen, harshly ending the call before dropping it to the counter behind him.

"Damn it, Kas."

Sitting back on my haunches, I look up at him innocently. "What? Just thanking you for last night."

Our eyes hold in a battle of wills, but I think we both know that right now mine is stronger. His cock bobs temptingly in front of me, and when I lean forward once more he doesn't do a thing to stop me. Instead, his fingers dive in my hair once more and he lets out a loud growl as I suck him as deep as I can take him. His head falls back as his fingers tighten, losing himself to the sensation.

"Fuck, my dirty little girl looks good on her knees."

His words send liquid lust straight to my core.

I work him slowly and drive him crazy with need before I up the pace and allow him to take the release he needs.

"Kas, fuck. Tiny," he grunts, his hold on me getting harder as his cock twitches violently between my lips.

I assume it's my warning, but I'm going nowhere.

His salty cum hits the back of my throat, and I swallow it down until he's finished.

Standing to full height, I find his wild, hungry eyes trained on me. His hand remains in my hair, but for a second, I have no idea if he's going to use it to pull me closer or to push me away.

"You shouldn't have done that, Tiny."

I shrug. "You know I'm not one for following the rules."

"Fuck," he barks, looking away from me. "Zach's coming over. He needs to see with his own eyes that you're okay."

Ignoring him, I push up on my tiptoes. "Kiss me."

"Kas." His voice is low, and it sends shockwaves through me.

"Kiss. Me."

He hesitates for only two seconds before his fingers twitch and he closes the space between us.

His lips press against mine before his tongue plunges into my mouth. I moan the second he finds mine. I need this so fucking badly.

My nails scratch at his shoulders as I try to get closer. Just being pressed up against his hard body isn't enough. I need more. I need everything.

Sensing my need, his hands drop to my arse and he lifts me onto the counter. I gasp when the cool of the marble bites into my skin. He uses the opportunity to deepen our kiss even further. It's wet, dirty, full of need, and utterly consuming. The exact distraction that I've been craving since he walked me out of that warehouse last night.

"Spike," I moan into his mouth.

"We've got fifteen minutes." His hands are

everywhere as he tries to take as much from me as I do him.

"Then we'd better be quick." He drops his lips to my neck, his hands cupping my breasts and pinching my nipples.

"I need to shower."

"Sounds perfect," I sigh, thinking of the water running down his skin as he slides into me. My thighs clench around his waist, my heels digging into his arse, forcing him closer.

"You're going to get me killed, Kas," he warns, kissing down over my collarbone. If it didn't feel so fucking incredible, his words and the reminder of last night might have been enough to cool things off. But that's the thing about when we connect: nothing else matters. Hell, nothing else exists.

"You're wasting time," I warn, although it pains me to do it when he laves at my nipple before sucking it deep into his mouth.

In a beat, he has me in his arms and is carrying me once again. In seconds we're in the bathroom and he's kicking the door shut behind us before turning the shower on. He doesn't wait for it to warm up. Instead, he stands us both under it before pushing me back against the tiles.

I don't notice the cold. I'm too consumed by him.

"Are you wet for me?" he moans in my ear.

"Yes. Please, Spike. I need you."

With my legs hooked up high around his waist and his hips pinning me to the wall, he releases one hand from my arse and teases my wetness with his cock.

My muscles contract, desperate to feel him pushing inside me.

After what feels like forever, he finally lines himself up with me before dropping me lower and impaling me on him.

"Fuck," I cry as the sensation of him stretching me open consumes me. "Yes, yes."

Taking both of my hands in one of his, he pins them against the wall above my head.

"You're fucking addictive, little girl," he grates out, his lips brushing against mine, his increased breaths fanning my face. "You're like my little drug. I try to resist. I know it's bad, but fuck, it's so fucking good."

His lips capture mine before I get a chance to say anything—not that I have a clue how to follow that up.

His thrusts get faster, wilder as his pelvis rubs against my hip in the most delicious way.

"Oh God, Spike. So good, so fucking good," I moan when he rips his lips from mine.

He releases my hands, allowing me to touch him. My fingers run over his hair, scratching at his scalp before I begin clawing at his shoulders once again when he grabs my arse and pulls my lower half from the wall.

The angle change is mind-blowing, and in only seconds I'm racing toward my release.

"Oh God, oh God," I chant before Spike thrusts into me one more time and sends me crashing head-first into an earth-shattering orgasm.

I cry out some unintelligible words as the sensations take over my entire body and I float away on the pleasure only he's able to give me. Just like I remember from last time, as I fly, I feel free, and the only two things that exist in the world are the two of us.

He's right about one thing: it is fucking addicting.

CHAPTER TWENTY

SPIKE

THE LAST THING I want to do is walk out of that shower without her and once again forget about our time together, but it's what's got to happen.

"Take your time," I whisper against her lips, allowing myself one more kiss before I turn my back on her and grab a towel.

The atmosphere in the room changes almost instantly, and despite the fact that it's full of steam from the hot shower, it feels icy cold as I break what we shared.

"Spike?" Her voice is quiet and broken, and I hate that I've got to do this. She needs support right now, someone to hold her, not for me to walk away. But I can't.

I've already made so many mistakes with her, and despite my best intentions, I just keep fucking up even more.

Maybe I should just admit to Zach what's been happening. I deserve the beating that's sure to follow, there's no question there.

Looking over my shoulder, I take in her small yet curvy body as the water streams down it.

Fuck, I don't want to leave her there looking so vulnerable and unsure of herself.

"Your brother will be here in a few minutes. Take your time."

With that, I pull the door open and sever the connection.

My heart aches the second the door closes behind me.

There is so much fucking wrong about all of this, but when we're together, when she's in my arms, it's the only thing that makes sense.

I'm fully dressed and making a fresh cup of coffee when there's a knock on the door. Kas still hasn't emerged from the bathroom and I've almost gone down to check on her a million times, but I can't.

"I brought breakfast," Zach says as a greeting, holding a bag up in front of me, but I don't miss how he looks around for Kas or anything else suspicious. I know how things looked last night. I know exactly what he's thinking.

The smell of bacon hits my nose and my mouth immediately waters.

"Thanks, I need this."

"Where is she?" he asks, stepping inside and looking down toward the bedrooms.

"In the shower."

"Are you sure she's okay?"

"As sure as I can be. She's not exactly an open book."

"She thinks she's a hard arse, but I think we both know it's all fake."

I mutter my agreement, but I'm on edge and worried about saying too much and giving anything away. His shoulders are already tense, as if he's come here for a fight, and there's a deepness to his voice that isn't usually there.

"How was she when you got her home?"

Broken. Traumatised. Scared.

"Exhausted. We cleaned her up, had dinner, and she crashed."

Okay so it's stretching the truth slightly, but it's all he's getting from me.

"*We* cleaned her up?"

"I ran her a bath. Although I wasn't sure if she should have had it. She's got quite a cut on her hip that I think might need stitches." Another half-lie. I swallow down my guilt and just focus on what's important right now, making sure she's okay.

Noise from down the hall has Zach looking up impatiently. For someone who used to stay as far away from his family as possible, he sure is protective.

"Do I smell bacon?" Kas asks, cutting through the tension building in the room.

Her voice has goosebumps erupting across my skin. I've not even seen her and she's affecting me in ways she shouldn't.

"Yeah, I brought bacon sandwiches."

Zach's eyes soften as she must appear behind me,

but I fight my need to turn and look at her. I'm already scared of what I'll find after walking out on her like I did earlier.

"Let me just get dressed and I'm there. Coffee, too?"

"I'm on it," I say, pushing from the sofa, glad of something to be able to do to try to rid myself of the nervous energy racing though me.

"She looks so pale," Zach comments once the sound of her door shutting signals that she's no longer in hearing distance.

"What did you expect? That fucker was going to..." I trail off. Neither of us need it spelled out.

"I know. I know. I was just..."

"Hoping it wouldn't affect her. I'm not sure that's possible, Zach. She might be strong, but even the hardest have limits."

He's nodding when I glance over, but his eyes are trained on the coffee table.

"Cruz's guys cleared the place after we left. Everything is sorted."

Shit, I hadn't even considered the evidence and dead bodies we left behind. What the hell is my life turning into?

The biggest thing to ever happen to me was when she... Nope. I shake my head, locking down any thoughts of that time in my life.

"That's... uh... good." I guess.

I'm sitting down with three fresh coffees when Kas' bedroom door opens and she emerges. This time I'm unable to keep my eyes averted and I glance up at her.

She's dressed in an oversized hoodie, her curvy legs bare and sticking out the bottom. Her hair hangs still wet around her shoulders, her face clear of makeup, but it's the redness to her eyes that makes my breath catch.

She's been crying.

"Hey," she says to Zach, totally ignoring that I'm in the room and walking over to him.

She drops down on the sofa beside him and accepts his embrace when he lifts his arm for her.

I watch them, feeling like I'm intruding when he drops his lips to the top of her head.

"How are you holding up?"

"I'll be okay."

My fists clench at her words. It's her answer for everything, and knowing that the people of her past have clearly accepted it pisses me off.

Has she ever had anyone looking out for her?

"Thanks for this," she says, reaching forward for the bacon sandwich.

"So, I was thinking. If you're up for it, you should come to the studio with Spike this afternoon. Get your training started." I don't miss the warning glance he shoots me. He's not happy about this, and I'm sure now he's really regretting his decision to allow me to mentor her.

"Yeah?" she asks, her usual spark returning to her eyes at the thought.

"Yeah. There's no point in you hiding here now, so you may as well make a start at your new life."

She swallows nervously. "You still want me, even though you didn't end up paying off my debt? At least, not with money, anyway."

"Kas, the money had fuck all to do with it. I'd have willingly paid that and more to keep you safe. You've got a talent and need a decent job. It's the perfect solution to getting back on your feet. And now all that is over with, I'll start looking for a place for you to live."

I half-choke on the mouthful of coffee I'd just swallowed, ensuring both of them turn their eyes on me.

"Sorry, wrong hole. Kas is fine staying here for as long as she needs."

Both sets of eyes narrow, but for very different reasons.

"I appreciate that, Spike, but I think it will be good for Kas to have some space to figure out what she wants from life." His words are sharp, making it impossible for me to miss his hidden meaning.

I look to Kas to find her lips pursed in frustration.

"I'm sitting right here. I can speak for myself, you know," she snaps at Zach. I almost smile at hearing her usual fire returning.

"You want to stay here?" he asks.

"Well..." Kas flicks a look at me, but the hardness in her eyes doesn't fill me with joy. "No, but I'd like to be able to make the decision myself."

"No?" I ask, disbelief dripping from that one word.

She shakes her head at me, I assume trying to tell me that we'll speak about this later, but it's too late. I'm already pissed beyond belief.

"Fuck this, Kas. You don't want to be here, you know where the fucking door is," I bark, standing from the sofa and swiping my keys, phone and wallet from the counter and storming to the front door.

In hindsight, I probably gave away too much about how I'm feeling about my new housemate and confirming Zach's suspicions, but the anger that's burning in my belly doesn't give a shit.

I run down the stairs, the red haze descending faster

than I should allow. I've done everything for her this past week, and she can just forget it all that easily at the mention of Zach finding her a new place to live. Well, fuck her.

Fuck. Her.

"Good morning," Louisa sings the second my foot hits the ground floor.

I have to give her a double-take when I look up. She looks good. Really good.

"M-morning," I grunt.

"You look like you could use a coffee. Is everything okay?"

I glance behind me, thinking about the two people I just left up in my flat as I consider her question.

"Yeah, everything's fine."

I might be frustrated with Kas' answer, but I think we all know it was the right one. The longer she's in my flat, the more I'm going to cave to temptation. The more I'm going to betray one of my best friends.

"Really? Want to talk about it? Freddie's asleep, we should have at least another..." she checks her watch, "fifteen minutes."

She takes a step toward her front door, which I now notice is open, and holds it wider, waiting for me to follow despite the fact that I haven't actually answered.

When I stormed out of the flat, I had no idea where I was heading. Into Louisa's definitely wasn't a part of my plan, but I soon find myself following her. Having a coffee with a friend sounds much more appealing than randomly wandering around the streets.

It's not the first time I've been inside her flat. It's almost identical to mine—the only difference is that there's kid stuff everywhere. And I mean literally everywhere. I've no idea how one little boy needs so much shit.

"Sorry about the mess. He's like a little whirlwind."

"It's nothing. You should have seen the state of my place before K—" My words falter at the almost mention of her name. "I'm not exactly a neat freak. It used to drive Titch crazy."

"He still living with his girlfriend?"

"Wife," I correct. It still feels kinda weird thinking about him being a married man, especially as he went from single to married in the blink of an eye.

"Oh yeah, how could I forget," she says with a laugh. "Black, right?" she asks, holding up a mug as I take a seat.

"Please."

"So, what's got you running from your own flat?"

"It's nothing."

I feel her stare the second the lie falls from my lips.

"Riight. Because it's such a normal thing for you to do. You always seem so... sure of yourself. No offence, but you look like a hot mess right now."

"Wow, thanks for that." I run my fingers through my hair, trying to tame it. I haven't looked in the mirror since our shower earlier, so I have no clue what state it's in.

"It's the girl, right? Kas?"

"Yes, no. I don't know."

She passes my mug over before lowering herself to the sofa in front of me.

She looks at me knowingly for a few seconds before saying words that rock my world.

"You've fallen for her, haven't you?"

"What? No, of course I haven't. She's Zach's kid sister."

"And that's meant to stop how you feel about her?"

I open my mouth to try to argue some more, but she beats me to it.

"We can't help how we feel, Spike. I of all people should know that. Look at how I ended up when I fell for the wrong one."

"And that's the exact reason I haven't. I'm not going there. Not with Kas. Not with anyone."

"Why?" she asks, her head tilting to the side much like a confused puppy. "I know I complain about this, but if I hadn't met him then I wouldn't have my Freddie, and I can't imagine life without him now. He's my world."

I shrug. "I have my reasons."

She sighs, and I hate that she's pitying me right now. I don't fucking need it.

"Just give it a chance, Spike. Who knows what could become of it."

Two broken hearts and a bleak future? No thanks.

I shake my head. "It's not meant to be."

"The fact that you're sulking about whatever's happened tells another story."

"Even without my own bullshit, she's Zach's little si—"

"Sister, I know. You mentioned... once or twice. If you spoke to him, I'm sure he'd understand."

"Oh yeah." I gesture to my face. "Does it look like he understands? And he did this without knowing anything happened."

"So something *has* happened." She raises a brow.

"Fucking hell."

CHAPTER TWENTY-ONE

KAS

AFTER TELLING Zach once again that I was fine, he finally took the hint and left after he finished his coffee. I'd be seeing him in a bit at the studio, but I got the feeling he didn't want me out of his sight. It was sweet, although totally overbearing and unnecessary. He confirmed that the threat has gone, that it was all over and that I could get on with my life. And that's what I intend to do.

I'm excited to embark on the next chapter of my life where I can hopefully have a job I love and finally know what it's like to live with my head above water with people who care if I float or drown.

That's not entirely fair. Jodie would have cared.

Feeling guilty that I've been too distracted with my

own disaster of a life to reply to the message she sent me checking in, I sit on the edge of my bed and tap out a reply, asking if we can meet up in the next few days. I might not spell out the recent events in my message, but I have every intention of telling her all about it. Hell knows, I need someone else's opinion.

I hit send just as the front door slams, followed seconds later by Spike marching past my room and to his own.

My teeth grind as I think about how he just stormed out earlier. He goes on and on about how he needs to do the right thing, not betray Zach or whatever—it's a little late for all that if you ask me, but hey—but the way he blew out of the place didn't exactly look like a guy who doesn't care.

"What the hell is wrong with you?" I shout, marching to his room and throwing the door wide open.

"Nothing, I needed a breather." I watch as he pulls his shirt off and replaces it with another.

"Really?"

"Really. I need to get to the studio. Are you fucking coming or what?" He spins and pins me with a hard stare. His jaw is tight and his lips pressed into a thin line. Whoa, he really is pissed.

"Uh, yeah. I'm coming, let me just change and—"

"Be fucking quick."

"Jesus, what crawled up your arse?"

He takes a step toward me, his dark eyes boring down into me. If it's meant to scare or intimidate me, then it falls far from the mark. I know him too well now to ever be scared of him.

His lips part like he's about to respond, but he must

think better of it because he closes them again and storms past me.

"It was nice talking to you too," I mutter as I make my way back to my room to throw some clothes on.

"Ten minutes and I'm leaving," booms through the flat.

I pull on a skirt and t-shirt before running a brush through my hair and shoving my makeup into my bag to do at the studio. I'm not sure pushing his patience by doing it right now would be wise.

"Right, let's go then," I announce, walking through the living room and pulling the front door open.

Spike pushes from where he was leaning against the kitchen counter, staring at his phone, and walks over.

At the last minute, his eyes lift and find me. They instantly narrow, a deep frown line forming between his brows.

"You're not wearing that," he spits.

"Err... I think I am." I jut my hip out and rest my hand on it, the cut making it smart a little.

His jaw pops as he stares at me. "This is the worst fucking idea ever," he mutters before blowing through the door. I assume I'm meant to follow, so after pulling the door closed, I run down the stairs after him.

He doesn't say a word to me as I climb on the back of his bike, suddenly understanding his issue with my skirt, and he speeds off into the city toward Zach's studio.

After parking out front and allowing me to get off, he kills the engine and immediately takes off for the building I haven't been inside since I had my latest ink done.

As I walk through the front door, the place feels

totally different. I was a nervous wreck during my only two visits here. I was terrified to tell Zach who I really was, terrified that he wouldn't believe me and that I'd be sent away like I didn't exist. That was the only time in my life I've ever been that nervous. The knowledge that my only living family member—that I know of—could turn me away like I was nothing has butterflies erupting in my belly. He probably thought I was a weak and timid little girl back then. I'm hoping he's learned that isn't who I really am now.

Thankfully, that didn't happen. Zach saw something within me—a little bit of him, maybe—and he took my words seriously. I don't think I'll ever be able to express how much his faith in me meant that day. After I lost Mum, I didn't think I'd have anyone close again. Yes, I had Jodie, but I knew that at some point she'd finish college and move on. She's a beautiful, intelligent woman, and any man would be lucky to have her. Unlike the rest of the arseholes I've met in the shitholes Mum moved us to, she doesn't deserve to be there or to have been dealt the shitty hand she has.

"Kas!" Biff says excitedly as she walks through a door at the back of reception. "It's so good to see you. How are you feeling?"

"I'm okay," I say and immediately wince, hearing Spike's warning not to say those words. "It'll take more than last night to break me."

"That's good to hear, but you don't need to put on a brave face around me." As she passes me, she runs her hand down my arm in support. "I know the guys can be a little..."

"A little?" a deep voice prompts from behind me,

and when I turn I find Titch standing in the doorway, wearing an amused smile.

"A little... rough around the edges, hard to talk to, arseholes," she explains with a smile while Titch shakes his head at her.

"You wound me, sis. Wound me."

"I told you to stop calling me that."

"What?" he asks innocently. "You're officially my little sister now." He throws his arm around her neck and messes up her hair.

"In-law, Titch. In-fucking-law, and you're barely a month older than me and a hell of a lot less wise, so knock it off, would ya?"

Titch turns his amused eyes on me. "She's just pissed because Danni has told her how much better I am in bed than Zach."

"Stop talking right fucking now," Zach booms from behind me.

"Jesus, I think I might have made a mistake agreeing to this," I say with a laugh.

"Nah, you're already part of this fucked-up family, kid. You may as well embrace it fully."

My teeth grind at his use of the term 'kid' again, but as he pulls Biff into his arms, he looks too damn happy for me to rip him a new one.

"Where's your mentor? Still got his knickers in a twist?"

"Something like that. He stormed straight down there the moment we arrived."

All three of them follow my finger and look down the hallway toward their rooms.

"You're fucking up his head good and proper there, girl. I've never seen him like this," Titch says—much to

Zach's irritation, if the colour of his face is anything to go by.

"Don't listen to him," Biff whispers in his ear, but the second she's finished she swallows nervously. It's good to know she's kept my secret, although it seems to be killing her. I wonder how long that's going to last.

"He just doesn't like having a female housemate. I'm ruining his game, I think."

"Well, if he should find it while you're still there, you'll know about it. The nights I had to listen to his fucking headboard banging." Titch rolls his eyes as my stomach twists uncomfortably.

It's not news to me that Spike's bedroom door may as well be a revolving one, but knowing it and hearing someone else describe it are two very different things.

"She'll be out of his hair soon," Zach says. "We're gonna find her a place of her own."

"Really?" Titch asks, his brows shooting up almost to his hairline.

"Why is that so shocking?"

"N-no reason. I'm just surprised."

"Okay well... I've got a client heading in at ten. I need to sort my shit out," Zach says, kissing Biff on the nose and disappearing down the hallway.

"What?" I ask when I turn back to find both Biff and Titch's stares burning into me.

"I don't know about my lil' sis over there, but I wasn't born yesterday. There's no way in hell Spike is letting you out of his sight anytime soon. The only other place he wants you sleeping is the other side of his bed, not in another flat on the other side of the city."

"Whatever," I say, waving off his comment as if it's nothing. "I should probably go find him."

I walk away, knowing that they're still both staring at me.

"I promise not to say I told you so when it turns out I'm right," Titch calls after me before barking a laugh when I flip him off over my shoulder. "He's in fucking trouble with that one," I hear him say to Biff before I knock on Spike's door and slip inside.

I'm expecting to find him brooding in the corner of the room or something, but when I look around, I find it's empty.

Making the most of my peace, I take everything in. Unlike his flat, this place is tidy—spotless actually. The two walls are covered in hand-painted designs, another has photographs of more artwork framed and arranged kind of like a huge mosaic, and the third wall holds a floor-to-ceiling bookcase with a built-in desk. It's impressive and totally not what I thought I'd find. I was expecting some dark and dingy room with crap everywhere.

I run my fingers over some of his art as I make my way farther into the room before letting my hand float up the soft leather of the tattoo chair and making myself at home behind his desk.

There's a half-completed design that he's clearly been working on, and I can't help but picture what he might look like while deep in concentration as he sketches.

I run my fingers over the intricate floral design, totally lost to the details of the piece, so much so that I don't hear him join me.

It's not until he speaks that I realise he's here and that he's right behind me.

"So you haven't changed your mind?"

"Jesus, Spike," I say, clutching at my chest where my heart is racing beneath. "A little warning would have been nice."

"I didn't exactly sneak in."

"Yeah, well. You scared the shit out of me."

With his hand on the back of his chair, he spins me around. His eyes drop to where my skirt is sitting high on my thigh. It's probably high enough to give him a flash of my underwear beneath, but I don't make any effort to cover up.

After long, tense seconds, his eyes find mine.

"You like what you see?" he asks, a twinkle in his eye that's been missing since our time in the shower this morning.

Fuck, how was that only this morning? My core clenches with my need to feel him inside me once again.

Biting down on my bottom lip, I make a show of checking him out.

"I think you already know the answer to that," I say in a voice that I hope is low and seductive.

"I wasn't sure about it," he says, leaning over me and swiping his sketch from the desk. "I think it's too dark for what my client wants."

My brain misfires for a few seconds as I try to switch lanes to talk about his sketch instead of telling him how badly I need him to fuck me again.

"J-just switch out a couple of those red roses for whatever these lighter ones are," I say, pointing to the flowers in question.

"Maybe. I guess we'll find out soon. She's in this evening to get started. I need to finish this off for her. Do you mind?"

"Oh... um... sure." I hesitantly stand, but the

arsehole doesn't move, so the second I'm at full height, I'm almost pressed against his hard body.

"Spike?" I question, trying to figure out what the hell kind of game he's playing. He blows hot and cold faster than I can compute.

"Kas," he counters, his voice deep and sending tingles right where I don't need them.

"My brother could walk in here any moment," I say, pointing out the obvious. "How do you think he'd feel, seeing you pressed up against me like his?" It's a low blow, but I can't help the words falling from my lips.

His eyes darken and his jaw pops with frustration while his scent fills my nose and makes me want to do things that would be a really, really bad idea in Zach's studio.

"Go and sit in the chair over there, and stay out of my way."

A shiver runs down my spine at his cold words. I might believe them if his eyes didn't betray how he really feels.

"With pleasure." I slip away from him, making sure I run my hand across his crotch.

"Motherfucker," he grunts when my fingers tease his already semi-hard cock.

I walk over to the other chair, where I dropped my bag when I first walked in here.

"Spike?" I ask, bending down to pick it up and ensuring my arse is in the air.

He clears his throat before answering, and I can't help but laugh. "What?"

"Where's the bathroom?" Standing to my full height, I spin toward him with a smile plastered on my face.

"Down the hall on the left."

I nod and duck out of the room. I can't help laughing to myself as I hear him cuss as I shut the door behind me. Although, I can't help but wonder if he was right as we left the flat earlier, because this could be the worst idea ever.

There are two cubicles in the room labelled as the bathroom, but I ignore them in favour of the mirror hanging above the basins.

Dragging my makeup bag out, I place everything I'll need on the counter before starting with my concealer. I might have slept better than I was expecting last night, but that doesn't mean I'm not rocking bags darker than most days.

I'm putting the finishing touches to my red lips when the door opens.

"Looking good, Kas," Biff says, taking in my face full of makeup.

"I got dragged out of the flat before I had a chance this morning."

"Men," she says with a roll of her eyes. "Seriously though," she says, her smile faltering. "How's it going after..." She trails off. I assume she means since I admitted to fucking Spike.

"Oh it's... going," I say with a sigh.

"Zach said you refused to let him look after you last night, that you only wanted Spike." The slight wince as she said it tells me all I need to know about how Zach feels about that.

"I wasn't in any kind of frame of mind to make sensible decisions."

"Kas," she warns. "They might buy your hard-arse bullshit, but I don't."

As I stare at her I feel some of my walls start to crumble. I like Biff, I have since that first day I walked in for my first appointment with Zach. I know I can trust her. She didn't go running back to Zach with details about me and Spike, despite the fact that I know it's killing her, but I really don't want to put any more of this on her shoulders.

"Spike just..." I blow out a breath. "He makes me feel safe in a way I've never experienced before. I know it's fucked-up, but it is what it is." I shrug. My movement pulls at the bandage I redid after my shower this morning, and I drop my hand to it.

"Are you okay?"

"Yeah, just a scratch from last night."

"Let me see." I lift my shirt, intending on showing her that it's wrapped and nothing to worry about, but the second her eyes widen, I know I made a mistake.

"Fuck, Kas. Let me look." She drops to her knees and, much gentler than Spike last night, pulls the tape from my skin. "This needs stitches. I'm taking you to the hospital."

"No, it'll be fine. It's just where it is. I keep moving and opening it back up."

"Exactly. It needs stitches. We're going now, or I'll get Zach involved," she warns.

"Ugh, fine. But it better be quick, I don't want to skip out on my first day."

"The boss won't care. Come on." She takes my hand and drags me out of there like a woman on a mission. She sticks her head into Spike's room and tells him what we're doing before doing the same with Zach, and before I know it we're on the pavement and climbing into an Uber.

CHAPTER TWENTY-TWO

SPIKE

I SHOULD HAVE BEEN RELIEVED that Biff was taking control and dragging Kas to the hospital to get that wound stitched up, but I wasn't. From the second the words fell from her lips, I was pissed off. I wanted to be the one to be looking after her.

I finished up my sketch for my afternoon client, although my head wasn't really in it. I was too worried about what Biff and Kas were going to say as an excuse for her having a random knife wound on her hip. It's not exactly an everyday kind of accident.

I get through two clients and three cups of coffee that I've got to make myself, seeing as the guys are also fully booked, before I hear the familiar sound of their voices out in reception.

Putting my pen down, I make my way out.

"Is everything okay?" I ask, looking between the two of them as they laugh together.

Seeing her genuine smile makes my chest constrict, but my joy doesn't override my concern.

"Yeah, why wouldn't it be?" Kas asks, her voice turning cooler the moment she shifts her attention onto me.

"No reason. I was just worried about what you'd say—"

"Oh, no need to worry about that. We got lucky," Biff says, winking at Kas.

"Lucky? Lucky how?"

"The nurse that stitched her up was a hottie. I think he'd have done just about anything she asked of him without batting an eyelid." As Biff smiles knowingly at me, jealousy and anger begin to swirl within me.

"He even gave me his number. Can you believe that?"

"Uh..." I start but soon find I have no other words. The thought of some guy having his hands on her is bad enough, but hitting on her? Oh, fuck no.

"Let's go." Wrapping my hand around her wrist, I pull her down toward my room.

"Watch out, we've woken the caveman," Biff calls from behind us, making Kas snort.

The second we're in my room, I back her up against the wall, pinning her hands above her head and staring down into her amused blue eyes.

"I hope you weren't planning on calling him."

"What if I already have?" My teeth grind at her words.

"Then you need to call him back and cancel."

"And why would I want to do that?" She tilts her head to the side, trying to look all innocent.

"You know why."

"Nope. Don't think I do. As far as I'm aware, I'm single and can hook up with hot nurses any day of the week."

A growl rumbles up my throat.

"Are you doing this on purpose?"

"What?"

I suck in a calming breath, forcing myself to reign it in and stay cool despite the fact that she drives me fucking crazy.

Dropping my lips to her ear, I try to stop myself from saying the words that are on the tip of my tongue, but I know it's futile.

"You're not going out with him."

"Give me one good reason why not, and I'll think about it."

I pull back so I can look into her eyes. They're already significantly darker than they were only moments ago, proving to me that she's as affected by our closeness as I am.

Tension crackles between us as she waits for my answer. Her eyes bounce between mine for a beat before dropping to my lips. It's then that I know I've lost any kind of restraint I should have when it comes to her.

I take her mouth, forcing my tongue past her lips in search of hers. My body presses hers into the door, until she gasps, and I remember that she spent the last few hours in the hospital.

That thought is like a bucket of ice water over me.

"Fuck," I bark, taking a huge step back and turning around so I don't have to look at her. Although my imagination is good enough to have a very vivid image of how she might look with her swollen lips and heaving chest. "Fuck."

My skin burns where she's staring at me. She probably thinks I've lost my goddamn mind with how I'm acting toward her. I'm starting to wonder if I have. I'm meant to be the oldest here, the wisest, the one with the most life experience to give me all the skills I need to do the right thing, but fuck, we may as well swap places because while she seems to know exactly what she wants, I'm the one fucking up and ruining everything.

I want her, I can't deny that. But I shouldn't have her. She's too young for me, too good for me. I'll end up breaking her heart, because I can't allow even the possibility of it being more than a bit of fun. The fallout would be too painful, and I already know I wouldn't survive it.

But I can't just play with her and have some fun like I would any other woman. She's Zach's little sister. She should be forbidden, untouchable. Yet I touched, and all I can think about is doing it again. Over and over.

"Spike, you need—" Whatever she was going to say is interrupted as a knock sounds out on the door.

"Spike, your client is here. Are you both decent?" Biff calls out.

I spin on the spot, pinning Kas in place with my hard stare.

"She knows?" I whisper, panic starting to build within me. If she knows, then there's no way she'll keep it from Zach. That's not how those two work.

Kas shrugs as if it's not a big deal.

"You told her?"

"Chill the fuck out, Spike. She guessed. I wasn't about to lie. So we fucked, it's really not a big deal."

A bitter laugh falls from my lips. "That's it? We just fucked?"

"Was that not what it was? If you were making love to me, then I didn't get the memo." She rolls her eyes and it pisses me off further.

A storm begins to swell within me. I shouldn't fucking care about any of this. I shouldn't care that she only thinks what we've shared was nothing more than a quick fuck to get what we both needed. At the end of the day, that's all it was, right?

"I don't make fucking love," I spit, taking a step toward her.

Instead of looking all intimidated by me, she takes one of her own, her eyes holding mine, heat still filling them. It makes my cock twitch.

"Well, there you go then. What the fuck are you trying to argue about? We fucked, it was fun, you were... okay."

"Okay?" I ask, my eyebrows almost shooting into my hairline.

"I mean, clearly you were good enough for a repeat, and probably a couple yet. But that might just be because you're easy. Accessible."

My chin drops. "You think I'm easy?"

She chuckles, and my blood begins to boil. "That's what all the dancers at the club said. Why do you think I tried it on in the first place? You didn't think I actually wanted you, did you, old man?"

Some unintelligible noise falls from my lips as our eyes hold. Tension crackles between us, but despite her words, I feel that familiar pull to her. I'm about to close the space and prove to her that she's wrong, that there's more here than just *convenience*, but I don't get the chance.

"Guys, seriously. I can only make excuses for so long."

"This isn't over," I warn, taking a step toward Kas who continues to hold her ground. Her eyes follow me until I stop right in front of her.

Reaching out, I slide my fingers around her throat. Her eyes widen at my possessive move and her lips part in preparation for my kiss.

Dropping down, I stop when our lips are a breath apart.

"Stop denying what we both know is true, Tiny. This..." my fingers tighten to the point I feel her pulse thunder beneath my fingers, "is anything but *convenient*."

"Spike," she moans, pushing forward and trying to take what she needs.

Spinning us, I push her backward. "I suggest you sit and watch. You might learn a few things."

She stumbles back when I release her, but it's not because I use any force, it's because of the effect I know I have on her.

Running my hand though my hair, I walk over to the door and rip it open, much to Biff's shock.

Her eyes widen as they run the length of me. If she was expecting me to answer the door naked or something, she must be bitterly disappointed.

Lifting up on her tiptoes, she looks over my shoulder before her eyes settle on Kas, who I can only assume has done as she's told for once and sat down.

When her attention comes back to me, her eyes are narrowed in warning.

"I'm watching you," she warns, pointing between her eyes and mine with two fingers. "You hurt her, and it won't just be Zach you need to be worrying about."

Pulling the door closed behind me so Kas can't eavesdrop, I force Biff to back up a bit.

"Have you told him?"

"Told him what?" she asks innocently, although I can tell it's fake. "Just figure your shit out, yeah? You want her? Fine. Just prove that you can do right by her. You don't, and this is all a bit of fun for you, then stop it right now. She can move in with us and it can be over."

"I know what I'm doing." It's a big fat lie, but I don't like how her suggestion of Kas moving in with them makes me feel.

"Riiight," she says with a roll of her eyes.

Great, I'm glad I'm convincing her just as much as I am myself.

"Just be careful. She's already been through enough. She doesn't need you shattering her heart."

"Who said anything about hearts?"

"She's not the kind of girl you fuck and chuck, Spike. And I'm not just saying that because of who she is."

Her warning hangs heavy between us as another door cracks open.

"Is everything okay?" Zach asks, looking between the two of us, concern written all over his face.

"Yeah, just having a little chat. Right, Spike?"

"Yeah, it was totally enlightening too. I should probably..." I point down toward reception and duck past Biff to collect my client.

I feel both of their stares burning into my back as I walk away. I chastise myself for allowing that kind of conversation to happen with Zach only a door away.

I should just admit to him what's happened and get the beating out of the way, but a huge part of me isn't ready to talk about it yet. I want to keep her to myself just a little bit longer. Is making her my dirty little secret wrong? Hell yeah, but I can't help myself.

"Hey, are you ready to get this show on the road?"

Hazel, my client, looks up with excitement etched onto her face.

"Yes, I'm so excited to see it."

She hops up, but not before openly checking me out. She was the same the last time she was here, but while I might not be too choosy about who I spend the night with, I've always made a rule never to fuck a client. That shit could get messy the next time they turn up for some ink.

"Come on then. I'm all ready to go."

Her eyes darken at my words, and I kick myself for playing into her hands. I'd usually say that shit on purpose, but today, to her, I have no intention of giving her any ideas. I might be about to get my hands on her body, but it's going to be another that I wish I'm touching, I already know that.

"Hazel, this is Kas. She's my new apprentice. Would it be okay with you if she sits in on the session?"

She looks between the two of us before nodding her head and agreeing, dropping her bag to the floor and hopping up in my chair like she owns the place.

I've met all sorts of people doing this job, all with different expectations for what's about to happen, and I can already tell that this woman has absolutely zero nerves getting this tattoo. Even some of the hardest guys I've worked on look more apprehensive than she does right now before a session, especially with a project as big as hers.

I glance at Kas as Hazel gets herself comfortable to find her eyes narrowed on the slim blonde waiting for me.

A smile curls at my lips. Karma is a bitch, and Kas might just be about to learn that rubbing that nurse under my nose not so long ago was a very, very bad idea.

"Okay, here's my finished design based on what we spoke about." I hand Hazel the sketch Kas was looking at when I first found her in here earlier, only I made the few changes she suggested.

"Oh my God," Hazel gushes. "I love it. It's totally perfect."

"Brilliant. I'm glad you like it."

"How could I not? You're a genius."

"I'm not sure that's true, but I appreciate it. Are you still set on where you want it?"

"Sure am."

I glance at Kas, who's watching the two of us with curiosity. She looks more nervous than Hazel, which is amusing.

"I'm going to need you to undress. There's a partition over there if you'd like to make use of... okay, or not," I mutter as she whips her top off without a care in the world. "There's a sheet there to cover up with, plus it'll stop you from getting cold."

I turn my back on both of them as Hazel faffs around, but I know Kas' narrowed eyes are trained on me. Tingles race beneath my skin, telling me that she's feeling much like I was when she mentioned the nurse. Good.

I grab what I need before confirming that Hazel is ready and not about to flash me, although I wouldn't put it past her.

"I'm more than ready," she breathes, her voice deeper. I'm assuming it's meant to be seductive, although it falls a long way from the mark for me.

Wheeling my station over along with my stool, I risk a glance up at Kas. As expected, she's staring at me with narrowed, angry eyes.

I shrug at her. This is my job, soon to be hers. She's going to need to get used to the idea of getting rather intimate with strangers.

"Okay, I need this sheet a little higher," I say gently tugging to expose the swell of her breast.

Hazel wants this piece to start on her ribs, wrapping around her left breast and up onto her shoulder blade. I can't deny that it's going to look stunning, I also can't deny that it's the perfect tattoo for Kas to sit and watch me do right now.

Some fat and hairy biker certainly wouldn't have the same jealousy swirling in her blue depths right now.

A sick part of me loves seeing her feelings so exposed. It tells me everything I need to know about how false the words she said to me not so long ago were.

At no point do I think about the fact I'm working on a half-naked woman. She's no different to a blank canvas to me as I trace out the part of the design I'm going to work on today before grabbing my machine and getting down to business.

The buzz settles me, grounds me in a way that nothing else I've ever found has. Tattooing is my happy place. It always has been, and it's what got me through the time in my life I refuse to think about. It allowed me to escape, to forget the betrayal, the heartache, and it helped me find myself again and allowed me to rebuild my life.

Time ticks on, but I don't pay any attention as the flowers start to come to life across Hazel's ribs. I don't notice the sweet scent of her perfume that was a little too overpowering when I first started, and I don't notice her looking down at me as if I'm the most interesting person in the world. I do, however, know that at no point do I lose Kas' attention. The desire that was simmering just under the surface from our short interaction earlier is still there, just waiting for the chance to explode once more.

"Kas," I bark, sitting back and giving Hazel a few minutes' reprieve from the bite of my machine.

"Yeah?" There's hope in her voice like I'm about to give her some wildly important job.

"I need coffee."

"Really?" she balks.

"Yeah, really."

"Great, that'll be right with you, Sir," she mocks. I can picture her eyes rolling in frustration as she walks to the door.

"Would you like anything?" she asks Hazel politely.

"A glass of water would be great. Thanks, sweetie."

I try to stifle my laugh when I hear a growl rumble up Kas' throat.

The second the door shuts, Hazel starts. "So, she looks like a fun kid to work with."

"She's not a kid." The words are out of my mouth before I've even realised I'm fighting for her.

"Oh, okay. She's kinda intense."

"Artists usually are, in some way."

"I guess."

"This is looking great," I say, changing the subject as I gently wipe at her skin with a cloth. "I think we'll go for another hour, and then you're going to need a break. It's going to really start getting tender as I get higher."

"I'll be fine. I have a high pain threshold."

That's what they all say, until they start squirming like a little bitch. I smile to myself. "That's great. But I don't want to push it too much for your first sitting."

Hazel continues to try to drag me into conversations about what I'm doing for the rest of the night and telling me about her plans. If she thinks she's getting through to me in any way then she really is dumber than she looks. I have no intention of spending any more time with her than necessary.

Thankfully, Kas returns soon after with two mugs of coffee and Hazel's water. As she comes to a stop beside us, she stares at Hazel with contempt in her eyes and I start to wonder if she's going to throw the water at her instead of passing it over for her to drink.

"Wow, that's looking incredible," she says instead after carefully handing it over.

"It's a good start, huh?"

"It's stunning."

I talk Kas through what I'm planning on doing next, seeing as I am actually meant to be her teacher and not ignoring her while making her jealous with my client.

"Pull that spare stool over," I say, although at no point do I actually look at her. I know it's too dangerous to do so. I can't see that jealousy swirling in her eyes once more and not do anything about it.

I talk to her about my machine, about the different angles and the way to achieve the different marks on the skin.

She's silent as she soaks up all the information. After a few moments, Hazel lies back down and the buzz of my machine fills the room.

We're practically shoulder to shoulder as I continue talking through everything I'm doing. I've never done it before, but I find it comes easily, although I'm not sure if that's because of who I'm explaining to, or not.

Kas leans in, watching my every movement, totally fascinated as I continue to bring Hazel's idea to life.

By the time I clean her up and wrap her new ink, the sun is setting outside my small window.

I book her in for her second session and allow Kas to walk her out while I tidy up.

I feel her presence when she re-joins me, but I don't look up. Now I'm done for the day, I just want to get out of here.

"You're really talented, you know," she says.

The second she shuts the door behind her, I swear she sucks all the air from the room. My movements falter as her footsteps get louder.

"I just do what I do."

"I can't wait for you to do me."

I cough as my breath catches in my throat at her words.

"Hazel was my last client of the day. Look," I say, ignoring her comment and pointing to my computer screen, "I'm off the next two days, but you can see my appointments for next week here. Biff is mostly in charge of sorting this out, but now she's training, we're starting to take over organising our own appointments again until we find a replacement.

"Adding one is easy." I click on the little plus symbol and show her how to put Hazel's next appointment in. "The client information is already in the system, so you just type the name in here and... done."

"Seems simple enough." I shudder as she runs her finger along the neckline of my t-shirt, my skin erupting in goosebumps. "So back to my previous comment." She leans forward, running her hands down my chest until her lips press against my ear. "Are you going to do me tonight?"

My body heats and my cock swells as I glance at my tattoo chair, imagining what it might look like with her laid out on it.

"Y-you've just had stitches, Kas. I'm not sure you need any more pain today."

"What about pleasure?" Her lips ghost over my neck, and I fight my need to spin on my stool so I can capture them with my own.

CHAPTER TWENTY-THREE

KAS

SPIKE WRAPS his warm hands around my wrists, keeping me pressed up against his back.

I want him to turn around. I want to sit in his lap and feel his arms around me as he kisses me again. I want to feel his tongue sweeping into my mouth, claiming me in the way only he can.

The words I spat at him earlier about us being convenient were bullshit, and I know he saw straight through it. That's the thing with him—he always sees. It's unnerving. I've managed to build up walls and keep everyone else out all these years, but he storms into my life when I least expect it and he just sees me. The real me, the vulnerable me that I try to hide from the world with my resting bitch face, dark makeup and tattoos. It's like my armour doesn't exist when I'm with him. And as much as I love it, I equally hate it because I know it gives him the power to hurt me like no other ever has.

"Let's go for dinner?"

"I'm sorry, what?" I ask, his comment giving me whiplash.

He releases me and stands. "Let's go for dinner."

"Dinner? Just the two of us? Like a... like a date?"

He barks out a laugh. "No, not like a date. I don't do those. More like two housemates going for food."

"Housemates? Housemates with... benefits?" I ask with a smile.

I step up to him, ready to run my hands up his chest, but he stops me.

"I would ask you what you fancy, but I think I know the answer. So I'll pick the restaurant."

"Fine by me."

"Grab your shit. Let's get out of here before you cause me even more trouble than you already have."

"Biff won't say anything."

"She won't need to if you carry on."

I shrug innocently. "Just having a little fun."

"Yeah, that's going to end with me in the fucking hospital."

"Give him some credit," I argue as I swipe my bag from the floor and throw it over my shoulder.

"I am. I could have said in a coffin."

"Dramatic much?"

"Only time will tell."

"Well, make sure you name me in your will. I want to take over your lease."

He barks out a laugh. "Fucking hell, Kas. You don't waste any time, do you?"

"My mum did actually teach me a few things," I say, then instantly regret it when he turns his sad eyes on me.

"Come on, I think you're going to love this place."

The second we're outside, he hands me my helmet and we climb onto his bike.

It's only a short drive, and although my stomach rumbles, I could spend so much longer with my arms wrapped around him and the cool summer evening air on my skin.

He guides me into a small Mexican restaurant, and it's not until we're seated that he finally looks up at me.

"So, did you enjoy your first day at the studio?" There's a twinkle in his eye. He knows exactly what he's asking.

"You mean, did I enjoy watching you get up close and personal to that woman's tits?"

"I didn't see her tits," he argues.

"She sure wanted you to, though."

"You noticed that, huh?"

I roll my eyes at him. "It was hard not to."

He nods slowly, a smirk tugging at his lips. "She was hot."

"She was," I agree, not wanting to get dragged into this. "You should call her."

"I should?"

"Why not?"

The waiter chooses that exact moment to interrupt us to take our orders. Neither of us has so much as glanced at the menu, but Spike clearly comes here often because he rattles off his order before turning his dark eyes on me.

"I'll have the same. It sounds great. Oh, and a pitcher of margarita, please."

"A pitcher? I'm driving."

"I know, it's for me."

"Long day?" *Like you wouldn't believe.*

"Plus, a little liquid courage might help me make that phone call later." I wink at him and it takes a few seconds for him to catch on.

Two can play at that game.

"You're not going to be making any phone call."

"Oh, and why's that? I could really do with ending the night with a little... stress relief." Stretching out my leg, I run my foot up his.

His eyes narrow on mine. "You're playing a very dangerous game, Tiny."

"One *you* started. So tell me, what were you trying to achieve, seeing as you keep telling me that you shouldn't touch me?"

His lips part, but he doesn't say anything, and I fear I may have just ruined everything by mentioning our reality.

Sitting forward, I place my forearms on the table and rest my breasts on top, ensuring he gets a great view.

His eyes drop almost instantly, and his tongue sneaks out to run along his bottom lip.

"Trying to make me jealous won't work, Spike."

"Oh no?"

"No."

"Care to explain why? Because you looked like you were about to blow a fuse earlier."

"It won't work, because you didn't look at her like you do me." I kick off my boot under the table and run my foot up his leg again, only I don't stop at his knee this time.

"Tiny," he warns, but I don't stop.

"And I know for a fact," he jolts as I press my foot to his semi, "that this wasn't interested in her." I rub him over the fabric of his jeans, and to prove my point he just gets harder.

As I continue, I suck my bottom lip into my mouth. His eyes darken with desire, and I know I've got him. His restraint is slipping faster than he can control. I love holding all the power.

Dropping his hand under the table, he wraps his fingers around my ankle, halting my movements.

"You're asking for trouble."

"I'm aware."

The air crackles between us as our eyes hold.

"Excuse me," Spike says, confusing me, but when a shadow falls over our table, I realise that he wasn't actually talking to me.

"Change of plans. Any chance we could get our order to go?"

"Oh... um... sure. I'll go and sort that out for you now."

At no point does he take his eyes from mine.

"To go?" I ask, a smile forming on my lips.

"To go," he confirms.

THIRTY MINUTES later I'm once again climbing off the back of his bike, but this time it's outside Spike's building and the anticipation that's crackling between us is almost unbearable.

I glance down his busy Saturday night street as he grabs our dinner from his top box and replaces it with my helmet.

There are people everywhere in their need to let go, but for some reason just one person stands out to me. A guy right at the other side of the street in a black hoodie. Unlike everyone else, he's not with friends, and he looks like he's far from enjoying himself. A shiver runs up my spine when I momentarily think that it could be Jet. But it can't be. He's dead, and I'm free. I think it's going to take a little while longer to adjust to not constantly having to look over my shoulder than I thought it might.

"What's wrong?" Spike's concerned voice asks from behind me, dragging me from my thoughts of the past.

"Nothing. Just waiting for you."

"You don't need to wait, Tiny. I'm right here for the taking."

"Right here on the street? Well, if you're okay with an audience." I make a show of crossing my arms in front of me, ready to pull my shirt over my head, but his low growl stops me.

"Don't even fucking think about it. There have already been too many motherfuckers who've seen you with too few clothes on. Get the fuck upstairs. Now," he barks. My feet are following orders long before my brain even processes the words.

The second we're inside, he's on me. His hands slide up my stomach, taking the fabric of my shirt with them until it's over my head and discarded somewhere behind him, my bra quickly following.

He pushes my hair over my shoulder and drops his lips to my neck as he continues pushing me forward, his already hard cock pressing against my arse.

"You drive me fucking crazy, Tiny."

"I like your kind of crazy," I moan as his large hands squeeze my breasts. "Oh God."

He licks up the length of my neck and my knees damn near buckle when his teeth graze my sensitive skin.

He directs me to his room, and the moment his door slams shut, my back is being pressed up against it and I'm lifted so we're eye to eye.

"Hey," I say when I find his dark, piercing stare.

"Fuck," he barks, diving for my lips. "Can't get enough," he moans into my mouth. I swallow down his words; the feeling is entirely mutual.

His tongue duels with mine as his hands trail around my body as if they don't know where to touch first. He squeezes my breasts and pinches my nipples, running them up my thighs so he can palm my arse, and it's not until he runs one of his fingertips over the damp lace of my knickers and I gasp that we break our kiss.

"Fuck, your hip. Does it hurt?"

My lips part, ready to tell him no, but he beats me to it. "Do not lie to me, Tiny."

"Yes, it hurts."

"Fuck." He releases me almost instantly, but he doesn't let me move from the door. Instead, he grazes his lips over my collarbone and slowly descends down my body, teasing me and driving me crazy the whole way.

He kisses and licks around both of my breasts, ignoring my nipples that are begging for attention.

Our eyes hold, and I swear it's the most erotic moment of my life, watching him playing me to perfection with just his lips.

"Spike," I plead. "I need—"

"Shush, Tiny. Let me take care of you."

Finally, he sucks me deep into his mouth, and my head falls back against the door with a thud as pleasure shoots around my body. I feel it right at the tips of my toes, it's so strong.

"More, Spike. I need more," I beg.

He drops lower, kissing down my stomach, tracing the lines of my tattoos with his tongue as if he's the one drawing them on my skin.

Images of me lying on his chair with his hands on me as he marks me permanently fill my mind. I almost put a stop to this to demand that we go back there immediately so he can do just that.

I don't care what happens next between us, if this thing is just a bit of fun while I'm here. I want a reminder of what he gave me. How he made me feel, even if it's for just a short time.

His fingers make quick work of the button on my waistband before he gently tugs it down my legs, letting it pool at my ankles. My knickers are next to go, and after tugging off my boots I'm standing naked before him.

He sits back in his haunches and runs his eyes over me.

"So fucking beautiful." Unable to take the honesty in his eyes, I have to look away. "Hey," he says, amusement in his tone. "You're not shy, are you?"

I suck in a deep breath and decide to go with a little honesty of my own.

"I don't think anyone has ever looked deep enough to notice before."

"Kas," he says on a sigh, torment flickering across his face. I know he hates what my life has been like, but there's nothing he can do to wipe it away apart from being part of my future.

I feel like at last I might have found my family, where I belong, and I want to embrace it as much as possible, even if it means this thing between us can't happen.

I might be enjoying myself with him, but I refuse to come between him and Zach, and when the time comes that Spike might have to choose, I'll ensure there isn't a choice to make.

He's already told me that he doesn't do tomorrows, and although I don't fully believe him, I'll make it reality for us if I have to.

"Don't give me that look."

"I'm not giving you any look other than one of complete awe. You amaze me, Kas. You totally disarm me and blow me away with your beauty and your strength."

I fight really hard to hold his stare this time, but it's a challenge.

He must be able to see that I'm losing the battle, because without saying any more words, he sits forward, taps my ankle, and lifts it to his lips.

"I'm going to fucking devour you, Tiny. I'm going to make you lose your damn mind like you do to me on a daily basis."

"Please," I beg as he kisses up my calf, slowly getting closer and closer to where I need him.

"If it hurts, tell me and we'll move."

"Okay," I breathe, although it's nowhere near true. With his lips on me and the anticipation racing through me right now, I barely feel anything else.

He licks and kisses up my thigh, and right before I

think he's going to move across to where I really need him, he sinks his teeth into my soft flesh.

"Oh fuck, Spike." That move, that claiming of me is almost enough to send me crashing into the release I so desperately need.

He pulls back slightly and looks at his handiwork, a satisfied smirk playing on his lips. "I guess it'll have to do until I get the chance to ink you."

I want to respond, but I don't get time, because after flicking a look up to me he forces my thighs wider and dives into me.

He sucks on my clit until I start to see stars.

"Holy shit, fuck. Shit."

The pressure, the speed, everything. He just gets it right every single time. It's like he's got a fucking instruction manual to my body.

His fingers lift when I'm almost on the cusp of falling just from his tongue alone, and one circles my entrance.

My muscles pull, desperate to feel him filling me, stretching me.

"Spike, please. More. More."

"As you wish," he moans against me, the vibrations from his low voice sending bolts of pleasure through me.

Two fingers surge up inside me and curl, finding just the right place. His teeth graze my clit before he flattens his tongue against it and works me until I'm screaming his name, my fingers pulling at his hair so hard that I start to wonder if it's going to fall out.

My orgasm hits like a tidal wave, threatening to send me crashing to the ground. My one leg holding me up starts to buckle, but before I fall, I'm in his arms.

I stare up into his dark brown eyes and my chest aches.

Fuck. I'm starting to feel way too much for this incredible man.

"I'll always catch you," he says, making me want to cry. Emotion burns the back of my throat but I force it down.

Witnessing yet another of my emotional breakdowns is the last thing he needs right now, I'm sure.

Unaware of how deeply his words affect me, he lays me down in the bed, his hands resting either side of my head as he hovers above me before his lips find mine once again.

I moan as my own taste explodes on my tongue.

"So fucking sweet," he groans. "I'm fucking addicted to you, Kas."

He once again kisses down my body. I start to think he's going to begin eating me once more, but after a brief kiss to my mound, he stands and begins pulling off his own clothing.

I watch his muscles pull and ripple as he pulls his shirt over his head before dropping his trousers and kicking everything away.

He stands with his hard cock jutting out in front of him so that I can take my fill.

After a few seconds, his restraint must snap because he takes himself in his hand and begins working his cock.

I groan at the sight of him taking what he needs, my core flooding.

"I need you," I admit.

"I fucking need you too, Tiny. A hell of a lot more than I should."

He takes a step forward and I scramble up the bed so he has some space. He settles between my thighs, running the head of his cock through my juices and sending little aftershocks from my previous orgasm shooting around my body.

"Stop teasing," I warn.

"I could say the same thing about you every fucking minute of the fucking day. All day I've been fucking hard for you, Kas. All fucking day," he admits, folding over me so his lips brush mine.

He finds my entrance, pushing in just enough to drive me fucking wild, but he pauses as my muscles clench, desperate to pull him deeper.

"All I could think about was laying you out on my chair and feasting on you, taking you, showing every motherfucker in that place that you belong to me."

"Oh God," I whimper as I acknowledge the serious tone in his words.

"You fucking slay me," he whispers as he surges forward, filling me in one thrust.

My back arches as he lifts my right leg so that he can get even deeper.

"Spike," I cry as he hits some magical place inside me that only he's been able to discover.

"Does it hurt? Are you okay?" he grates out through gritted teeth.

"Yes, yes. Just... move, please."

A pained laugh falls from his lips before he pulls all the way out of me and flips me over so I'm on all fours with my arse in the air.

"Fucking addicted," he mutters almost to himself as he pushes back inside me slowly.

"Spike," I moan as he pushes—deeper than before.

"Fuck, yes." His palm connects with my arsecheek. It stings like a bitch, but I can't deny that it doesn't make me wet as fuck.

"You like that, dirty girl?"

"Yes, yes," I pant, earning me another slap.

I try to look back over my shoulder, desperate to see him, but he doesn't notice. He's too busy staring at where we're connected.

I'm jealous. I want to see it.

After a few seconds, his eyes lift to mine. The heat, the emotions within them has my breath catching.

"Kas?" he whispers, but he doesn't say any more. Instead he wraps his hand around my throat and drags me up so my back presses to his front and he captures my lips in a punishing kiss as his hips continue to piston in and out of me.

It's too much. It's not enough. It's fucking everything.

My head spins as I feel every single one of his movements inside my body.

He was wrong earlier. This isn't just fucking. This, right here, right now... it's so much more.

My nails scratch at his thighs, needing to brand myself on him just like he does every time he so much as touches me.

His lips trail across my neck and shoulder until he sucks my earlobe into his mouth.

"You feel like fucking heaven, and I never want to leave."

"So don't," I whisper back. "I'm here. I'm yours. Take whatever you need."

"Fuck, Kas."

His movements get more and more erratic as we both start to chase our releases.

"Can't get enough. Fucking addicted," he mutters in my ear between his heaving breaths. "So fucking good, my dirty little girl."

"Spike," I moan as my body begins to tighten with my impending release.

He sits up, his fingers finding my clit to help push me over the edge.

"Come, Tiny. Come all over my cock and show me how fucking good this is."

"Oh shit. Fuck, fuck, fuck, Spike," I scream as he pinches my little bundle of nerves and sends me crashing over the edge.

"Fuuuuuuck," he roars only a second later before his cock twitches violently inside me as he fills me, marking himself on me in yet another way.

Once he's finished, he falls down onto my right side, making sure to stay away from my bandage, and tucks his face into the crook of my neck as we both fight to catch our breaths.

Long minutes pass with just the sounds of our heavy breathing filling the room.

"This shouldn't be happening," he admits quietly.

"I think we both accepted that it is, a while ago."

"I'm not talking about you being Zach's sister."

"Oh?"

His hand skims up my body, causing goosebumps to erupt in his wake before he cups my cheek and turns my head so I have no option but to look at him.

"How I'm feeling. It shouldn't be happening. I promised myself I wouldn't ever let it happen again."

My breath catches in my throat as I allow his admission to sink in.

"W-what are you feeling?" I ask, although I'm not entirely sure I'm prepared for the answer.

"I'm..." He hesitates, breaking our eye contact for a beat before he seems to get a grip of himself and looks me in the eye once again. "I'm falling for you, Tiny, and no matter what I do, I can't seem to stop it."

"Fuck," I breathe.

To my utter shock, my response makes him bark out a laugh. "Yeah, that's about how I feel too."

"Spike, I don't know–"

"Shhh, enough talking. I'm not done with you yet."

"Oh?" I ask, a salacious smile appearing on my lips.

"I need to make the most of my time before you disappear, on me."

"Who says I'm disappearing?"

"You did. You told Zach earlier that you didn't want to live here."

I think back to my brother's visit. How was that only this morning? It feels like a fucking year's passed since then. I remember him storming out and not knowing what his issue was. It's only now I realise what I said.

My eyes soften as I look at his concerned face. This time it's my turn to cradle his cheeks in my hands.

"You don't think I want to live here?"

He shrugs. I've never seen him so unsure of himself. It's totally endearing that this big, confident, self-assured man can show me this side of him. I'm not sure many people have seen this Spike before.

"I only said that because it's what he wanted to hear. I'll stay here as long as you'll have me."

A little of his previous sparkle brightens his eyes.

"But across the hall?"

"If you want me to."

"And if I want you right here? In my bed with me every night. What would you say then?"

"I'd say that I'd certainly consider it."

"Oh, it's like that, is it?"

He pulls me on top of him, my core lining up with his already hard cock. I rock down on him, making his eyelids flicker with pleasure.

"I'm not one to make life easy. You should know that by now."

"Don't I fucking just," he mutters, lifting me with ease so I can sink down onto him. "Fuck. I swear it gets better every time you surround me."

I smile down at him before circling my hips, causing his fingers to tighten on my thighs.

"Hmmm... I think I might need some more evidence before I form an opinion on that."

"I've got all the time in the world for evidence, Tiny." He stretches his arms out to the side. "Now ride me. Show me just how dirty my girl can be."

CHAPTER TWENTY-FOUR

SPIKE

I LOOK up to find Kas staring at me as if I'm a puzzle she's trying to work out.

"What?" I ask hesitantly.

"When you said earlier... that this shouldn't be happening. What did you really mean?"

I shove the food on my fork into my mouth, mostly just to give me a bit of thinking time. I hadn't intended to say those things to her earlier, they just kind of fell from my lips in the moment. My need to be honest with her about how she makes me feel too much to deny.

My heart begins to race as I consider the possibility of talking about my past and laying everything out on the table.

"Why shouldn't it happen again? What happened

before?" she prompts when she must sense that I'm trying to figure out a way out of this.

"There was... um... someone."

"I knew it," she says, a little too excitedly. "That first morning when you told me that you don't do tomorrows or whatever bullshit you spat at me, I knew it was bollocks."

"Forget it," I mutter, pushing my half-eaten dinner away from me, my appetite long forgotten.

Standing, I walk to the kitchen in the hope of losing some of the tension pulling at my muscles just from thinking about that time in my life.

I pause with my palms on the counter, hanging my head low and closing my eyes.

I don't hear her move, but I sense when she's close. She slips between me and the counter, forcing me to stand straighter.

Her small hands run up my chest until they lock behind my neck.

"It's okay," she soothes. "You don't have to tell me. Pasts can be... painful, I get that better than most."

Dark shadows fill her eyes, and I'm taken back to the night she had a nightmare.

"One day, Tiny. One day, I'll tell you everything."

She smiles. "Me too."

She lifts up on her toes and brushes her lips against mine.

"Have you finished eating?"

"Yeah, you?"

She nods, lifting higher so her lips are next to my ear. "Take me back to bed, Spike."

WHEN I WAKE the next morning, it's to a cold and empty bed. I sit up, thinking that she's done a runner in the night, but the second I hear a noise coming from the living room I relax, feeling stupid that she might have gone anywhere.

"Hey," she says when I join her. "I thought it was my turn to treat you to breakfast."

Walking up behind where she's standing at the stove, I wrap my arms around her waist. The pull I constantly feel toward her is stronger than ever after last night.

"Morning," I whisper, dropping my lips to her neck.

"Morning," she giggles. "You're in a good mood."

"Why wouldn't I be? I've got you standing in only my shirt," I say guessing as to what's missing beneath it, "and you're cooking. You know that's the way to a man's heart, right?" I still the moment the words are out of my mouth.

She doesn't miss it. Flipping the pancake she's cooking from the pan, she turns in my arms.

"Funny, because I thought it was blowjobs."

I bark out a laugh and immediately feel the weight of my past, my fears, leave me.

"Yeah, those always help too."

"Did you sleep well?" she asks, looking up into my eyes as if the answers will be within them.

"I did, although my bed mate is a wriggler."

She shrugs. "I wouldn't know. I haven't slept with anyone before."

"You've never slept in the same bed as someone else?" I ask in shock.

"Well, Mum, yeah. But she was usually too strung out to notice she was even in a bed let alone that I was with her. Don't," she warns. "Don't give me those sad puppy eyes."

"Well, I'm glad I was your first." I bite down on my tongue to stop from telling her that I'd like to be her last too. I fear I already said too much last night about where my head is.

"Me too." She spins back around to make another pancake, successfully rubbing her arse against my already semi-hard cock in the process.

"Tiny," I warn, my hands holding onto her hips to keep her in place.

"Yes?" she asks with an innocent look over her shoulder. "I'm just making you pancakes."

"Sure you are."

"Go sit down, they're nearly ready."

Reluctantly, I do as I'm told. But I soon realise that being able to watch her do her thing in only my shirt is totally worth it.

"What are your plans for the day?" she asks as she plates up.

"Well, I usually go to the gym on a Sunday morning. But I'm sure I can find us a much more fulfilling means of exercise."

"I need to meet a friend," she says, ignoring my comment as she walks over, although the heat in her eyes tells me that she heard it loud and clear.

"Okay, where?"

"I'm not sure. I'm waiting for her to wake up and reply."

"Invite her here." The words roll off my tongue faster than I can control. Kas' eyes meet mine and they look as shocked as I feel.

"H-here?"

"Sure. I mean, if you want to. This is your place now, too. I want you to treat it as such."

"You really want me here?"

"Of course I do."

"Because you get regular access to my pussy?" she accuses.

"I mean, that's definitely an added benefit."

She pauses with a piece of pancake halfway to her lips. "Spike, what are we doing here?"

"No, no, please. Don't do that."

"Don't do what? I'd just like to know where I stand here. Am I your housemate or your live-in bed partner until you get a better offer and kick me to the curb?" she asks, successfully proving that her comment about us just being convenient yesterday was utter bullshit.

My chin drops that she thinks I could possibly see her that way. Reaching across the table, I take her spare hand in mine.

"I'd never kick you to the curb, Kas."

She shrugs, sadness washing over her. "Why not? Everyone else in my life has. I've started to wonder if that's where I belong."

Lifting her from her seat, I place her on my lap and brush her hair from her face.

"No. Everything about that statement. Just... no. I want you here, with or without the pussy," I wink.

She drops her head to my shoulder, thinking for a moment.

"I need..." She sighs. "I need to rebuild my life, Spike. I need to start over, and I need to take it seriously. That means I need to be somewhere that is going to be permanent for a while at least. I need to find my footing, discover who I am, because I'm not *that* girl. I know you don't want to talk about tomorrows or that kind of stuff, and honestly, nor do I. I've been here a week and already it feels like so much longer. I don't want to pressure you or for either of us to make decisions that are too hasty in whatever this is. But I need to know if this is my home or if I need to find another."

I know the sensible thing to say would probably be to suggest she finds her own place, just like Zach has, but the thought of letting her go, of having to find someone else to live here with me, fills me with dread.

I make a snap decision, one I hope I'm not going to regret down the line.

"This is your home, Kas." I cup her cheek and lift her head so she has no choice but to look at me. "If you want it to be."

"But..." She blinks at me, chewing on her bottom lip and making me want to make it my own. "Which bedroom?"

"Do we have to define it?"

"I guess not."

"We can both just live here, and the rest we can make up as we go along."

Her eyes bore into mine with an intensity I'm not used to. She wants to know why, why I'm so closed off to the idea of a future, of committing to anything.

"I was engaged." The words tumble from my lips without permission and she stills in my arms, sucking in a surprised breath. "We were young, we'd been together since we were fourteen. She was my best friend, my first, my everything.

"We'd lived together all through uni. Our families thought it was a bad idea, but we were determined. It was... everything. Every day I fell in love with her more and more. Everyone thought we'd grow apart, but we never did.

"I'd been saving my arse off so that we could put a deposit down on a flat on the outskirts of the city. It was in a really shitty area, the flat was tiny, but I didn't care. I just wanted us to be together, and thankfully my gramps helped to make it a possibility.

"I'd bought an engagement ring, and on our last day at uni, I took her to the flat and proposed. She didn't see it coming at all. It was priceless." I can't help smiling as I think of that day, of the happiness I felt at knowing she was finally going to be mine.

Kas must see my face change, because she reaches out and cups my cheek, her thumb gently caressing my stubbled jaw.

"We never moved in." Kas gasps, probably thinking that she died. Over the years, I wondered if it would be easier to deal with if she had. "She started an internship the following week, met some guy, and within six weeks she told me that she no longer loved me and walked away from everything we had."

"Oh my God." Kas' hand lifts to cover her mouth. "Spike, shit."

"I was left with a flat I couldn't afford alone, and an engagement ring that was worth fuck all to pawn."

"And a broken heart," she whispers.

The ache in my chest I'm all too familiar with pulls tightly, making my breathing falter.

"Broken doesn't even begin to describe it."

"Jesus, Spike." Leaning forward, she captures my lips with her own and kisses me so sweetly that it helps to release the pull in my chest, replacing it with a much scarier sensation.

We're both breathless when she pulls back, her eyes dark with dirty intentions.

"I'd love to be your housemate if you want me. No labels, just... us."

A smile twitches at my lips as I look down at her. "That sounds pretty perfect to me."

"There's just one problem," she says with a wince.

"Yeah?"

"Zach."

"I'll talk to Zach."

"And tell him what? That we're some weird mash-up between housemates and friends with benefits?" The colour drains from my face at the thought. How the hell am I meant to explain this to someone else if we don't even know what it is?

"I'll figure something out. In the meantime, stop distracting me from the incredible pancakes my girl made me." I push her up from my lap and grab my fork.

I stuff a syrup-covered slice of pancake into my mouth and look up at her when I realise she hasn't returned to her seat.

"What?" I mumble around the food.

"You called me your girl."

"I did, didn't I?" Weirdly, I don't feel the panic I thought I would at that slip.

"Yeah. I liked it."

"Good. Now eat. I've got plans for you later."

ONCE WE'VE FINISHED, I reluctantly drag on my gym clothes and throw my duffle over my shoulder, ready to set off.

"Sure I can't convince you to join me?" I ask, stopping in the doorway to Kas' room where she's rummaging through her drawers to find something to wear.

"At the gym? No fucking chance. You're all the workout I need." She wiggles her thong-clad arse at me, and I groan.

"Is your friend coming?"

"Jodie? Yeah. She's on her way now."

"Okay, well, have fun."

"Spike," she calls, running after me as I head for the door. "Don't you dare leave like that."

"Like what?"

"Without this." She launches herself at me, forcing me to drop my bag so I can catch her instead.

Her lips slam down on mine and she kisses me until I almost forget about my trip to the gym and just take her back to my bed instead.

"Okay, you can go now," she says with a wink as I let her slide down my body.

Her eyes drop to where my cock is now tenting my sweats. "It's an all-male gym, right?"

"Whatever helps you sleep at night, Tiny."

"Good, because that's mine, and I'd appreciate every other hussy who wants a taste to know that."

"Jesus, Kas. I may as well just hand my balls over now."

"I think I'd prefer them exactly where they are."

Chuckling at her, I pull the front door open and head out.

CHAPTER TWENTY-FIVE

KAS

"WHAT HAPPENED?" I ask the second I open the door to find my best friend standing on the other side with a black eye and cut lip.

"Ugh," she says with a roll of her eyes as she pushes past me and into the room. "Some arsehole decided to jump me last night. It's nothing, it barely hurts."

"It looks sore as fuck. Have you iced it?"

"It'll be fine. It's not my first, and I doubt it'll be my last."

"Sit your arse down. I'm sure Spike's got peas or something we can use."

I rummage around his freezer and I do find the standard bag of peas crushed at the back. I bash them against the counter to loosen them up a little, making

Jodie complain before I wrap a towel around them and pass them to her.

"Thanks," she mutters sarcastically, taking them and placing them to her eyes nonetheless, although she looks anything but happy about it.

"I brought pastry. And coffee, obviously," she says, nodding at the tray she walked in with.

"Ooooh," I say, reaching for the paper bag. I might have just had a stack of pancakes with Spike, but I'm not one to turn down a sweet treat.

I pull out a chocolate twist and settle back on the sofa.

"So who was it? Anyone you recognised?"

"Nope. Just some guy in a hoodie. Fucking arsehole. He didn't even steal anything, it was weird."

A ball of dread forms in my belly as she says those last few words.

"He didn't want your phone or purse or anything?" I ask, sitting forward once again.

"Not that he said."

"D-did he say anything?"

"No. He was probably wasted or high or something. It's not like it's unusual where we come from."

"I know, there's just usually some kind of motive." The ball continues to grow in my belly.

"Why do you look so concerned?"

"Um..." It's a good question. They're all dead. D's brother took care of them. Didn't he? "I'm sure it's nothing."

"You think it might have been Jet, don't you?"

"Jet? No, probably not. The last time I saw him he wasn't exactly... breathing."

"What?" She blanches, her eyes as wide as saucers.

"If I tell you this, you have to keep it zipped."

"You got it."

I explain the details of Friday night, although I leave out any names or anything that might lead back to people other than Jet and his gang of arseholes.

"Holy shit, Kas. Are you okay?"

"Yeah, just a little scratch on my hip."

"So why do you look so concerned? If they're all gone, if it's over, then you've no reason to think that has anything to do with it."

"I know. I'm just being cautious. It's kind of ingrained at this point. You're probably right, just some guy who'd had it out with his girl and needed a punching bag."

"Exactly, there are more than a few of them around our parts."

"Ain't that the fucking truth. So... this place is nice. Where's your new housemate?"

"At the gym."

"Damn, I was hoping I'd get to meet your hero."

I open my mouth to argue and tell her that he's hardly that, but I can't because it's kind of true. Spike might be aware that he took me away from my previous life, but I don't think he can ever appreciate just how much he really did save me. I'd wanted out for years, but men like Jet would always have kept me down, ensuring that I owed them for whatever reason. People don't leave that place usually, unless it's in a body bag.

I got lucky, and I owe it all to him.

"You've got that look on your face."

"What look?"

"The one of a girl in love."

"Fuck off, I'm not in love with him."

"You've fucked him again though?"

"Uh, yeah. Once or twice."

"Girl, you are in trouble here," she laughs.

"How so? I'm pretty sure this place is the opposite of trouble."

"Zach know you're banging his mate yet?"

"Er... not exactly."

"What's that meant to mean?"

"He hit him for thinking that he had. I have no idea what's going to happen when he finds out he really has been."

"You need to talk to him."

"I know," I mutter.

"He's your brother. You need to take control of this situation."

"Ugh, why do you have to be the sensible one?"

"One of us has to be."

Silence falls between us as we both eat and drink, lost in our own thoughts.

"I'm working at the studio. Zach wants to train me up."

"That's awesome."

"Yeah, I think it could be. I watched Spike do this crazy design on a woman yesterday. I want that. I want to spend my days doing that."

She shakes her head.

"What now?"

"Nothing, it's just... your voice changes when you talk about him."

"Ugh, enough." I ball up the paper bag in my lap and launch it at her.

As always, once we get into setting the world to rights, the time seems to go at lightning speed, and before I know it, there's a key being pushed into the door and Jodie's eyes widen in delight.

I've no idea why, if it's excitement to see him or anxiety about what Jodie thinks of him, but butterflies erupt in my belly.

He pushes into the flat and throws his gym bag into the direction of his room before running his hand through his still wet hair to pull it back from his face.

"Holy shit, girl," Jodie breathes, her eyes locked on my man.

A wide smile spreads across my face. My man, hell yeah!

"Oh shit," he says, his eyes flying to us. "Hey, J-Jodie, right?"

"Sure, but I could be anything you like," she says with a wink, making me bark out a laugh. Jodie has never been backward in coming forward when it comes to what she wants, although I can tell by her eyes that she's joking right now. She's too good a friend to even consider going after my man.

Spike coughs, covering up his shock at her words. "Right, well. Are you... okay?" he asks, his eyes narrowing on her dark, swollen one.

"You should see the state of him," she jokes.

"She got jumped last night," I say, when the concern doesn't leave Spike's face.

"Shit, are you okay?"

"Seriously, you two need to stop worrying. I'm fine, he didn't steal anything. This'll be gone in a few days and I'll be as beautiful as ever."

"You want another coffee?" I ask, getting up and walking straight into Spike's arms when he opens them for me.

"You two are sickening, you know that, right?" I shrug while Spike stiffens in my arms slightly.

"So, coffee?"

"No, I'm good. I'm going to head off before you start panting like dogs."

"What? We will not–"

"You fucking should, girl. Make the most of him." I watch as she collects up her stuff and dumps her rubbish in the kitchen as if she lives here herself.

"Call me in a few days with updates, yeah?"

"Sure thing. Please try to be safe?"

"Always." She blows me a kiss and then she's gone.

"Whoa, she's a bit of a whirlwind. I can see why you're friends."

"You calling me a whirlwind too?"

"Fucking right, Tiny. You blew in here and turned everything upside down in only a few minutes."

"Huh." I look around at the tidy apartment. It wasn't a total mess when I first arrived, but it was obvious that a single guy lived here. "I guess I did."

"Go get ready, we're going out."

"Oh? Where?"

"It's a surprise."

I smile at him, loving the cheeky glint in his eye before rushing to my room to do as I'm told.

"What are we doing here?" I ask when I climb off his bike outside of Rebel Ink.

It's in darkness, the usual bright pink light no longer illuminated like the other times I've been here.

"Thought it was the perfect time to get some teaching in."

"You've got a client today?"

"Nope. The studio is closed, and I just so happen to

know that the flat above is also empty right now and for the next few hours." He winks.

"What are you suggesting exactly?"

"Come on." He laces his fingers through mine and we run across the road together so he can let us inside.

I look around as he fumbles with his key. I'm still feeling a little uneasy after learning that Jodie was attacked. I know it's crazy, I know I'm safe now, but I just can't shift the fear.

"Everything okay?" Spike asks when he glances at me.

"Yeah, just being nosey."

I follow him through. He doesn't turn any lights on until we get back to his room.

Just like yesterday, my eyes land on all his artwork. I'm just as in awe now as I was the first time I saw it all.

"You're really talented, you know that?"

He doesn't respond. Instead he starts moving stuff around behind me.

"Did you always want to do this?"

"Pretty much, yeah. As a kid, all I used to do was draw. It used to drive my grandad crazy because I'd stick them to all the walls. Then I went to uni, got my art degree. I had a job all lined up before... all that happened," he says, referencing what he told me earlier. "I screwed it up, though. I started drinking heavily. I fucked everything up, really.

"Once I sorted myself out I managed to get a job, but I didn't really love it. I was worried that everything I'd spent my life doing was for nothing. I moved around a bit, and tried to find my place in the industry. I knew I had the skills, it was just a reminder of everything I now wasn't going to have. Tattooing was part of a dream that had been long shattered. I didn't really know how I felt about it all.

"But then I found this place, and everything in my life started to make sense once again. Zach, D and Titch pulled me into their little dysfunctional family, and as far as my career is concerned, I've never looked back."

"Do you still miss her?" I spin around so I can see the look in his eyes as he answers.

"Yes and no. I don't think I miss her as such. I miss the life, the security, safety and contentment of knowing she'd always be there. That makes me sound like a right pussy, doesn't it?"

I step up to him, taking his hands in mine. "Not at all. It makes you human."

"Have you forgiven her?"

"Yeah, I think so. It's been ten years. Over time, I've realised that if she wasn't happy then she was right to do something about it. I would have hated for her to feel trapped. I'd lived my entire life with just my grandad. I think I was just desperate for a normal life."

"What happened to your parents?"

"Okay," he says with a laugh, pulling me into his arms and wrapping them around my waist. "I think question time is over for now."

He drops his lips to the top of my head before releasing me once more.

"So what now?" I watch as he steps away from me and starts undoing his jeans. "Spike?" I ask curiously.

"Lesson time."

"You're not going to let me..." I trail off, because other than him demanding I get on my knees—not that I'd complain—I can't think of another reason why he'd drop his trousers in here.

"Ready to lay down your first ink, Tiny?"

My chin drops as he hops up on the chair.

"You're joking, right?"

"Nope. Deadly serious. Now, grab the stool. You'll probably need to raise it up and get over here."

"Oh my God," I breathe, my hands already starting to tremble with the thought of putting something permanent on his skin.

"You look like you're about to faint," he says with a laugh.

"I think I might."

"It's fine. Just relax. Plus, if it's shit, I'll just get one of the guys to go over it with something better."

"Hey," I argue, not happy with him covering up my art. "You'll wear it with honour, even if it's shit."

"We'll see." He winks.

"So what do you want?"

He reveals a folded piece of paper and hands it over for me to see. The second I open it, I gasp.

"You stole this?" I ask, pretending to be offended that he ripped one of my designs from my notepad.

"I prefer the term borrowed. You can glue it back in later if you like."

"I love this," I say, running my fingertip over the ink staining the page.

"Me too. It's why you're about to redraw it on me."

"Spike, I can't..."

"You won't know unless you try. Anyway, you can start on my arse, that way if you fuck it up, I don't have to look at it."

I splutter a laugh but when I look up at him, I see he's serious.

"I guess you'd better turn over then. You can talk me through it."

He smiles at me before turning the chair into a bed, flipping over and lowering his boxers so I get the fine sight of his arse in front of me.

"Aww, your arse is a virgin. I get to be your first." I don't think about the words that fall from my lips until he barks out a laugh.

"Now, now. I'm here for some ink, not any funny business."

"I didn't mean it quite like that. Good to know how you feel about it, though."

Shaking his head, he rests it on his forearms and gets comfortable.

"You look just a little too relaxed about this for my liking."

"I trust you."

His admission hits me like a truck. My breath catches and emotion immediately burns the back of my throat.

I try to cover how his words affect me, but I think he sees it nonetheless. Thankfully he doesn't ask. I'm not sure I want the look I know he'll give me if I were to admit that I don't think anyone has ever said that to me before.

"Okay so where do I start?" I ask, changing the subject before he decides he wants to start digging.

He talks me through the first steps, and before long I have the first part of the design traced onto his skin.

"You keep moving," I complain as I work on one of the snake's tails that wraps around one of the many skulls in my design.

"Yeah, that kinda comes with the territory of working on people. You'll get used to it."

I put it off as long as I can, but eventually he realises what I'm doing because he turns to look at me.

"You ready?"

"No."

"Come on, I know you can do it. Remember everything I said yesterday. It's just a pen, and I'm just paper."

"Okay," I whisper, picking up his machine and holding it like he showed me yesterday. I might have some very limited experience with an old machine over the years when people realised that I could draw, but they were nothing like this.

The moment I turn it on, I feel the vibrations right down to my toes.

My hand trembles as I lower it to his skin, but the moment I make my first mark, I relax—which is crazy, but he's right. It's just a pen, and he's just the paper.

"Just focus on the outline. You're more than capable of doing that. We can work on filling in and shading later."

I nod despite the fact he can't see me. I'm too focused to reply.

I have no idea how much time passes, but the muscles in my shoulders and neck ache from the unusual angle I'm sitting at.

I turn the machine off and place it on Spike's table before standing and stretching out my back.

"You done?" he asks, watching me with heat in his eyes.

"For now. It hurts."

"You'll soon get used to it. How's it look?"

"Umm..." I look at his arse, focusing more on the roundness of it than my sketch.

"I guess I'll look myself then." He pushes from the bed and walks over to the mirror hanging on the opposite wall. "Kas," he says, looking over his shoulder.

"You hate it?" I ask, hating the vulnerability in my tone.

"Not at all. It's incredible."

"Really? You're not just saying that to make me feel better."

Leaving his arse exposed, he turns his stare on me. I close the distance between us, the pull I feel toward him too much to deny.

His hands cup my face and he drops down so his nose is almost touching mine.

"I'll never lie to you, Tiny."

I smile, the satisfaction that he really does think I did okay washing through me.

"You're sure, though? It's okay?"

"It's more than okay. Over the next few weeks you can draw the rest and then start practicing on me. I'll be your canvas."

"Don't people usually start on grapefruits or some shit?"

He laughs. "Back in the day, yeah. I'm sure we could pick you a couple up if you'd prefer to work on one of those."

"Never."

"Awesome. Wrap me up, then it's time to swap."

"Swap?"

"Yep. You didn't think I was the only one leaving here today with some new ink, did you?"

CHAPTER TWENTY-SIX

SPIKE

SHE LOOKS at me as if I've just spoken to her in a different language.

"Okay, well... unless you don't want—"

"I do, I do. I just wasn't expecting it. What were you thinking?"

"I borrowed another one," I admit, reaching back into my jeans that are currently in a pile on the floor and pulling out the second drawing. "I assume it's the one."

I unfold it and show her. She nods, confirming that I'm right. I knew it was the design she'd mentioned to cover the inevitable scar on her hip the moment I saw it.

"We can start on your thigh, and we'll work our way up and then do the final bit once you're healed."

"Sounds perfect. I don't want to look at that for any longer than I have to."

Stepping up to her, I twist my fingers with hers and pull her flush against my body.

"All that's over, Kas. This right here is a new start."

She swallows nervously before nodding. "For both of us?" I know what she's asking. She's telling me that it's time to let go of the past, of my heartbreak, and take another chance.

She makes it feel so easy, sound so tempting, that without much thought, I think I could dive in headfirst with her. The realisation has my heart racing and my head beginning to spin.

Of all the women, why her? Why the one I shouldn't be anywhere near? But others haven't made me feel the way she does. I realise that could be because I never gave any of them the chance, but I know it's not that. I knew Kas was different the moment my eyes landed on her all those weeks ago at Zach's birthday. I just didn't realise quite how much until I dragged her from that stage and forced her into my life.

I nod. "For both of us." She smiles up at me and I swear my entire world shifts on its axis. "Ready for your new ink?"

"I can't wait."

Before I have a chance to think, her jeans are on the floor with mine and she's climbing onto my chair.

"How do you want me?"

'Naked with your legs open' is on the tip of my tongue, but even for me, that feels a little dangerous. I know that Zach and Biff are out at an Abbott family meal along with Titch and Danni, but they've got to come back at some point.

Stepping forward, I lift the back of the chair so she can sit and show me where she wants this tattoo to start.

A wicked smile curls at her lips as she widens her legs and points to the inside of her thigh. "I thought it could start about here, wrap around and continue up here." She trails her finger along her skin in a way I wish I could do with my tongue right now as she lifts her shirt, stopping just shy of her ribs.

"That's going to take quite a while," I say, glancing at her intricate design.

"It's a good thing I've got all the time in the world then, isn't it? Make me your masterpiece, Spike."

A growl rumbles up my throat. She can't possibly know what words like that do to me.

She would never let me ink her, no matter how much I begged. It was wrong of me back then, and probably just as bad now, for me to want to mark Kas' body the way I do, to make it mine. She'll have my art on her, probably forever after today, a constant reminder of what we had here.

I let her get comfortable and then grab my machine.

"A-aren't you going to trace it on?" Her voice wavers.

"Tiny, are you nervous?"

She swallows harshly. "I... uh... I'm not great with needles."

I run my eyes over her exposed skin before me which is covered in ink. "Riiight."

"I can't help it," she shrugs. "It'll get better. Just get started."

"Okay." The buzzing of my gun fills the room, and I lower it to her skin. She flinches when I first make contact, and when I glance up at her, all she does is laugh at herself. The sound immediately makes me feel lighter.

I work on the first few flowers on the inside of her thigh, losing myself in the art, in the softness of her skin, in the scent of her sweetness surrounding me.

Time races past as we both stare at her skin, watching the design emerge with every stroke and movement of my hand.

I'm so lost that I don't hear any noise from outside the room. That all stops, though, when the door flies open.

"What the—what the hell are you doing?" Zach barks, his eyes wide as he looks at the two of us half-dressed and in a somewhat compromising position with me practically between Kas' legs.

"Teaching," I say as innocently as possible.

"With my sister on her back and you in your boxers?"

"Uh... yeah. Look..." Dropping my machine back to the table, I stand and show Zach Kas' handiwork.

"Mate, seriously," Zach complains with a wince when he figures out where this is going.

"Quit being a pussy."

He rolls his eyes before dropping them to my exposed skin. "That's not bad. Well done, Kas." He flicks his eyes to her before they come back to me. Anger is simmering just under the surface. As we stare at each other, I can't miss the silent warning he's giving me. It's just a shame he's about a week too late. "Your arse, really?"

"What? Where did you let Biff do her first one?"

A smile twitches at his lips, and I know I've got him. "Okay, fine. But I should warn you that this wasn't what I had in mind when I suggested this. I knew I should have asked D," he mutters.

"You don't need to protect me, Zach. I'm a big girl and can make my own decisions."

His eyes narrow at her. "What are you trying to tell me?"

"N-nothing. Just that I'm an adult and you can't control me or what I do. You try, and you'll only push me away."

Zach looks between the two of us suspiciously, but his gaze lingers on me longer than necessary. Guilt bubbles up inside me, and I have to bite my tongue not to blurt out what's been going on.

I need to, I know it's the right thing to do, but I can't. Telling him could ruin everything that Kas and I are building, and I can't risk it. Not yet. Just a few more days and we might have discovered what we really are. I might have grown a pair of balls and been able to admit to myself that I'm willing to really give this a go with her. The thought of accepting it myself makes my heart race, let alone telling someone else that I've opened myself up to the possibilities of more heartache.

"I guess I'll leave you to it then," he mutters, backing out of the room.

Just before he disappears from our sight, Kas calls for him.

He looks back to her, his eyes softening and telling me that all he's trying to do right now is protect her in a way that no one has before, in a way he's been unable to. I'm desperate to tell him, that is all I want as well, but I don't think he'll see my honourable intentions. All he'll see are all my past conquests and questionable decisions.

"You can trust me, Zach. I'm not going to screw all of this up. I promise."

He nods at her before ducking out of the room.

"He's going to fucking kill me when we tell him."

"No, he won't. He'll understand." She reaches for me and brushes her fingers against mine.

"Let me finish this section up, then let's get out of here."

"MMM... I could wake up to this every morning," Kas moans, arching her back as I lick at her clit. Her hands thread into my hair as I slide two fingers inside her and bend them in a way that I know will make her scream. "Spike," she cries, her grip on me tightening.

I up my pace, playing her until she shudders against me, her muscles pulsating around my fingers.

"I need a shower. Fancy it?" Lifting my head from between her thighs, I look up at her dark, lust-filled eyes.

She bites down on her bottom lip, making me want to suck it into my own mouth.

"You naked with water running all over you..." She pretends to think for a few seconds. "I'm sure I could get on board with that."

"Good." Pulling her from the bed, I drag her behind me as I head for the bathroom before lifting her into the bath and turning the shower on.

"Fucking hell, that's freezing."

"Let me warm you up then." I pull her into my body, my already hard cock pressing against her stomach, desperate to slide deep inside her, and my lips find hers as my hands work their way over her curves.

I push my tongue between her lips, telling her everything I'm feeling with my kiss alone, or I hope that's what I'm doing.

"How's your hip?" I ask as I kiss my way across her jaw and down her neck.

"I can't even feel it."

"Good. Turn around and place your palms on the tiles."

Immediately, she does as she's told, shoving her arse out for me to take advantage of.

"You know, you're getting awfully compliant with my requests." My palm connects with her arse, the slap ringing throughout the small room.

"I tend to follow orders better if I think they're going to end in orgasms."

I laugh, dropping my hand to her core, finding her still dripping wet from her last release.

"Keep your arms locked," I order, taking myself in hand and running the head of my cock through her folds.

"Spike," she moans impatiently.

I tease her for a few more seconds before surging forward, filling her in one thrust of my hips.

Her heat surrounds me and I have to reach forward, pressing my own hand against the wall next to hers to hold myself up.

"So fucking good," I groan as I start to move inside her.

My thrusts become frantic as I push us both toward our releases, but at no point does she release her arms.

"Come, Kas." Slipping my hand around her

stomach, I find her clit and pinch, forcing her over the edge.

I follow seconds later, emptying myself inside her before pulling her up and wrapping my arms around her body as our hearts fight to return to normal.

"I always visit my grandad on a Monday morning," I admit while we're both getting dressed.

"Don't let me stop you."

"I'm not. I was wondering if you..."

"If I?" she prompts.

"If you wanted to come with me."

"To meet your grandad?"

"Y-yeah."

"Sure, if you want me to."

I nod. "I do. I've never taken anyone before," I admit. "Well, not since..."

"Spike," she says softly, walking up to me and wrapping her arms around my waist, "are you nervous?"

"Yeah, I am. It's a big deal."

"Why, don't you think he'll like me?"

"No, I think he'll love you." *Just like I do.* By some miracle, I manage to keep those final words to myself.

"I'VE NEVER MET anyone's parents before," Kas says as we walk toward the entrance to where Gramps lives. "Should I have worn something a little more... conservative?"

I run my eyes over her crop top and ripped jeans. "No, not at all. Just be yourself. He'd see right through you anyway."

"Okay. Fuck. I'm nervous." She shakes out her arms and blows out a breath.

Wrapping my arm around her shoulder, I lead her inside and toward where I know he'll be waiting.

As we round the corner, I spot Maureen at the table with her puzzle first, before movement from the chair where I know he'll be catches my eye.

"Well, well, well. What do we have here," Gramps says excitedly, his eyes firmly locked on Kas and totally ignoring that I've walked into the room.

"Hi, I'm Kas," she says nervously as she steps up to him and raises her hand to shake his.

She squeals in shock when he tugs on her arm and pulls her into his body for a brief hug.

"Morning, Spike," Maureen says to me as Gramps drops his lips to Kas' ear and whispers something to her. Something embarrassing about me, no doubt. That thought is only confirmed when she throws her head back and belts out a full belly laugh.

"Uh oh... looks like someone's caught the love bug," Maureen says with a wide smile playing on her lips.

"I...uh..." *Fuck it.* "Yeah, I think I might have."

Tears fill her eyes as she smiles at me. I've no doubt that she knows my story. She and Gramps seem pretty tight.

"Well, it seems she's won his old heart over too." Her eyes flick to where my gramps is now laughing at whatever Kas said, and my chest constricts in a way I realise I've missed so much.

I stand and watch them for a few seconds, acknowledging that I didn't need to be nervous about bringing her here. Just like everything else with her, it's just right.

As if she can feel my stare, she looks up at me. She has a wide smile on her face, and I accept in that moment that despite all my fears, I've fallen, and fallen hard.

"You'd better get over here before Gramps tells me all your secrets," she mocks, but I don't miss the way she calls him Gramps. Why am I not surprised that he's already demanded that?

Rolling my eyes at the pair of them, I walk over. Gramps' hand lands on the back of my neck. "You've got yourself a little firecracker here, son," he whispers, quiet enough so that only I can hear.

I nod, smiling at him.

"So, Kas. Tell me everything," he demands when the three of us sit down.

"Err... not much to tell, really," she says, a sadness in her tone that I hate hearing.

"She's training to be an artist," I blurt out, focusing on the future, not the past.

"Is that right? You any good?" he asks her.

"He seems to think so. He's so confident he ensured I start on his arse."

"She's going to be an incredible artist."

"Awesome, so maybe you'll ink me?" Gramps asks, making me groan.

"Your own grandson is refusing you some ink?" Kas asks in mock horror.

"I know. I think it's damn right disrespectful if you ask me. One of the best artists in the city shares my DNA, and he won't ink me."

"Give me a few months to get a feel for it and I'll give you whatever you want," Kas offers with a wink, once again making him belly laugh.

"Spike," he says, his face turning serious for a second. "I like this one. She's a keeper."

Kas' eyes burn into me, waiting for my response.

"You think? She's a pain in the arse, if you ask me." I can't help laughing when her small hand connects with my shoulder.

CHAPTER TWENTY-SEVEN

KAS

I'M STILL RUNNING over the morning and in meeting Spike's gramps around my head later that afternoon while we lie on one of Spike's sofas watching the TV. Well, he's watching it, I've no clue what channel it's even on.

Propping my chin on his chest, I look up at him, taking in his features for a second before a smile twitches at his lips

"What?" he asks, not taking his eyes from the TV.

"Nothing. Just looking."

"Okay." He continues staring ahead, but I know he's not paying any attention now. "Whatever it is, Tiny, just ask."

"Will you tell me about your family?"

He blows out a long breath. "There's not really much to tell. My grandparents basically brought me up. My mother, their daughter, was a mess by all accounts. She fell pregnant with me when she was fifteen. I don't remember her. She left some time before my second birthday. We've no idea where she went or what she did. It was almost ten years later when Gramps got a visit from a police officer with the news he'd been dreading for years. She'd overdosed on heroin."

"Jesus, Spike."

"See, we're not so different really."

"What happened to your gran?"

"She died the year before we found out about my mother."

The words *I'm sorry* are right on the tip of my tongue, but I know from experience that they're the most unhelpful words ever.

"Your poor gramps."

He shrugs. "The two of us did okay. He made sure I had every opportunity to follow my dreams, and we figured shit out together. Although I probably should have listened to him when he told me things were too serious with Marissa." My breath catches at hearing her name. It's the first time he's used it, and although I know the story is very true—his pain every time he talks about it makes it abundantly clear—being able to put a name to the woman who shattered his young heart makes it seem so much more real.

"We have to make our own mistakes sometimes."

He nods at my words, lost in his memories.

I desperately want to change the subject in the hope of wiping the sadness from his face, but before I come up with anything both of our phones vibrate on the coffee table.

Our eyes meet as if we're both asking the other who it is before he reaches forward and grabs them both, passing mine over.

He laughs before I even get the chance to look at my screen. Intrigued, I wake up my phone and look at it to find a group message.

Pear Tree. 8PM. Time to welcome our newbie Rebel to the family.

"Who's this from?"

"Titch. I should have expected it."

"And I'm assuming the newbie is me?"

"Yep. Consider it an initiation of sorts."

"What the hell? Is he planning to get me drunk and make me run naked around the streets?"

He tenses beneath me at my suggestion. "I should fucking hope not, although there will probably be shots involved."

"Shots I can do."

As the next hour passes, our phones continue to light up as everyone agrees to meet.

"I guess I should go and get ready then," I suggest when we've only got an hour left before we need to be at the bar.

"Maybe we should just stay here?"

"And invite a ton of questions from Zach?"

He looks to me, scrubbing his hand down his face and over his jaw.

"What's wrong?"

"We need to talk to him."

"I know, and we will. But maybe not tonight. Tomorrow?"

He thinks for a minute. "Tomorrow," he agrees.

Pushing from him, I head for my room.

"Kas?"

"Yeah?"

"You're going to need to be on your best behaviour tonight."

"What are you trying to suggest?" I ask, wiggling my arse as I disappear into my room to decide what to wear.

I put some music on and set about getting ready for our night out.

"THAT WASN'T what I had in mind when I told you to behave," Spike states as he fills the doorway with his wide frame.

"What?" I ask innocently, spinning around for him so he can get a proper look. I'm wearing a pair of black denim shorts that show off the tattoo Spike started—along with a little too much of my arse, if the look on his face is anything to go by.

"Tiny," he warns, his voice deep and raspy, causing tingles to erupt in my lower belly.

Tucking a lock of my now curled hair over my shoulder, I reach for my bag and shove my phone inside it.

"Ready?" I ask innocently.

"If I end up in the hospital tonight, it'll all be your fault."

Stepping up to him, I slide my hand up his chest and grip onto the back of his neck.

With my high shoes on, I'm that much closer to his lips. Reaching forward, I stop millimetres away from his. "Just think, you'll be the one who peels it all off me later."

"Tiny, you don't play fair."

"What would be the fun in that?"

Stepping around him, I slip from the room.

"You coming, old man, or would you prefer I make you a hot milk and tuck you into bed?"

"If anything happens tonight, it's on you." He steps up behind me, his hands cupping my arse as he tucks his face into my neck. "Fuck, you smell so damn good."

"No time for that, they're going to be waiting."

"Fucking hell." He makes a show of rearranging himself before following me from the flat.

"There's an Uber waiting," I inform him as we descend the stairs.

"Oh, I was going to—"

"Enjoy yourself," I finish for him.

"If you call watching every other guy in the room eye fuck you, then yeah, it should be a great night." I smile to myself, glad he can't see how happy his little jealous streak makes me.

"Fuck them, Spike. You're the only one I'm going home with."

"Damn fucking straight."

We climb into the awaiting car and head off to meet the others.

Spike explains about the Pear Tree being their local, and I realise just how true that is when we walk in and the guy behind the bar greets him by name. Without looking, Spike directs me to a booth at the back of the huge bar.

Zach, Biff, Titch, Danni and D have already started without us, from the looks of the empty glasses littering the table. All of them look happy to see us—apart from Zach, who assesses both of us as we walk toward him.

"Here she is, our newest little Rebel," Titch announces before getting up and walking to the bar to get the round of shots that Spike already warned me about.

"Why are you so late?" Zach barks.

"Don't look at me," Spike says with his hands up in surrender. "I wasn't the one curling my hair." He flicks me a look that makes me laugh as I slide into the booth beside my brother.

"Shots are up," Titch says, returning with a tray full of neon green drinks for everyone. Well, everyone aside from Danni, it seems.

"Work night," she says with a shrug, but while the guys ignore her comment, I don't miss the look between her and Biff and the small smiles on their lips. It seems there's much more to her work night excuse than she wants to let on.

Before they notice my attention, I turn back to the guys.

"So, you haven't changed your mind yet, then?" D asks me.

"No way—as much as I'd love to leave him with a half-done tat on his arse."

D's eyes widen. "He let you ink him? That fucker's never let me anywhere near his skin."

"I guess I'm lucky then."

"Show us," Titch pipes up, much to Spike's horror.

"I'm not showing you my arse in the middle of the bar," Spike sulks.

"Fucking pussy, get that shot down your neck and show us. It won't be the first time we've seen your naked arse, although usually it's while you're ploughing your cock into some randomer."

"Carter," Danni gasps, slapping his shoulder.

"What? It's true," he argues, while Spike pales.

I shake my head at him. His past is his past, just like mine is mine. There's nothing we can do to change it, no matter how much we might not like it.

"Now, drop your pants, man. We want to see her handiwork."

"For fuck's sake," Spike mutters, but he clearly decides against arguing because he stands and shows everyone at the table the top half of his arse.

"Oh damn, girl. That's a hell of a lot better than the first one I did," Titch says, making my chest swell with pride.

"Really?" I try to fight my smile, but I can't stop it from forming.

"Hell, yeah."

"What about your first, Biff? I assume Zach is sporting the evidence," I say, turning the attention away from the two of us.

"Of course. You gonna show it off?" she asks, turning to Zach.

Shifting away from her side, he lifts his shirt, showing off the fresh ink on his ribs.

Everyone around the table bursts out laughing at the sight while Biff smiles.

"You inked a fucking pussy cat on him?" D asks, his eyes wide in shock.

"It's part of a bigger design, but yeah, I put my stamp on him." She winks.

"Fucking hell, you're so fucking whipped," D complains, looking at Zach before briefly flashing a glance to Spike.

The guys launch into stories about their first times and their tattoo horror stories from over the years. As if by magic, our drinks are continuously refilled, and by the time someone suggests moving on, my head is spinning nicely.

"The Avenue?" Titch asks, although from the way he says it, I already think the decision's been made. We make our way outside before heading to the club.

"See, I told you it would be okay," I say to Spike once we're outside the club, waiting in line.

"The night is still young, Tiny."

I glance over at my brother where he has Biff backed up against the building. "I don't think we're his main focus right now."

"Fucking hell," Spike mutters, turning his back on the love birds.

"You're just jealous," I say with a smile.

He's silent for a moment before he drops his lips to my ear. "I've been hard since I saw you in those shorts earlier. All I can think about is sliding deep inside you, feeling your pussy contract around me and teaching my little girl a lesson. So yeah, I'm fucking jealous that he gets to do that, and I can't so much as touch you."

I whimper, my need for what he just described sending my alcohol-fuelled brain right into the gutter.

"You're already wet for me, aren't you, Tiny?"

"Maybe you should find out," I taunt, taking a step forward and toward the bouncer who, predictably, asks for my ID.

I hand it over, feeling like a child hanging out with

all these adults, before he nods and allows me inside. I really didn't need a reminder of the age difference between me and Spike, but as I walk inside beside him, I don't think it's been any more obvious to me.

"Going down?" Titch shouts over his shoulder, although he doesn't wait for a response, he just heads for the stairs.

We find a patch of space at the opposite end of the bar and Titch sets about ordering us more drinks.

We all down two shots before Biff and Danni take my hands and drag me out to the dancefloor.

Thankfully, they don't make any attempt to talk. Biff knows what's been going on between Spike and me, so I have no reason to think that she hasn't shared all the details with Danni.

The three of us form a small circle and start dancing.

I can't remember the last time I went out with friends and just let go. All I do know is that it's been far too long.

I forget about everything, about those dancing around me, and lose myself to the music. My arms lift above my head, I roll my hips, and I let the beat flow through me.

The only other person I'm aware of is the burning stare I feel. I don't look for fear of being caught, but I know he's watching me.

"He's got it bad for you, girl," Biff shouts in my ear.

I shrug, trying not to make a big deal out of it. The last thing we need is Zach noticing tonight and causing drama.

A few more songs pass and both Zach and Titch join us so they can dance with their girls.

Disappointment floods me when I don't feel his hands slip around my waist and his body pressed against my back.

With Zach distracted, I risk a glance over my shoulder.

I immediately find him lifting a drink to his lips and downing it in one. The second he looks forward, his eyes find mine. They widen slightly before a mix of anger and hunger fills them.

Every muscle south of my waist clenches with need as our connection holds.

Sadly, D slides another drink over to him and our contact is lost as he takes it and once again drinks it in one.

With the weight of our secret weighing down on me, I excuse myself from the happy couples and head for the ladies' for a breather.

Thankfully, with it being a Monday night, there's no queue and I walk right inside. There are a few women perfecting their hair and topping up their makeup, but none of them pay me any attention as I make my way down to the final cubicle in the hope of a few minutes of quiet.

That all changes as I walk inside the small space and a few gasps and squeals sound out. I'm about to look to find out what the fuss is about when a large pair of hands grips my waist and continues pushing me inside.

My heart jumps into my throat as old fears of Jet rush to the forefront, but I relax the second his scent fills my nose.

"Spike, what the hell are you doing?"

He spins me around, presses my back up against the wall and slams his lips down on mine.

His tongue forces its way inside—not that I would have denied him entry—as he stakes his claim on me.

One hand threads into my hair, tugging so he can deepen the kiss while the other skims up my side and slips under my top to find my naked breast.

A low growl rumbles up his throat when he finds my bare skin. He pinches my nipple, making me gasp.

"Spike," I moan as he tugs my hair harder, exposing my neck and dropping his lips to the sensitive skin.

"I fucking need you," he groans, his fingers dropping, popping open the button on my shorts and disappearing inside. "Fuck," he barks when he finds me wet and ready for him.

"Spike, please."

The fabric drops from my hips and I eagerly kick it off, my need for him all-consuming.

His eyes bore into mine. They're wild, the chestnut almost black with desire.

"Fucking hell, Kas." He stills, and I panic that he isn't going to continue.

Reaching out, I open his fly, pushing his trousers and boxers down his hips, taking matters into my own hands.

I'm about to wrap my hand around his solid length when he growls once more and my feet leave the floor.

"Oh fuck, Spike," I cry out when he finds my entrance and drops me down onto him. The sensation of being stretched open and so full of him, his all-consuming touch and the alcohol racing through my veins, is a heady combination.

His hands grasp my arse with an almost painful grip and he pistons in and out of me.

"I was watching you," he groans in my ear. "I

wanted to be pressed up against you, dancing with you, showing everyone in here that you're mine."

"Oh God," I whimper, racing toward a mind-blowing release all too soon.

My nails claw at him as I try to get more.

Our heavy breathing and moans of pleasure fill the space around us, but I don't give anyone who might be listening a second thought as he continues moving, giving me everything I need.

"So good, so fucking good," he moans in my ear before once again taking my lips on his and swallowing down my cries for more.

Our kiss is wild, dirty, and messy, I can't get enough of it. He sinks his teeth into my bottom lip and my entire body explodes, that tiny bit of pain sending me flying over the edge I was teetering on.

"Spiiiike," I cry out, fighting to catch my breath as pleasure takes over my body. My limbs become heavy as tingles continue to race to my toes.

"Kas," he groans, it's so low and rough it threatens to send me headfirst into a second release as his cock twitches inside me.

"Oh God. Oh God. Fuck." My head falls back again as my second orgasm hits me all of a sudden, and I drag much-needed air into my lungs.

After a few seconds, Spike lifts his head from my neck and pulls out of me. I miss him immediately and almost demand that we go again, until my surroundings come back to me and I remember where we are.

Fuck.

"I shouldn't have done that," Spike says, tucking himself back into his trousers, suddenly sounding much more sober than only a few seconds ago.

"Don't," I say, reaching out to cup his cheek. "Don't regret anything when it comes to us. You need me, I'm right here."

"Fucking hell, Tiny. You fucking slay me."

"The feeling is entirely mutual," I whisper, reaching up to brush my lips against his.

"Get cleaned up. We should probably head back out."

"They won't have noticed," I say, praying that my words are true.

I do as I'm told before pulling my clothes back on and running my fingers through my hair to tame it.

"Stop," I cry out when Spike is about to open the cubicle door.

I pull a wipe from my bag and lift it to his face to wipe away my red lipstick that's covering him.

"Thanks," he mutters before pulling the door open and marching from the ladies' toilets almost as quickly as he entered.

The women who are now at the basins watch him leave before turning their eyes on me.

I don't give them the time of day and move to a basin of my own to fix my makeup.

A smile tugs at my lips as their attention remains on me.

Their jealousy is so strong I can almost taste it.

He's all mine, I think as I reapply my makeup, but a loud scream from outside forces me to stop mid-application when a huge ball of dread fills my stomach.

I don't know how I know, but I do.

CHAPTER TWENTY-EIGHT

SPIKE

THE EYES of the interested woman follow me from the ladies' bathroom, but I don't look at any of them. Why would I when I have Kas?

My head is still back in that cubicle, so I don't even notice the man loitering outside the door—well, not until I feel the crack of his knuckles against my jaw.

Motherfucker.

My back collides with the wall from the force of the hit, but it seems that wasn't enough.

As I look up at one of my best friends, his fist flies toward me once more, connecting with my cheek and making my vision blur.

"Fucking liar. You're a fucking liar," he bellows, taking his anger out on my face.

I could fight back. I could probably hold my own to an extent, but what's the point? He knows the reason he just watched me walk out of the ladies' toilets, and in a few seconds Kas is going to emerge, making it even more obvious.

My clenched fists remain at my sides as I let him take what he needs.

Women scream and run, but no one stops him.

Not until the inevitable happens.

"Zach," Kas screams, running toward us as fast as she can. "Stop it. Fucking stop it," she squeals, wrapping her small hands around his forearm, but he's too focused on his next hit because he pulls his arm back with such force that Kas flies backward and collides with the wall before falling to a heap.

I move to get her, but I'm not quick enough, because Zach's fist sinks into my stomach and I double over in pain, dropping to my knees.

Kas recovers quicker and crawls over to me.

"Shit, Spike. Fuck. Are you okay?"

"Yeah, yeah. I'm good. You need to get out of the way."

"Fuck that, Spike. I'll stand right beside you."

"There you are... what the fuck have you done?" Biff screams as she rounds the corner, taking in the scene before her and standing in front of her husband in the hope of stopping him.

I stare up at Zach. His eyes are blown, his chest is heaving, and his fists are clenched and covered in blood —mine or his, I have no idea.

I've never seen him like this before. This angry and uncontrollable.

Biff pushes at his chest to make him back up, but he doesn't move. In fact, I'd swear he only gets closer.

It's not until two bouncers come running around the corner that he backs up, and that's only because they take an arm each and practically drag him away from the scene.

"I fucking trusted you," he screams back at me as he attempts to fight the two guys holding him.

"Fuck. I'm so sorry," Biff says, dropping to her knees on the other side of me to Kas.

"It's not your fault."

Lifting my hand, I wipe away the blood trickling down my chin.

She looks back in the direction Zach went in before her concerned eyes come back to me.

"Go to him, it's okay."

"Are you sure?" I've never seen her look so torn.

"Yes. He's going to need you."

"Spike, for once will you stop thinking about everyone else and concentrate on yourself," she snaps. "Anyway, he's not going to want me anywhere near him when he discovers that I already knew about this."

I wince, knowing that she's right.

"Don't worry about me, I can handle him." She winks.

"Just go," I say as I notice a member of staff heading our way.

Pushing from the floor, I manage to get to my feet with the help of Kas' arm around my waist.

"One of my colleagues is about to call the police. If you'd like to follow me, then—"

"No," I bark, much to his surprise. "No police. We're leaving."

"But you need to press—"

"I need to do fuck all."

The guy—who doesn't look a day over eighteen—pales at my tone.

"Excuse us," Kas says, taking a step forward with me and forcing him to stand aside.

"But—"

Kas stops when we're in front of the guy. "Nothing happened here. You got that?"

He swallows nervously but eventually nods and allows us to leave without any further drama.

"Fucking hell," D shouts when he sees the two of us trying to make our way to the exit. "What the fuck were you thinking?"

"Don't start," I mutter. I don't need him playing dad right now.

I fucked up tonight. Hell, I fucked up the first time I laid a finger on Kas, but it's a bit late to regret any of that now because I'm in too deep.

"There's a car on its way," Kas says

"They're not going to let him in like that."

"They're going to have to."

"Jesus. He really didn't stand a chance with you, did he," D says as if I'm not even here.

"Nothing wrong with going after what you want. How much did you give him to drink?"

"Few shots, some whisky. I wasn't fucking counting."

I lose focus on what they're saying by the time the cool night air hits me. Thank fuck D came to help, because there's no way Kas would have been able to hold me up.

I have no idea how we get home, but the next thing I know, the softness of my mattress hits my back.

"Thank you for helping."

"You sure you don't want me to stay?"

"No, you get off. Try to enjoy the rest of your night."

"Make sure you lock the door behind me." My brows draw together at his strange words. D's not usually one to say shit like that. Or maybe it's just because he's talking to Kas and not one of us.

I don't get a chance to think much more about it, because the room spins before I drift off again.

"Ouch," I complain when a sharp pain wakes me back up.

"Quit being a pussy," Kas whispers.

"I'm okay, you don't need—"

"Shut up. He did a fucking good job on you."

"I know, I can feel it." She might be cleaning my face up as gently as possible, but still, it aches like a motherfucker. The only consolation is that Zach's hand must be pretty messed up right now. "I fucked up tonight. I'm sorry."

"It's not just your fault. We should have spoken to him days ago."

"Yeah, but I didn't need to follow you to the toilets."

"Didn't you?" I crack an eye open to see a wicked smirk playing on her lips. Despite the pain I'm in, my cock swells at the memory of fucking her in that cubicle.

She's right, it did need to happen.

"Fuck. He was a mess, I've never seen him so angry."

"He'll get over it," she says with much more confidence than I feel.

I rest back, allowing her to continue what she's

doing. Her touch feels too good, and my head is spinning way too much to argue about it.

"This is going to hurt like hell in the morning."

"It hurts pretty bad now. Are you okay?"

"Spike," she sighs.

"He threw you into the wall." My entire body tenses as I remember her body flying like nothing more than a rag doll.

"I'm fine. Can you sit up? I need to get this shirt off you?"

"Trying to get me naked?" I tease.

"Always," she deadpans.

"Hmm... are you going to kiss it all better?"

"You're a nightmare."

"Yep, but I'm all yours."

ROLLING OVER, my cheek presses against the pillow and my eyes fly open.

What the fuck...

The image of Zach's fist flying at me emerges, and I groan. Fucking hell, it wasn't a nightmare.

"Are you okay?" Kas says, sitting up, concern filling her face as her eyes flit over mine.

"Yeah," I manage after clearing my throat.

"Here, take these." Sitting up, she passes me over a couple of painkillers and a glass of water.

"Thank you."

"I'm not sure what hurts worse, my face or my hangover."

"You had way too much to drink last night," she points out helpfully.

"I had to watch you from a distance. What else was I meant to do when all I wanted was to walk up behind you and hold you?"

"Spike," she sighs, laying back down and carefully tucking herself into my side.

After a few minutes, I manage to drift back off to sleep.

"HMM... I could get used to this," I mutter, cracking my eyes open again to find Kas sitting beside me on the bed in only her underwear.

"We... uh... need to go to work," she says with a wince.

"Fucking hell," I groan.

"Biff's offered to cancel your clients if you can't make it."

"How's Zach?"

"She said he was okay, but I'm pretty sure she was lying."

I nod. He has every right to still be furious with me. I lied to him about the one thing I promised I wouldn't do.

"I need to go. I need to talk to him."

"No, Spike," she says, taking my hand in hers. "*We* need to talk to him."

I stare at her, taking in her beauty. "I don't deserve you."

"Yet here I am anyway," she jokes.

"He might never be okay with this," I say, voicing my biggest concern.

"We'll cross that bridge if it comes to it. First, we need to hold our heads high and get on with it."

She pushes to stand so she can finish getting ready, but I tighten my grip on her fingers and pull her back.

"I..." My voice cracks with nerves and Kas' brows draw together. Blowing out a breath, I force out the words that I really need to say to her. "I really want this... us. You know that, right?"

A genuine smile curls at her lips. "I do. I feel it. I know this scares you—hell, it scares me too. But you don't need to doubt that I don't know how you feel. I do."

I nod. "Good. That's good."

"Whatever happens, we'll fight it together, yeah?"

"Yeah." I smile for the first time in what feels like days, although I instantly regret it because the split in my lip opens up and stings like a bitch.

"I guess I'd better attempt to make myself look presentable."

"Good luck with that," she laughs.

"Fuck, is it that bad?"

"I think it's sexy." She runs her eyes from my face and down to my exposed chest and stomach.

"Kas?"

"No time. Go get in the shower, then we need to head out."

I roll my eyes at her but do as I'm told.

Thankfully, the painkillers she gave me earlier have taken the edge off and I'm able to shower and dress almost like normal.

"Well aren't you a sight for sore eyes," she says when I join her in the living room where she's been waiting for me.

"Ready?"

"I've called an Uber. You're not driving like that."

I want to argue, but after getting a look at myself in the mirror, I know I don't have a leg to stand on.

Hand in hand, we head out, ready to discover what's waiting for us at the studio.

CHAPTER TWENTY-NINE

KAS

I TELL myself that I'm not going to look when we step outside the building, but it all goes to shit when my eyes take on a life of their own and start scanning the area for the guy who was loitering last night.

Just like the dark figure at the other end of the street the other day, he scared me.

I tried not to react, but D noticed where my attention had drifted, and he also saw the guy in the shadows watching us as we carried a passed-out Spike into the building.

I spent most of the night staring at the ceiling, attempting to convince myself that it was a coincidence. That he was hiding for any other reason than waiting for us… for me.

I tell myself time and time again that the threat is gone. Jet is dead, along with his goons, and all of that is over. Mum's gone, her dealer is gone, and I have a new life.

Only, things aren't ever that simple, are they?

I hate doing it, but old habits die hard, and after I'd dressed for a day at the studio, I slide my flip knife into my boot.

Until I moved here there wasn't a day that passed where it wasn't on my body somewhere, just in case something happened.

I'd witnessed people get jumped on almost a daily basis, and fuck if I wasn't going to be prepared for it to happen to me.

"What's wrong?" Spike asks, his eyes drilling into me. So much for being discreet.

"It's nothing."

"Don't fucking lie to me, Kas. Who are you looking for?"

"N-no one. There was just this guy last night."

He stares at me before his eyes widen as if he's remembered something.

"That why D told you to lock the door after him?"

"Uh... yeah. It's probably nothing. Just some scumbag hiding in the shadows."

"You keep saying things like that."

"Well, it's probably true. This is London. There are arseholes on every corner. It's probably nothing."

"Or it might not be."

I shrug, trying really hard not to make a bigger issue out of this than it needs to be.

"All that's over, right? It's nothing. I'm just being paranoid."

He studies me for a beat before our car pulls up and we climb in.

I fight not to stare out the window to continue looking for someone, but I can't shake the feeling that something's not right.

Discreetly, I lean down to scratch my ankle, but really I'm just making sure my knife is in place and putting my mind to rest somewhat.

Rebel Ink is still in darkness when we pull up. We're early, in the hope of talking to Zach before clients start arriving.

My heart pounds in my chest and my palms feel a little sweaty as Spike lets us both inside. The place is in silence as we walk through reception.

"Upstairs," Spike says before walking through the kitchen and toward the stairs that lead up to Zach and Biff's flat above the studio.

Silently we make our way up, the atmosphere already making it hard to breathe.

The moment we're at the top, Spike reaches out and knocks on the door.

Movement inside is almost instant, but when the door is pulled open, it's Biff who stands on the other side, looking exhausted.

"Hey," she says softly. "How are you?"

"I'll live. Is he here?"

"Um..." She glances back, telling us both that he's obviously inside and hiding. "No?" I don't think it was meant to come out like a question.

"Just let us in, we need to talk."

"He's still angry. At all of us," she adds quietly.

"I expect him to be, but he needs to hear what I've got to say."

"Not yet, just give him a little more time."

"What good is that going to do? This isn't going to go away."

Biff blows out a knowing breath.

"Zach, get your fucking arse out here," Spike barks, making Biff jump.

Silence follows.

"I refuse to do this through a fucking door, man."

"Just go and do your job, and be fucking glad you're good at it, or you might not have one right now."

"You don't mean that, man."

"Don't I?" he spits back. "Stay out of my way. Both of you."

Biff winces at the fierceness of his tone.

"We'll be downstairs," I say to her, giving her a sympathetic smile and placing my hand on Spike's arm to encourage him to move.

His lips part to argue, but after a second he must realise that I'm right because he turns and heads down the stairs with a sigh.

"Just give him some time. He'll come around."

"And if he doesn't?" he asks again.

"He will. Now, what delights do you have for me today?" I ask, trying to turn his thoughts from my pig-headed brother and toward his clients.

He smiles at me, clearly seeing what I'm doing, but he goes over to his computer nonetheless and powers it up.

He talks me through his clients, tells me what I can expect, and sets me up to do a few jobs. Before we know it, his first victim is walking through the door.

"Jesus, mate, that looks sore," he comments when I stand aside and allow him to join Spike.

"Nah, you should see the state of the other guy," Spike jokes as he sets about doing his thing.

I watch, I listen, I take everything in that he tells me until my fingers are twitching to have a go once again.

The sound of movement outside Spike's room has me on edge all day. Every time a door opens, I tense, thinking that Zach's going to come storming in. But he never does. Every time there's a knock at the door, it's anyone but him. All the others poke their heads in to make sure that both of us are okay after what went down.

I didn't have Zach down as the kind of person who hides away from an issue, so it makes me wonder just how angry he really is if he feels the need to stay away while knowing we're right here, waiting to talk to him.

Despite the fact that I'm engrossed watching Spike work, the day still drags, knowing that we've still got to deal with it.

"I'm hungry," Spike complains when his penultimate client for the day leaves. "You fancy some dinner?"

"Sure. What do you fancy?" I ask, jumping from the sofa where I was sketching, eager to get out of the studio and get some fresh air. The atmosphere in this place is kind of depressing.

He rattles off his order, but he calls out to me before I get to the door. "Don't go alone," he warns, clearly remembering my trepidation this morning. "Take Biff with you, or ever better, just send her."

I agree and head out with the intention of finding Biff to do as I'm told, but reception is empty, as is the kitchen.

Not wanting to disturb her, whether she's in with

Zach or upstairs, I leave it be and push through the front door.

I only need to go up the street a bit. It'll be fine. I'll be back in a few minutes.

It's getting late. The sun is beginning to set, casting the street in orange shadows.

Sucking in a deep breath, I make my way down the street to get the burger Spike requested.

WITH BOTH OUR orders in hand, I make my way back toward the studio. The sun has dipped below the buildings, and what was a relaxing soft hue on the walk here has now turned into a slightly eerie darkness, making me wish that I had done as Spike suggested and got Biff to come with me.

Tugging my jacket tighter around myself, I set off on the short walk. My legs move as fast as I can make them go as the dread I've been feeling for the past few days quadruples in my belly.

I tell myself over and over that I'm just being paranoid as I hurry back.

I'm almost there. I can see the neon Rebel Ink sign in the distance when I sense someone behind me.

My foot shoots forward, ready to run, but I don't get the chance.

A large hand covers my mouth as an arm wraps around my middle, hauling me back into a hard body. The bag in my hand falls to the floor as all the panic, the fear, the anxiety I've been feeling recently slams into me.

I try screaming in the hope of alerting someone, but

unlike my earlier journey, there's no one on the street to watch this play out.

I'm dragged into the shadows of an alley as I kick, bite, and attempt to scream.

"Fucking bitch," the guy grunts when I manage to connect my boot with his crotch.

My heart pounds in my chest as my head spins, desperately trying to figure a way out of this.

I hiss in pain when I'm pushed up against the wall, the rough bricks scratching at my skin as his hard body presses into my back.

"What the fuck do you want?" I bark the second he releases my mouth.

"You have no idea who I am, do you?" His fingers wrap around my hair and my head is violently pulled back so I have no choice but to look at him.

I narrow my eyes, studying him as he waits for me to make whatever connection I'm meant to.

His eyes are somewhat familiar, but I have no idea where from.

"Am I meant to?"

"You fucking should. You've got my money."

It takes a few seconds longer than it probably should, but realisation dawns eventually that he's obviously got some connection to Jet.

Fuck, fuck. *Fuck.*

"I don't have any money." My head is ripped back once again, and an excruciating pain shoots down my neck and back at the vicious move.

"Where is it?"

"I don't have it."

"Don't fucking lie to me," he bellows, forcefully

spinning me around and slamming my back up against the wall.

My head collides with the bricks, and for a few seconds I see stars.

I should be screaming, trying to alert someone, but with his cold, evil eyes staring down into mine, I'm frozen.

"Who are you?"

Instead of responding, he lifts his arm, backhanding me across the cheek.

"Motherfucker," I mutter, feeling my healing lip split back open.

"Where's the fucking money?"

"I don't have any fucking money. Do I look like I have the odd fifty G hanging around?" I spit.

"You turned up with a bag. Where did it go?"

"Read my fucking lips, arsehole." His hand grips me around the throat and he squeezes enough to scare me but not to cut off my air supply. Not yet, anyway. "I. Don't. Know."

His grip tightens as his lips purse in anger.

"This is going to go two ways," he warns. "Either you tell me where that money is, or you're not leaving this alleyway breathing."

His eyes hold mine, but if he's hoping to see fear in them, he'll be bitterly disappointed. I've dealt with arseholes like him my entire life. He can threaten to kill me all he likes—hell, he can do it if it's going to make him feel better about himself—but I won't give him any details that might lead him to Zach, which is where I assume the money is.

"No wonder Jet had such fun with you," he says, a smile full of evil intentions appearing on his lips.

"Maybe I should get in on the action before putting you out of your misery."

His arm lifts once more and I brace for the hit that sends me crashing to the ground. My head ricochets off the concrete, a piercing pain spearing down my neck at the same time my shoulder begins to burn.

Seconds before he drops down to me, I have the briefest opening to reach down for my ankle with the arm I didn't land on.

I breathe a sigh of relief when my fingers wrap around the cool metal handle of my knife. I knew there was a reason I slid it in here before leaving the flat earlier. If I learned one thing from my mother, then it's to always trust my gut, and my gut has been screaming at me for days that something's not right. I'm so fucking glad I listened.

He practically dives for me, wanting to take advantage of me being in a heap on the ground, but the second he's in reaching distance, I flip my knife and drive it into his neck.

I have no idea where I hit. All I care about is that I did.

His eyes go wide as realisation hits him.

"You're going to fucking pay for that," he gargles, blood flying from his mouth as he spits each word.

I pull the blade from him as fast as it entered, and I manage to use his momentary distraction as he reaches for his neck to scramble out from under him.

He looks up at me as I stand above him, my knife still firmly in hand in case he tries anything more, but the longer I stand there, the only thing I witness is the life draining from his eyes.

CHAPTER THIRTY

SPIKE

"ZACH. SPIKE." Biff's scream fills my quiet studio. The panic within it turns my blood ice cold.

Pushing my stool out behind me with such force it crashes against the wall behind, I run for the door and rip it open.

Looking as concerned as I feel from only those two words, Zach appears in his doorway.

He looks at me for the briefest of moments before he runs toward reception. I follow right behind him and collide with his back when he grinds to a halt in the entryway.

"What the fuck?"

Looking over his shoulder, my entire world seems to crash around my feet at the sight before us.

"Kas," I breath, pushing a frozen Zach aside and running toward her.

My eyes flick over her. The amount of blood covering both her face and her clothing have my heart threatening to beat out of my chest.

"I-I'm okay," she whispers.

Stepping up to her, I reach for both of her hands. I find one clenched tight with something in it.

Lifting her arm, I drag my eyes from hers to see what she's holding.

My eyes widen when I find a blood-covered knife in her grip.

Prising it from her fingers, I place it on the coffee table behind me before taking her face in my hands.

"Are you hurt?" I have no idea if the blood is hers or someone else's, but the fact she's standing here and talking is a good sign.

"N-no."

"What happened?" Zach barks, coming to stand beside me, having dragged himself from his shock.

"A... a guy j-jumped me. H-he..." she blows out a breath, her body trembling beneath my hands as her adrenaline starts to subside.

"Sit down," I encourage, dropping down before her and pulling her onto my lap.

"We need to call the police," Biff says, coming to sit on the edge of the coffee table with a bowl of bubbly water and a facecloth.

"No," Kas cries. "Fuck," she mutters, dropping her face into her hands. "He was one of Jet's guys. He wanted the money."

"Fuck," Zach barks.

"Dawson," I shout, making Kas jump on my lap. "D, get out here right now."

In seconds, a door opens and heavy footsteps head our way.

"What the—"

"Call your brother now," I demand. "They missed one."

He doesn't need any more explanation than that. He pulls his phone from his pocket and barks orders down the phone.

"Where is he?" he asks Kas.

"In the alley down there." She lifts her arm, her trembling hand pointing in the general direction. "I... I stabbed him... in the neck. I think he's... I think he's..."

"Don't worry," he soothes. "We've got it covered."

The second he hangs up, he pockets his phone and dashes back to his room before emerging with whoever his client was and the two of them go running out the door.

"Fucking hell, Tiny." I pull her into my arms, rest her against my chest and hold her tightly as her body continues to tremble.

She doesn't say anything. None of us do as the atmosphere continues to almost suffocate the four of us.

"Where's your client?" Kas finally asks, breaking the silence.

"No show. But don't worry about that right now." She looks up at me with her huge blue eyes, and I fear I lose the last padlock I'd fused in place around my heart all those years ago.

"Jesus, fuck." Zach barks, marching to the other side of the room with his hands threaded through his hair.

He paces back and forth for a bit while the three of us watch him with curiosity.

Eventually, he draws to a stop and stares between the two of us. His brows pull together, but some of the anger that was surrounding him when he first marched out here with me has vanished.

"You fucking love her, don't you?" he barks at me.

Kas startles in my arms. "Zach, please," she begs. "Don't do this now."

A beat passes, but before I know I'm even doing it, my lips part and I say the most honest thing I have in years.

"Yeah, yeah I do."

Kas gasps while Zach barks a curse.

"Y-you do?" she whispers, looking up at me with disbelief in her tear-filled eyes.

"Yeah, Tiny. I do."

"Oh my God," she gasps, her small hand coming up to cover her gawping mouth. Her tears spill over, and despite the fact that she's clearly got a smile on her face, the sight guts me.

Pulling her into my chest once more, I drop my lips to the top of her head as she cries.

"Take her the fuck home and look after her," Zach demands.

My eyes lift to his. His anger and frustration are right there in his familiar blue depths, but there's more. There's understanding, compassion, acceptance.

"Thank you," I mouth.

"Let's clean you up first," Biff says, wringing out the washcloth as I release Kas so she can get to her.

Once she looks a little better, she stands—quietly thanks both Biff and Zach—before tucking herself into my side and allowing me to walk her out to the waiting Uber.

As we set off down the street, we pass a cluster of bikes parked at the side of the road. Both of us crane our necks to see what's going on, but it's too dark.

"Come here." Releasing my seatbelt, I slide over beside her and pull her into my arms. "I'm so fucking proud of you."

"Yeah?" she asks.

"Yeah, and maybe a little scared," I admit with a laugh. "Do you always carry a knife?"

"Shit, my knife," she gasps, sitting forward in panic.

"It's with Zach and Biff. It's okay."

She looks at me for a beat before resting back against the seat. "I always used to. When you live in the places I have, you need to be able to protect yourself when the inevitable happens."

"Have you ever—"

"Used it before? No. I can honestly say that was a first."

"Shit."

"Yeah."

"Did he hurt you?"

"It was just a slap." I narrow my eyes at her. I know her tells now, and I know she's lying. "Please, Spike. I'm okay, I promise."

"Okay," I agree, because she looks too vulnerable right now to do anything else.

The second we're inside the flat, I start pulling off her bloodstained clothes. By the time we're in the bathroom, both of us are just standing in our underwear.

I twist the taps and pour in a generous amount of bubbles that fill the room with a relaxing floral scent.

Turning to her, I brush the hair from her face and take her cheeks in my palms.

"This is the last bath we're having like this," I tell her, staring into her eyes.

She nods, her eyes heavy with exhaustion. An idea hits me, and my fingers twitch to do something with it, but I need to wait. I need to look after my girl before I start making any plans.

Removing our last few items of clothing, I step into the hot water and reach out for her to join me.

Just like the last time, she settles between my legs and nuzzles into my chest as the soothing water surrounds us.

Silence stretches between us. I'm desperate to ask her what happened, but I know that I need to give her the time to process. I can't even imagine what's going through her head right now.

"I thought he was going to kill me," she says quietly after the longest time. My hold on her tightens, but my lips remain sealed, allowing her to say what she needs to. "His eyes. They were... they were so cold... dead. If I didn't do what I had, then I would have been the one leaving that alley in a body bag."

"Fucking hell," I breathe, not really believing what I'm hearing. "I'm so proud of you," I repeat, needing her to know just how fucking brave, how incredible she is.

"For killing someone?" she asks, sounding confused.

"No, for standing up for yourself. For taking control of the situation. For being so fucking brave."

"I just did what anyone would do," she says quietly, not making a big deal out of this.

Dropping my hands to her waist, I lift her and spin her until she's sitting astride my hips.

"No," I say firmly. "What you did was incredible. You're so fucking strong, and I'm so fucking gone for you."

She gasps, but I don't allow her time to say anything. Instead, I slide my fingers into her hair and pull her forward. My lips brush hers, testing the water, but the second I feel her tongue sneak out, I know she's on board.

I part my lips, and she hungrily slides her tongue in search of mine.

Our kiss is slow, passionate, and I try to pour into it everything I feel as I attempt to ignore the fact that she hasn't said anything in response.

I'd be lying if I said it didn't bother me, but I know I'm being selfish. She's just been through something huge. Hell, she's been going through something unbelievable since I first dragged her off that stage. However she's feeling about me shouldn't be her biggest concern right now.

"Spike," she moans into my mouth, her hands gliding over my chest and stomach until one of them wraps around my length.

"That's not—" I start, wanting to tell her that sex wasn't where I was intending this to go.

"Shhh," she soothes, as if she's suddenly the one looking after me as her hand gently strokes me.

She kisses across my jaw and down my neck as she continues working me.

Part of me wants to tell her no, that she's injured and should be relaxing, but I know better than to try to stop her when she wants something.

So instead of taking her hand in mine and forcing her to lie back down, I stretch out a little more as she kisses across my collarbones, enjoying the feeling of her touch.

After a few minutes, she lifts up, her eyes burning into mine as she sinks down on my length.

My eyes threaten to close as the sensation takes over me, but I fight it, my need to keep our connection stronger than my need to drown in the feeling of her.

"Fuck, Tiny."

"No talking," she demands, pressing two fingers to my lips before dropping her palm to rest over my heart. "Just feel."

I nod. It's all I'm able to do as she lifts up and slowly sinks back down again.

Needing to give her the escape from reality that I'm sure she needs right now, I reach down and begin to rub slow circles against her clit.

She moans in pleasure, her muscles clamping down on me as her back arches.

It's a fucking fine sight, despite the blood that's still covering some of her skin.

"Come, Kas. Show me just how good it feels."

After only a few seconds, her body tenses and her eyes slam shut as pleasure races through her. Her pussy squeezes down on me so tight that I have no choice but to fall over the edge of the cliff with her.

Pulling her down onto my chest, I run my fingers up and down her back as she catches her breath.

"Spike," she whispers.

"Yeah, Tiny?" When I look down, she's staring up at me with awe in her eyes.

"I think I love you too."

My breath catches at her words before a smile curls at my lips.

"You think?"

She shrugs. "I've never loved anyone before. But I've also never felt like this before either." She draws circles around my heart as she speaks causing goosebumps to prick my skin despite the hot bath we're in.

"It's scary, isn't it?"

"A little. Mostly, it's kinda exhilarating."

"Yeah?"

"Yeah." She looks away for a moment.

"What's wrong?"

"Can you... can you wash my hair, like you did before?"

"For you, anything."

AFTER I FINISHED WASHING HER, I wrapped her in a fluffy towel to dry off before tucking her into bed. She could hardly keep her eyes open, so after forcing her to take a couple of painkillers, she curled up and almost instantly fell asleep.

I'd hoped I was wrong about her being injured, but the second I started massaging her scalp as she asked me to, she let out a loud gasp and I knew it was wishful thinking.

Finding my phone in my jeans that I'd dropped on our way to the bathroom, I discover numerous missed calls from Zach, Biff and D.

Going for Zach first, I lift the phone to my ear and listen to it ring.

"Is she okay?"

"She will be. She's sleeping. I don't think it's really hit her yet."

"Fucking hell," he mutters. I picture him tugging at his hair and spinning around the way he does when he doesn't know what to say down the line. "I've only known about her for a couple of months and she's already aged me a few years."

"You don't need to worry about her, Zach. I think she's more capable of looking after herself than we are."

"I know. Fuck," he barks. "But it shouldn't be that way."

"I know, man. But it is what it is."

"I fucking hate that I haven't been able to help," he admits.

"You've helped more than you think you have."

He blows out a long breath. "D sorted everything."

"Was he..." I trail off, but Zach clearly knows where my question is heading.

"No. Although he is now."

"Who was he?"

"Jet's brother. Cruz didn't think he was involved anymore. He hadn't been seen for months. Seems that he might have just been working in the background."

"Is that it now?" I ask, almost pleading for this to finally be over for Kas.

"Yes. Well, they're pretty confident."

"That's not exactly reassuring."

"They thought they had them all last time, so..." he trails off. Neither of us need a reminder of tonight's events.

"D's going to call you. He's got a friend or something who Kas might want to talk to about all this.. A shrink of some sort."

"I've already had a missed call from him."

"Okay, you should probably call him back then," he suggests awkwardly.

"Yeah..." Silence hangs heavy between us. "Zach?"

"It's okay, Spike. Everything's okay."

"I... um... What I said earlier, it's tru—"

"I know," he interrupts. "I know. Just... just promise me something."

"Sure."

"Make sure her future is a fuck load better than her past."

"You got it. She's one of us now, Zach. We're not going to fail her."

"Maybe so, but you're the only one with her heart."

My breath catches at his words. "Fuck," I mutter.

"Trust me, I know how you feel. Just for the love of God, don't fuck it up."

"I'll do my best, man. I'll do my best." I hear Biff in the background asking about Kas and I make my excuse to hang up so I can ring D.

He tells me a slightly more detailed version of what Zach did, seeing as he was there with Cruz when they found the motherfucker who jumped my girl. He also explains about his friend and tells me he'll shoot her number over so I can give it to Kas, should she feel she needs it.

After thanking him for once again bailing her out of his fucking disaster, I hang up and crawl into bed beside her.

Wrapping my arm around her waist, I pull her warm back against my front and breathe in her sweet scent.

"I love you, Tiny."

"I love you too. Thank you for saving me."

CHAPTER THIRTY-ONE

KAS

"MORNING, TINY." I blink a couple of times to get my eyes to focus.

"What are you doing?" He looks down at the small bag he's currently packing before looking back up at me.

"Uh... packing."

"Going somewhere nice?"

"We sure are."

"We?"

"We, Tiny." He winks. "And if you want to find out where we're going, then I suggest you get your cute arse out of bed."

"What do I need?" I ask, excitement starting to bloom in my belly.

"Normal stuff."

I raise a brow. "You're talking to a girl here."

He chuckles. "Just normal stuff. Clothes, underwear, you know."

"For how long?"

"A few days."

"Wow, you're full of details."

"That might be because it's a surprise."

"Would now be a good time to tell you that I don't have a passport?"

"We're not leaving the country, don't worry."

"So, we're not going on the run because I killed a guy. Good to know." His movement stops at my words and his eyes find mine.

"Kas, I—" The seriousness in his tone has me cutting him off. I really don't want to do serious right now, especially if he's planned something for us.

"It's okay. It was a joke. I'm not sure anyone will miss that scumbag, just like his friends."

"I know, and I agree. I was just going to say that you didn't actually kill him. When D and Cruz got there, he was still alive."

"Shit, that must have hurt then."

He shrugs. "He was Jet's brother."

I nod, acknowledging that would be why I recognised something about him.

"They sorted it?" I ask, wanting to confirm what I already know.

"Yeah. And..." Spike hesitates, making dread start to push away my earlier excitement. "D gave me a number for a shrink friend, should you want it."

I smile at him. "I appreciate that, but I'm good."

He flashes me a knowing smile. "As I thought. I'll forward it to you anyway, just in case."

I want to argue, but I don't have it in me. All he's trying to do is look after me, and I appreciate it more than he could possibly know.

"So where are we going?" I ask, changing the subject back to something a little lighter.

"Not telling you. But the sooner you get up and pack, the faster you can find out."

Scrambling from the bed, I falter when my head starts to ache and my muscles pull, reminding me of what happened last night. Pushing it from my mind before Spike notices something is wrong, I head to my room.

In the middle of my bed is a brand new suitcase with a couple of bags already inside.

"What's all this?" I shout but startle when his hands slip around my waist and pull me back into his body.

"Presents."

"Why?"

"Why not?"

I bite onto my bottom lip. I don't need to tell him that people don't just buy me presents because they feel like it. He already knows, and presumably it's why he's done it.

"Pack what you need, and don't look inside the bags. You've got fifteen minutes."

He leaves me to it, and after running my fingers over the bags that are practically calling to me, I rip my hand away and do as I'm told.

Spike isn't anything like the people of my past. There are only nice things, thoughtful things inside those bags.

Ten minutes later, I pull the wheelie case down the

hallway toward where he's waiting for me in the living room.

"All set?" he asks, looking up from his phone.

"I think so, although I have no idea if I've got everything I need."

"You have," he says confidently, making my brows draw together.

"What are you planning?"

Pushing from the sofa, he walks over and holds out his hand. "Pass me that. I'll carry them downstairs."

I nod and follow him out, watching as he locks up the flat and then trails behind me as we make our way down the stairs.

As we hit the ground floor, a door opens. Louisa steps out, her eyes flying to both of us. If she didn't look so shocked to see us, I'd think she was waiting. "Jesus, are you two okay?"

It's not until I see the horror in her eyes that I really remember just how we look.

"Yeah, we're good," Spike says, as I say, "You should see our opponents."

The reality of my words hits me hard. The guy who did this to me is gone. It may not have been me who dealt his final blow, but I've no doubt he'd have bled out in that alleyway if D and Cruz hadn't got there so fast.

"O-okay," she says, her eyes flitting between the two of us, looking totally unconvinced by our words.

"We're heading out of town for a few days. We'll be back at the weekend," Spike tells her, but I look up at him, soaking up any clue he might give as to where we're going.

"Okay, well... have fun."

"Oh, we will," Spike says, picking up both cases in

one hand and pressing his other to the small of my back. Tingles race across my skin at his suggestive tone, and heat blooms in my lower stomach.

"I can't believe you just said that," I chastise him as the main door closes behind us.

"Why not?"

"She wants you. It's just mean, flaunting what she can't have."

"That's very thoughtful of you. You'll be suggesting sharing next."

My teeth grind. "Um... I think not."

Dropping the cases, he grips the nape of my neck and pulls me against his body.

"Jealousy looks good on you, Tiny."

"I'm not—"

"Don't bother trying to argue. I like it," he says, brushing his lips against mine and giving me the sweetest kiss that only makes the ache between my legs worse.

"All in good time, Tiny."

He pulls away from me all too soon, before stepping toward a car I recognise.

"Is that Zach's?"

"Sure is. He owes me a favour or two after rearranging my face."

I stand awkwardly on the pavement as he places our cases in the boot and holds open the passenger door for me.

"Come on then."

I hop inside, and in only a few seconds he joins me.

"You said we're going out of town. Are we leaving London?"

"Yeah, is that okay?"

"Yes," I answer eagerly. "I've never left the city."

"You serious?"

I nod sadly, not really wanting to admit just how sheltered I am when it comes to travelling.

"Well, sit back and enjoy a little of the country, then."

I do as he suggests and get comfortable as he changes the radio station and pulls out of the space on the side of the road.

With the windows down and the music blasting, I suck in deep breaths of fresh air as we make our way out of the city.

"How far away is it?" I ask after a long stretch of silence.

"About an hour and a half."

I nod, turning my head to look at him. He's got one hand on the wheel, his fingers tightly wrapped around it, his strong forearm flexing, making his ink ripple as he keeps control of the car.

"See something you like?" he asks cheekily.

"Hell yeah. You look hot behind the wheel."

"Yeah?" He flashes me that heart-stopping smile of his, and I squirm in my seat. "Don't do that," he warns.

"Do what?" I ask innocently.

"Make me fuck you in the back of your brother's car. That won't help," he chuckles.

"He must be somewhat okay with this, or he wouldn't have loaned it to you."

"I think he had a bit of a reality check."

"What? When I almost died?"

He swallows like hearing the words causes him physical pain. "Yeah, something like that."

Turning away from him, needing to end the

conversation I stupidly started, I look back out to the greenery surrounding us.

"It's really beautiful out here."

"It is."

"Do you always want to live in London?"

"I... um..." He hesitates, making me look back to him. "The plan was always to move out before starting a family."

"With her?" I can't help the bitter tone that fills my voice. A huge part of me is grateful that she left him, because I've got him now. But equally I hate her for hurting him something fierce. I really hope I never meet her.

"Yeah. After that..." He shrugs. "I've never really thought about the future too much. I'd been living day to day until..."

"Until?" I ask when he trails off.

"Until you."

"And now what?"

"I still have no idea, but I'm up for thinking about it again."

A smile curls at my lips. "You want to plan our future?"

"Yeah, if you want to?"

I nod, the thought of tomorrow not scaring me as much as it once did. "Yeah, I think that would be good."

"So, what do you want, Kas? Have you always seen your future in London, or did you want to head off elsewhere?"

"Well I always dreamed of a sunset somewhere, but mostly, I was just happy to wake up the next day."

"Kas."

"Don't give me the sad voice. It's over."

He nods.

"And now… I want a career, I want to actually be good at something and make myself a life. I want a home, a place where I feel safe and want to return to. I want to not look over my shoulder every five seconds to see if anyone is trailing me. I want to look forward and not wonder if I'll even have a future to worry about."

"And me?" The vulnerability in his tone makes my heart ache.

"You? I want you right by my side." Wide smiles spread across both of our faces as he reaches over and laces his fingers with mine.

"I like the sound of that."

One of my favourite songs starts playing on the radio. Resting my head back, I belt out the lyrics like I have no cares in the world as the warm air whips past my face.

"I like you like this," Spike says once I've finished my terrible rendition.

"Like what, making you go deaf?" I ask with a laugh.

"Relaxed. Happy."

"It's nice to have forgotten most of my worries, I must admit."

"Well, let go of the rest. You've got nothing to worry about for five whole days."

"Five days?" He nods. "Are you going to tell me where yet?"

He tilts his chin to point out of the windscreen, and I turn to look.

"Holy shit. Don't joke," I say with amusement when the rolling hills before us drop away to reveal the most stunning manor house in the distance.

"I'm not joking."

"Spike," I squeal. "I can't go in there. They'll think I'm one of the cleaners."

"Only you're not. You're a guest with everything the place has to offer at your feet."

The car draws closer, past all the perfectly tended lawns and bright blooming flowers.

Spike brings Zach's car to a stop beside the others that would look more at home in a fancy showroom, and I stare up at the impressive building.

"I thought places like this only existed on the TV," I mutter, not entirely sure how I feel about walking inside as a guest. "Why here?"

"I have it on good authority that this place is one of the best."

"Who from?" I ask, my brows drawing together as I try to think who he might know who has the money to stay here.

"Biff. I called in a favour," he admits with a shrug.

"I don't want their charity, Spike."

"It's not. She just got me a good rate. The rest is all me. I want to spoil you, let you have a few days out and... thank you."

"Thank me. What for?"

He turns to me, his eyes softening as they bounce between mine. "For showing me that just because I've been burned, I don't need to hide. For bringing meaning back into my life. For giving me a chance."

"Spike," I whisper, leaning into his touch when he lifts his hand to my cheek. "I should be the one thanking you. You've saved me over and over in only a few days."

"I guess that makes us even then," he says with a smile.

"I guess so."

"So, do you fancy it? Or I can drive us back to the city."

I think of the delights that might be hiding for us inside that building. I imagine us both in fluffy robes, having a couple's massage, drinking champagne for breakfast, and late nights watching the sun go down over the countryside beyond.

"Oh, I fancy it."

"Good. Let's go." He kills the engine and shoulders the door before jogging around the bonnet and opening mine for me.

He helps me down before getting our cases from the boot, and with his arm around my shoulder, we walk toward the entrance.

The inside is like nothing I've ever seen before. My eyes flick around, not knowing where to look first.

I expected the member of staff who greeted us to look us up and down and turn her nose up like we didn't belong, but from the second she looked up from her desk, she was nothing but welcoming.

"Would you like some help with your bags?" she asks softly after handing over our key and giving us all the instructions we might need.

"No, we're good."

"Okay, the lift is just over there. You're on the fourth floor, room 402. If you need anything at all, just call down."

"Thank you," we say simultaneously before turning the way she pointed.

"This is insane," I whisper, looking around at the most luxurious lift I've ever stepped foot in.

"It looks good on you, though."

"You think?" I ask as he stalks toward me.

"I do."

The lift dings before he manages to back me up against the wall, and although I'm disappointed not to have his hands and lips on me, I don't want to get caught before we've even stepped inside our room.

"This way," he announces, taking off down the hallway with our bags.

"Whoa… this isn't just a room, it's a…"

"Suite. I know." He turns on me, a shit-eating grin on his face.

"Spike," I breathe. "This is all too much."

The plush carpet, the rich ruby red walls, the huge sofas and the open fire. I don't know where to look first.

"It's nowhere near enough, Kas. I don't have much. This isn't normal life for me either, but it's time for a fresh start, for both of us."

I smile up at him, my heart thundering in my chest in a way it never has before. The fear I've been all too used to is gone, replaced by just how strongly I feel for this incredible man who's looking down at me like I'm the only woman in the world.

"I love you so much."

"I love you too, Tiny. Now…" he says, reaching down to take my hand, "fancy checking out the bedroom?"

I giggle like a schoolgirl when he winks and drags me in the direction of a door, a naughty glint in his eye that I know I'm never going to tire of.

EPILOGUE

KAS

ONE MONTH LATER...

THE BUZZING that fills my ears now feels as familiar as my own heartbeat. My eyes stare at Spike's hand as he adds the finishing touch to my new tattoo that covers one of the many scars of my past.

My chest heaves as he works on my hip, so close to where I'm desperate for him.

After we spent an incredibly relaxing five days at that fancy hotel, we returned back to his flat and set about moving me into his room. For someone who was adamant that he didn't want a woman or even consider a future, he was very keen to start our new life together.

We'd not spoken about anything to do with the future aside from that brief conversation we had in Zach's car, but I know he's thinking about it. I can see it in his eyes when he looks at me. And I can't deny that the idea of him asking the question I know is eating at him, even this early into our relationship, doesn't fill me with excitement.

I might not have all that much experience with love and all the things that come with a serious relationship, but I know what I want, and I've never really been one to back down from a challenge.

I know I'm young and have all the time in the world to think about settling down, but I know Spike still thinks about our age difference, and although it doesn't bother him, I don't think he really wants a girlfriend. He wants more, he wants what Zach and Titch have, and I can't help but feel the same when I see them together.

I lose myself in thoughts of my future as he works, his fingers flexing, the ink on his hand and forearm pulling as he moves and making me even hotter for him.

"Okay, I'm done," he announces, sitting back and looking proud of himself.

"Yeah?"

I push myself from the chair so I can see and stare down at his artwork. He's done an incredible version of my own design, but I can clearly see the little additions and tweaks he's made.

"What's this?" I ask, pointing out the pocket watch he's added into my design. It's the exact same as the one that adorns his side.

"Something sentimental."

"Why, what's it...?" I stare down at it, looking at the

time he's put on it. "Is that the time you pulled me off the stage?"

A smirk pulls at his lips, and I know I'm right.

"You're an idiot," I laugh.

"I was so fucking pissed at you that night. If I'd have known how you were going to change my life, I might have been a bit nicer."

"Nah, it was hot."

"It was? You never told me that."

"Why would I? Your ego doesn't need stroking."

He shrugs, looking back down at my hip.

"What else is there?" I ask, straining to see the ink that disappears around to the bottom of my arse and thigh.

"I'm not telling you, you'll have to find it."

"You're a pain in the arse." I narrow my eyes at him and all he does is laugh.

"Let me wrap you before I start on my next job?"

"I thought you were done for the day."

"I am. But you're half naked on my chair. I'm not letting you off until—"

"DAD!" a high-pitched voice screeches on the other side of the door.

Our eyes collide as my brows pull together.

"Excuse me, you can't just..." Biff shouts, sounding as shocked as I feel as footsteps stomp down the hall.

Spike is up and off his stool in seconds. He has the door open before I have a chance to get off the chair.

I grab a towel that he's thrown over the arm of the sofa and wrap it around my waist so I can follow him out without flashing everyone. I might want to show off my new ink, but not quite like that.

"Emmie, what the hell are you doing?" D barks,

standing in his doorway, his large frame looking even more terrifying as he stares down at the young girl.

"I'm moving in with you," she sasses, dropping a giant bag at his feet. "She's a fucking bitch, and I can't live with her anymore. I fucking hate her," she seethes.

"Emmie," he sighs, his hand lifting to run through his hair as he tries to switch lanes from bad boy tattoo artist to father.

"I didn't know D had a kid," I whisper to Spike, who's standing beside me, watching the show.

"He tries to keep his lives separate."

"Why?"

"Because what Emmie is saying isn't entirely false."

"Oh."

"Please don't talk about your mother like that," D says, although his face is pulled tight, telling me that while he might want his daughter to be more respectful, he clearly agrees with her.

"Why? You can't stand her either. Please, Dad. You either let me stay with you or I'm taking off."

"Em—"

"No, don't *Emmie* me. I'm sixteen. I can do what the fuck I like, and you know it."

"Jesus fucking Christ," D mutters, looking up for the first time to see us all staring back at him. "I guess you'd better come in, then."

He stands aside and allows her to slip past him, bending down to collect her bag before glaring back at us all.

"Get back to fucking work. The show's over."

Are you ready for D?

PLAY YOU is now live!

Need more of my Rebel Ink boys?
Make sure you ONE-CLICK INKED my K Bromberg
Driven World/ Rebel Ink crossover novel about Corey,
who you first met in Hate You.
Keep reading for a sneak peek!

ACKNOWLEDGMENTS

I can't believe that book number three in this series is done. I loved Kas from the moment she appeared in *Hate You*. I knew she was hiding a little firecracker under her nervous façade when she arrived to make her announcement to Zach. I've had so much fun with her defiance. And Spike, gah, he's so damn sweet.

This book took a much darker turn than I was expecting and opened up so many new avenues that have been spinning around in my head, driving me crazy!

I love these tatted up bad boys so much, and I'm so excited to dive into the fourth book in the series. I've been dying to discover more of D from the moment he welcomed Biff to Rebel Ink.

As always, I need to say a massive thank you to so many people for helping me to make this possible.

Michelle and Sam for alpha reading, and my incredible team of beta readers for falling in love with Kas and Spike with me.

Evelyn, as ever for whipping both me and the story into shape.

Darlene and Athena for proofreading and polishing it up for me.

And finally, my readers for allowing me to create these worlds and spend my days immersed with my crazy characters.

Until next time,

Tracy xo

ALSO BY TRACY LORRAINE

Falling Series

Falling for Ryan: Part One #1

Falling for Ryan: Part Two #2

Falling for Jax #3

Falling for Daniel (A Falling Series Novella)

Falling for Ruben #4

Falling for Fin #5

Falling for Lucas #6

Falling for Caleb #7

Falling for Declan #8

Falling For Liam #9

Forbidden Series

Falling for the Forbidden #1

Losing the Forbidden #2

Fighting for the Forbidden #3

Craving Redemption #4

Demanding Redemption #5

Avoiding Temptation #6

Chasing Temptation #7

Rebel Ink Series

Hate You #1

Trick You #2

Defy You #3

Play You #4

Inked (A Rebel Ink/Driven Crossover)

Rosewood High Series

Thorn #1

Paine #2

Savage #3

Fierce #4

Hunter #5

Faze (#6 Prequel)

Fury #6

Legend #7

Maddison Kings University Series

TMYM: Prequel

TRYS #1

TDYW #2

TBYS #3

TVYC #4

TDYD #5

TDYR #6

TRYD #7

Knight's Ridge Empire Series

Wicked Summer Knight: Prequel (Stella & Seb)

Wicked Knight #1 (Stella & Seb)

Wicked Princess #2 (Stella & Seb)

Wicked Empire #3 (Stella & Seb)

Deviant Knight #4 (Emmie & Theo)

Deviant Princess #5 (Emmie & Theo

Deviant Reign #6 (Emmie & Theo)

One Reckless Knight (Jodie & Toby)

Reckless Knight #7 (Jodie & Toby)

Reckless Princess #8 (Jodie & Toby)

Reckless Dynasty #9 (Jodie & Toby)

Dark Knight #10 (Calli & Batman)

Dark Princess #11 (Calli & Batman)

Dark Legacy #12 (Calli & Batman)

Corrupt Valentine Knight

Ruined Series

Ruined Plans #1

Ruined by Lies #2

Ruined Promises #3

Never Forget Series

Never Forget Him #1

Never Forget Us #2

Everywhere & Nowhere #3

Chasing Series

Chasing Logan

The Cocktail Girls

His Manhattan

Her Kensington

ABOUT THE AUTHOR

Tracy Lorraine is a *USA Today* and *Wall Street Journal* bestselling new adult and contemporary romance author. Tracy has recently turned thirty and lives in a cute Cotswold village in England with her husband, baby girl and lovable but slightly crazy dog. Having always been a bookaholic with her head stuck in her Kindle, Tracy decided to try her hand at a story idea she dreamt up and hasn't looked back since.

Be the first to find out about new releases and offers. Sign up to my newsletter here.

If you want to know what I'm up to and see teasers and snippets of what I'm working on, then you need to be in my Facebook group. Join Tracy's Angels here.

Keep up to date with Tracy's books at
www.tracylorraine.com

INKED SNEAK PEEK

A DRIVEN WORLD / REBEL INK CROSSOVER NOVEL

INKED

CHAPTER ONE

Harlow

"What the hell do you think you're doing?" Bailey, my best friend and roommate, asks the second she finds me sitting on the couch with a blanket over my lap, a tub of ice cream in hand and a rum and Coke on the coffee table.

"Err... Friday night in?" I say, my brows drawing together, trying to figure out if I've forgotten something. The look on her face and the way she's standing impatiently with her hands on her hips sure points to that.

She's just finished a twenty-four-hour shift at The House, caring for her boys, so I was expecting her to take up residence on the other couch with her wine while we caught up with *The Bachelor*.

"It's Austin's birthday," she says with a roll of her eyes.

"Right."

"We're going out. We're meeting everyone at Rush

in..." she pulls her cell from her back pocket and looks at the time, "in like... an hour, so we need to get our shit together."

Before I have a chance to argue, she's standing before me and pulling the ice cream from my hand.

"Come on, H. Move that sexy ass and go and find a hot little dress to wear."

After depositing the tub on the coffee table, she rips the blanket from my lap and attempts to pull me from the couch.

"Really?" I sulk. "Austin won't care if I'm there or not, I barely know the guy." We might work for the same company, but it's not like we spend any actual time together, other than the odd night out.

"I told him you'll be there."

"But you didn't think to tell me," I mutter, eventually going easy on her and standing.

"I could have sworn I'd mentioned it."

"When could you? You've hardly been home this week."

She shrugs. "Well, you know now. It's going to be a great night."

She ushers me out of the living room—thankfully after I grab my drink. I have a feeling I'm going to need it.

When we get to my room, she allows me to get ready alone, which is a relief. The last thing I need is a Bailey makeover for tonight.

Smoothing down my silk top, I add a layer of gloss to my lips and slip my feet into my shoes.

Bailey's still sitting in front of her mirror when I join her in her room thirty minutes later.

"How are you ready al—no, no, no. You can't wear that," she says looking at me over her shoulder in the mirror. I look down at my skinny jeans and black blouse.

"Why not? It's perfectly fine."

"Yeah, for an afternoon with your aunt."

Minus the height of my heels, I can't argue with her.

She spins on her chair, and I get a look at her dress—if it can even be described as such. It's fire-engine red; I swear I've got underwear that covers more skin.

I run my eyes over her, suspicion beginning to stir in my stomach. "I feel like I'm missing something. This isn't just a night out for Austin's birthday, is it?"

"His cousin's coming."

And now, it all starts to make sense.

"The British one?"

"Yes! I can't wait to hear him say my name," she swoons, getting this far-off look in her eye.

I shouldn't be surprised—she's been telling me about him for quite a few weeks now and trying to convince Austin to introduce them.

"You mean moan your name," I mutter.

"Harlow, I'm not some easy piece of ass, you know."

"Really?" I ask, my brows lifting, my lips curling in amusement.

"Okay, so maybe I am, but only for the right guy."

"Riiight."

I watch as she gets up from her seat and walks toward her wardrobe, thankfully pulling her ridiculously short dress down in the process so I don't have to see her easy ass.

"Now, let's see what I've got."

"Oh no, B. You're not getting me in one of your dresses. They barely fit you, they'll never cover my ass and tits."

"Have faith, girl. Have faith."

Sadly, I have very little. I love Bailey, but at times she has questionable taste. Our styles are opposite in every way, not just with how much skin we deem acceptable to expose.

"Yessss..." she squeals, and my stomach drops into my heels. "This will look killer on you."

She pulls out a scrap of navy fabric and holds it up in front of me with a wide smile on her face.

"B, you won't catch me dead wearing that."

"Just try it on. It's a little big for me." I don't see how that's possible, seeing as it looks like it's a size zero from this distance, but I keep my mouth shut. "It'll be perfect. And," she adds, an idea hitting her, "it might help with that little situation you're in the middle of."

"I'm not in the middle of anything," I say, swiping the hanger from her because I already know that fighting with her on this is pointless. I may as well just try it on, prove it doesn't fit, and then hope she'll allow me to revisit my wardrobe for a dress that will cover what God gave me.

"It's been what? A year since a guy so much as touched you."

It's been almost a year and a half since my last failed attempt at a date, but I refrain from correcting her.

I shimmy my jeans down my legs and carefully pull my blouse off before laying them out over Bailey's bed. "What?" I ask when she shakes her head at me.

"You know it is okay to sometimes leave clothes in a pile on the floor, right?"

"I'm a neat freak. You could have to deal with a hell of a lot worse than me following you around and tidying up after your messy ass."

She rolls her eyes and hands me the dress once I'm in only my underwear. Deciding that pulling it up might be the easiest option, I step into the fabric and attempt to drag it over my hips. The material has more stretch than I gave it credit for, because it skims happily over my curves. I pull the straps up my arms and put them into place over my shoulders before looking down.

"Okay, you are *so* wearing that. Have you seen your ass?"

"Weirdly, no," I sass, looking over my shoulder at the mirror behind me. I nod, because I can't deny that the fabric hugs it pretty nicely.

"You gotta lose the bra though."

"Nope. Not happening."

Bailey's hip juts out and she rests her hand on it as she stares at me in a 'go on, try and argue' stance.

"There's enough support in the dress."

"I'm sure it'll hold them up just fine, I'm more worried about flashing someone."

"Making your mission a sure success."

"I'm not on a mission. I'm perfectly happy as—"

"Nope. You need a man-induced orgasm. End of."

I know I've been a little uptight recently, but it's not my lack of male attention that's causing it, and I doubt a night with one will solve the issue.

Bailey must see my shoulders drop, because she walks over and takes my hands in hers. "I know you're worried about her. I am too. But sitting around the house feeling guilty about not being able to do more isn't going to help in any way. No matter the results, you still have a life. You may as well at least attempt to enjoy yourself."

"I guess." I don't feel all that enthused, but I know she's right.

"Now, drink this," she says, handing my glass back to me. "Then let the girls free, and we're out of here."

I tip my glass to my lips and swallow what's left before doing as I'm told. I'm soon following Bailey out of the house toward the awaiting car. Despite my earlier disinterest, tingles of excitement start to ignite in my belly. I can't deny that the dress looked good once I turned and got a proper look at myself in the mirror. I also can't deny that I'm currently showing more boob than I have to anyone outside the bedroom in a lot of years.

Shaking thoughts of my past from my head, I climb in the car as Bailey begins flirting with the driver. Just because I'm dressed up and showing a little skin, it doesn't mean I'm going back to a time in my life I'd rather forget. I'm just going out for a night of drinking and dancing with my best friend. It's exactly what I should be doing. I'm young with no ties, a Friday night out for a colleague's birthday should be a normal thing to do.

Pushing aside my worries, I look at Bailey, who flashes me a wide smile, and I try to relax.

"Tonight's going to be great. Did I tell you that Rylee managed to secure the VIP section for us thanks to her... connections," she says, wiggling her eyebrows. I groan as I think of her boss, Rylee and her famous boyfriend.

My heart starts to race. "A-are they going to be there?" I try to ask as casually as I can.

"Please don't tell me you're still scared of being in the same building as him?"

"I'm not scared, B," I argue, although I'm not entirely sure that's true. "I just always make myself look like an idiot every time I'm anywhere near him. I turn into a fumbling teenager with one glance in his direction." My cheeks heat at my admission. I don't need to tell Bailey this—she's witnessed my mortifying behavior, time and time again when it comes to him. Colton Donavan. My teenage heartthrob, incredible Indy driver, and all-around nice guy. It should be illegal to be that good looking, kind and generous. I was obsessed with him in my former years, thanks to discovering a trashy magazine on the coffee table after school one day with him on the cover. No matter how many years have passed, it seems the second I'm in his vicinity, I return to that time in my life where I had no idea how to control my raging hormones or to keep a leash on my mouth.

"Oh, I know. Why do you think I demanded you come? You're tonight's entertainment," she says with a laugh.

"B," I squeal, swatting her shoulder playfully as she teases me. "I've no idea what's wrong with me."

"I get it. He's... captivating." Her eyes darken as she relives the one moment of her past that she'll never let me forget. "And his kiss," she says on a sigh.

"Oh, get over yourself," I chuckle. "You know full well that you got passed up that night for Rylee and haven't stood a chance since."

"I know, and I still stand by the fact that I rocked his world so much that night that he lost his mind a little after. I mean, why wouldn't he want more of this?" She gestures to herself with a pout.

"No idea, B. No idea."

"Well, I'm over it." I laugh; with the number of times she brings it up, I beg to differ, but I'm not going to point it out again. "I've got my sights set on a British banger tonight."

I bark out a laugh. "Do you even know what this guy looks like?"

"Only in my imagination."

"So he could be an old cockney with a beer belly and a bald head?"

"Yes and no. He's still in his twenties, so I'd like to think he's not bald."

"Still leaves a lot to go wrong, don't you think?"

"Nah, it's all good. I can feel it in my blood."

"I'm pretty sure that's the wine."

"Meh, tonight is my night, H. Just you wait and see. I'm gonna snag me a Brit, and I'm not letting this one out of my sight."

"If you say so," I whisper, looking out the window and seeing the neon lights of the club coming into view.

After saying the right words in the bouncer's ear, he stands aside and allows both Bailey and I to enter the club, although not before he gets his fill of her scantily-clad body.

"You offering up sexual favors again, B?"

"Not necessary this time. Come on, stop dawdling, the bar and the Brit are calling."

She grabs my hand and together we make our way through the crowd and toward the roped-off stairs that lead to the VIP section.

As we move, the loud bass from the music vibrates

through me, and even though being here tonight was the last thing I wanted to do after a long week at work, I can't help a little excitement and the desire to get up on the dancefloor creeping in. It's been a long time since I've let go with my best friend and forgotten about the world for a few hours.

After sweet-talking the second bouncer in as many minutes, we're climbing the stairs and away from the masses of people.

We're only three-quarters of the way up when I first see him. My nerves hit me like a sledgehammer and my body starts to tremble. It doesn't matter how many times I see and talk to him. It doesn't matter that I hear stories from Rylee about what a 'normal' guy he is. To me, he's still the man I had pinned to my teenage bedroom walls and said goodnight to before falling asleep.

I focus on my feet as I climb the stairs, the gems on the front glinting in the spotlights above and giving me a distraction from the man I'm walking toward.

I've got one more step to climb. Thinking I'm safe, I look up, but the second I meet his piercing green eyes, my feet falter. The platform of my shoe connects with the step, and I go tumbling forward.

Closing my eyes, I reach my hand out in the hope that it connects with something to break my inevitably painful collision with the tiled floor. Thankfully the pain never comes. Instead, my hand hits something warm and soft.

Finding my feet, I drag my eyes open to see what stopped me.

The second I see what I used to stop my fall, I gasp in horror and stumble backward into someone else. Large hands grip onto my waist to steady me as I keep my eyes locked on the floor. My cheeks flame so hot I swear they're going to catch fire any moment.

"Jesus, Harlow, that was some entrance," Colton says with a laugh as I continue to die a thousand deaths at embarrassing myself once again.

"Are you okay?" A deep, smooth voice washes over me from behind, making me wish the ground would just swallow me up. I nod, but not before I hear the laughter of my best friend behind me.

"I'm fine. I'm fine," I mutter, looking up but only so I can see which way the bar is so I can get a drink and hopefully wipe this disaster from my memory. "T-thank you," I whisper to the man behind me who's still holding me upright, probably thinking my legs don't work correctly.

"Anytime." I push to move away, but his voice makes me pause. It's deep, rough, and his accent is... I don't have time to try to figure it out. I just need to get away from him and Colton's green eyes that turn me into a fumbling moron.

"Oh my God, Harlow. That was classic," Bailey howls beside me as I wait for the bartender to notice me. "I mean, Colton's used to women falling at his feet, but using his cock to save yourself from breaking your nose on the floor? That was fucking—"

"Enough," I bark. "This is all your fault." Turning to her, I narrow my eyes in the hope it'll shut her up.

"Me?" she asks, innocently pointing to herself.

"Yes. I should be on the sofa right now with my second tub of ice cream and watching others falling in love on some shitty reality TV show."

"Oh yeah, that sounds like a winning way to spend

your Friday night, H. I'll call you a cab right now to return to your evening of fun."

"Really?" I ask hopefully, missing her sarcasm.

"No. Harlow. No. You embarrassed yourself, so what? Colton doesn't care, so neither should you." She waves and the bartender comes right over—of course he fucking does. One look at her and he's like putty in her hand. Me? He barely even saw me standing here. Rolling my eyes at myself, I listen as Bailey orders us four shots of tequila.

"Tequila?" My lip curls in disgust.

"Yes, hopefully it'll give your confidence a boost and loosen you up a little."

"Here's hoping," I mutter, more to myself than her as I pick up the first one and knock it back before immediately going for the second. The alcohol burns my throat, but it's only seconds before it starts warming my belly. Maybe it will have the effect Bailey intended.

"Oh, the birthday boy's here. Let's go and wish him a happy birthday." I look over to where Bailey's focus is and see both Rylee and Colton standing before Austin.

"It's okay, you go. I'll order some more drinks."

"He's just a guy, H. You can talk to him like any other."

"I know. And I will talk to him... them. I just... I need another drink first. I can only embarrass myself so much every hour."

Shaking her head at me, she takes off across the room, her heels clicking against the black polished tiles and her mile-long, tanned legs eating up the space. I don't need to look around to know she's got the attention of at least a handful of men as she moves. Bailey has this aura surrounding her, one that turns all attention on her. Something that I most definitely don't possess. I'm just the best friend who makes an idiot of herself as often as possible and only helps to make Bailey look so much more desirable.

Blowing out a long breath, I turn back to the bar, only to find that the bartender has once again vanished to serve someone else. Sitting myself up on a stool, I watch as he gets farther and farther away from me before turning to play on his cell.

Fantastic.

Thinking that I'll just order a cab home, I turn to slide from the stool but come to a stop when I find a guy standing before me. One side of his mouth curls up in an unsure smile.

"Hey, how are you doing?"

His deep voice is immediately recognizable. My eyes drop to his hands that are tucked into the pockets of his pants, but as I do that, I feel the warmth of one of them against my waist from not so long ago.

"Oh yeah. I'm sorry about that. I'm a bit of an id..." My eyes run up exposed forearms that are covered in ink. I find the rolled fabric of his white shirt and my mouth waters when I discover his muscular biceps beneath. It's open one button too many at the neck, showing even more art, but it's when I find his light blue eyes that it feels like my world tilts slightly.

His lopsided grin turns into a megawatt smile, exposing perfectly straight white teeth beneath, and my entire body sighs.

"Can I buy you a drink?"

It takes me a few moments to register that he's said anything, but once I do, I tilt my head to the side and look at him once more.

"Y-you're the Brit?"

That lopsided smile returns, but this time a dimple pops up in his cheek.

"What gave me away?" I bite down on my bottom lip and his eyes drop to focus on it. "It's Corey. And you are?"

"H-Harlow."

"Well, it's a pleasure to meet you, Harlow. Shall we?" he asks, gesturing toward the bar before lifting his hand to call the bartender over.

Ignoring the vacant stool beside me, he chooses instead to stand next to me. Just close enough that his warmth heats my side and his scent fills my nose. This guy knows what he's doing. It should be a turn off, but I can't help but fall for his charm. Maybe Bailey was right. I bite down on my bottom lip as I attempt to remember what it feels like to be touched by a man.

Bailey's going to kill you for talking to him first, I think as I look up at him once more, my cheeks burning with my previous thoughts. When I glance over my shoulder, I see she's still preoccupied with Austin and a few of the other counselors from The House along with Rylee and Colton. That's enough to tell me that I'm not heading over there anytime soon.

INKED

CHAPTER TWO

Corey

Tonight is my first night out—night off, actually—since setting up the studio over here. But Austin gave me little choice about it. He first mentioned it a few weeks ago, and, assuming he'd forget about it, or at least forget about me, I pushed it aside. But when he called again at the beginning of the week and told me that I had to be here and reminded me that he'd given me prior warning, I didn't stand a chance. Part of my moving here was so that I could spend time with this side of my family, something he used against me to ensure I attended. Turns out though, he didn't need to try quite so hard; all he had to do was mention the quality of the women who would also be here, and I'd have followed orders in a heartbeat.

I realised just how right a decision that was when I found myself following a curvy redhead up the stairs to a VIP area that's been reserved for my cousin tonight, courtesy of his famous friend.

I've been so busy that women haven't been on my radar all that much since I arrived in LA. I mean, I've spent my fair share of time inking them, but that's about as close as I've got. And my lack of action hasn't been more obvious to me than those few seconds of watching her arse sway before me as she climbed the stairs.

"So, you know Colton?" I ask once we've given the bartender our orders. A pint for me and a rum and Coke for her. I must admit, I was surprised. I was expecting her to order a glass of bubbles like I've seen the other women drinking, or at least a glass of wine, but it seems this woman has been sent to surprise me tonight. First, her fine arse, swiftly followed by her damn near falling into my arms not long after, and now this.

"Thank you. I need this," she says, swallowing a generous mouthful before turning to look at me. "I work with Rylee. I've spoken to Colton several times."

"Same. Although from the number of hours I've spent watching him fly around a track, I like to think I know him quite well."

"Hmmm..." she hums, her cheeks flaming almost as red as her hair.

"So you work for Corporate Cares? Are you a counsellor?"

"No, no." Her eyes go wide like the idea in itself is shocking. "I support the organisation wholeheartedly, but me and kids don't mix." I open my mouth to tell her that that can't possibly be true, but she beats me to it. "I'm in charge of fundraising."

"Sounds like fun."

"I love it. It's important for me to give back."

I nod at her, finding myself lost in her chestnut eyes as she stares back at me.

She coughs, clearing her throat and breaking the tension between us after a few seconds, and I'm forced to look away.

"So what is it you do?"

"Harlow, there you are. I thought you were coming to talk to the birthday boy," a high-pitched voice says from behind me before a blonde wrapped in the smallest dress I've ever seen stands so close to me that I have to take a step back.

"Yeah... I... uh..."

"Oh, are you still embarrassed about that? I'm sure Colton's already forgotten." She waves her friend off with a swish of her hand, and my eyes widen in shock. "Who's your new friend?" She turns to me, her eyes running over my face as what I guess is supposed to be a sexy pout appears on her lips. She falls a little too far from the mark for me. That and all the effort she's putting in to look so good.

"Corey," I say politely, holding my hand out for her.

"Oh, my Brit." *My Brit?* My eyebrows rise at her assumption. "Austin didn't say you were here yet." Ignoring my hand, she steps right into my body, pressing her breasts into my chest and stretching to drop a kiss to my cheek. "I've been so looking forward to meeting you."

"Oh really?" I ask, placing my hands on her shoulders and trying to remove her from me. "I'm not sure Austin's ever mentioned you."

Harlow snorts a laugh and when I look up, I find the most breathtaking smile lighting up her face.

"Oh, that can't be true. I'm sure you've just forgotten. I can only imagine that you've met so many new people since you arrived. I'm Bailey. I work with your cousin. He's told me all about you."

"Is that right?"

"Sure is. So tell me about yourself, I can't wait to get to know you better."

"Well, actually, I was in the middle of a conversation with your friend here."

Bailey stands back and looks over her shoulder. "Oh, okay, well..." She sounds dejected, making me wonder how many guys turn her down. Not a lot, I'm guessing.

"Would you like a drink, B?"

"I'd love one, thanks." I stand and watch both of them as Harlow orders Bailey a sauvignon blanc. They're both stunning, Bailey more so now I don't have everything thrust in my face, but to me, Harlow stands out by a mile. Her soft red hair, her large dark eyes that just ooze innocence... I bite down on my bottom lip as I study her while she talks to her friend. She must sense my stare, because her eyes flick to mine and she startles when she finds me looking back. Colour hits her cheeks, and it only makes her more alluring. It looks like coming here tonight was more than worth it.

My cock stirs behind the fabric of my jeans, desperate to end the evening with a little action.

Bailey lifts her drink from the bar and takes a sip while looking between the two of us suspiciously.

"So... I'm just going to go..." she trails off before disappearing off into the crowd.

"Good friend of yours?" I ask once I'm confident she's well out of earshot.

Harlow laughs and excitement shoots through me. She is exactly what I need tonight.

I take a step closer, her perfume filling my nose and making my mouth water.

"Yeah, actually. My best friend."

"Really? You seem so..."

"Different?"

"Yeah," I say, relieved that I'm not the only one who sees how opposite they are.

"Don't let her front fool you. She's a great person. She just comes across a little—"

"Desperate?"

She laughs. "I was going to say full-on, but desperate works too. Everyone around us seems to be coupling up. Austin, Colton," she says flicking a look over to where they're standing with their girls. "She's just feeling left behind."

"And she thought I might get her up to speed."

I watch her lips, enthralled as she purses them to take a sip of her drink. "You've no idea. She's been going on and on about meeting you since Austin told her you'd first moved here."

"Why? She's never met me. I could be a right arsehole." A smile curls at her lips.

"The accent," she says like it should be obvious. "She was hoping you'd talk all sexy to her." Harlow rolls her eyes at her friend's insanity. "So, are you?"

"Am I what? Going to talk all sexy to her?" I drop the tone of my voice and delight when the roughness of it makes her pupils dilate. My brows pull together as I cast my mind back over our previous conversation, trying to figure out what she's asking me.

"No. An *arsehole,*" she says, adorably trying to mimic my accent.

"Some would probably say I was. Others not so much."

"Cryptic."

Closing more of the space between us, I reach out and tuck a lock of her hair behind her ear. "Maybe you'll just have to find out for yourself."

Her lips part but no words come out as my fingertip brushes the shell of her ear. "I... um..." I search her eyes, trying to read her. She seems reluctant, yet there's something in her eyes. Something wild that I know is screaming to get out.

Our connection holds before she sucks her bottom lip into her mouth and my gaze drops to watch.

"Harlow," that familiar voice calls from somewhere. "We're going to dance. You coming?"

My eyes jump back up to hers. I want to ask her to stay here with me, but I've just met her; I've got no right to even suggest keeping her away from her friends and colleagues.

After another second, she rips her eyes from mine and looks at Bailey, who holds her hand out.

"Yeah, just coming."

I stand back, allowing her some space. She downs her drink before giving me a small smile and walking towards her friend.

Her arse sways as she makes her way over, and my trousers suddenly seem a little too tight as I imagine what, if any, underwear she's got on beneath. When I look up, I find Bailey watching me. Her eyes are narrowed, and I'm not sure if it's jealousy or a warning.

Make sure you PRE-ORDER to keep reading. INKED releases on 10/15